King of Detroit

Written by

Dorian Sykes

RJ Publications, LLC

Newark, New Jersey

The characters and events in this book are fictitious. Any resemblance to actual persons, living or dead is purely coincidental.

RJ Publications

www.rjpublications.com
Copyright © 2012 by RJ Publications
All Rights Reserved
ISBN-10: 0981999883
ISBN-13: 978-0981999883

Printed in the United States

August 2015

2 3 4 5 6 7 8 9 10

Dedications

This book is for every nucca that played the game raw, and took his like a man when adversity struck.
And to my co-defendant, Rolo, may we use this time to strengthen our resolve.

Acknowledgements

Ma Dukes- as always, thank you much! Without your steady belief in me none of this would have been possible. From start to finish, Ma', you've held me down and I love you more than life!

Nephews 'RJ' and 'Dee' – May you continue to grow and have a close relationship with God. I love both of you and pray that both of you become a great success. - May ya'll never play this game because it ain't even worth it.

Big Bro Ron, Sr. – What up dough, Lil' Bro making moves man. Thank you, man, for holding down the fort in my long absence, looking after Ma Dukes and being a real father. I truly commend you. Bro, your time is coming.

Linda Huddleston – thank you so much for preparing this book. You've been with me since my first book and it's been nothing short of a pleasure working with you. You really get it done. (Midnight Express Books) – check 'em out!

Unc Gene – What's up man! Nephew making power moves again, baby...

Mojo – I know you're holding it down in the best possible fashion and making noise. We shall cross paths soon my nucca – full embrace. Tell Sha' Boggy I send nothing but luv.

Piwi – Cleveland's finest. What up my dawg. Won't be long now til you touch them streets. You walked it on down like real nuccas do, holla at ya' boy. I won't be too long.

And to the man who made this project possible, COACH – Good lookin' Big Homie for the opportunity. You could have sold your story to a number of big publishing houses, but you kept it gully and I thank you for that. We should do a sequel???

Intro

Interview with Author D. Sykes and Corey "Coach" Townsend April 2, 2010.

D. Sykes – Man just let me start by saying that it is an honor to work with you on this.

Coach – The feeling's mutual young dawg.

D. Sykes – So let me ask you, after all these years why have you choosen now to break your silence?

Coach – For the longest I would never entertain the thought of putting out a book because to me it's like dry-snitchin' in a sense. I know that people read them for entertainment and excitement, but we're not the only ones tuned in, feel me?

D. Sykes – So, why now?

Coach – I just believe that the record needs to be set straight on a lot of things. And the only way to do that is for me to speak – when real nuccas speak, muthafuckas tend to listen. For me it's the lesser of two evils. I am not doing a tell-all book like some other rats did and have all my men indicted. Nah, I am helping you with a fictitious story line.

D. Sykes – WOW! I love this shit, keep going please.

Coach – Like Eminem, he's not from Detroit. He got the whole world thinking we're on some clown shit in the 'D.' Nuccas don't battle rap in Detroit. That's not our sound or swagger. We promote real nuccas like Rock Bottom, Chedda Boyz, Street-lordz – real nucca shit. Em, ain't did nothin' for the 'D' besides put them D12 clowns on and

Obie Trice garbage ass. 8 Mile is not the heart of Detroit like nuccas seem to think. It's borderline for the other folks and their suburbs.

D. Sykes – So, Em, is not from Detroit?

Coach – Young dawg, don't sit there and try to keep a bias standpoint on this shit. You from the 'D" and you know dawg is from Ferndale, Michigan.

D. Sykes – (laughing)

Coach – You got me soundin' like the 'mad rapper' and shit. (laughing) But nah, on a more personal level as to why I decided to share my story, I wanted it to be told accurately. When I die, I don't want nuccas who've never met me doing documentaries on me, lying and shit... that shit irks me when I watch these documentaries on fallen soldiers, and nuccas be tellin' the life story of that man. How you gone tell a man's story unless you've walked in his shoes, felt his pain, and saw things the way he did? You can't create reasoning as to why a man lived the way he did, and that's why I'm giving you my own story from start to finish.

D. Sykes – So, let me ask you – who's the King of Detroit? (Long Pause)

D. Sykes – I never once heard you personally claim that title, the streets crowned you. But I, along with millions of readers want to know who is the real King of Detroit???

Coach – I am!

D. Sykes – Well, then take us back down memory lane.

Chapter One

-1987-

I remember the last time I saw my father alive, that day will forever be stuck in my memory. We were sitting at a red light on 7 Mile and Conant with the top down on my Pop's new triple black Benz. We were listening to Frankie Beverly and Mayes, sounds pumpin', when out of nowhere a black van rammed us from behind. An old silver Chrysler pulled on the driver's side and tried boxing us in, but just as two masked gunmen exited the van, the light turned green and Pops smashed out, jumping the curb and making a hard right turn down Conant.

"Get down!" King David yelled, pushing me down.

The gunmen let off a few shots, one hitting the dashboard and another cracking the windshield. Pops lifted the top on the Benz while plotting our escape route. Seeing that the Chrysler was only a few cars behind and the van not too far behind them, Pops smashed the gas trying to get enough distance to make a turn down a side street.

"Son listen, I am going to turn this next corner, and when I do, I want you to jump out," Pops said scanning the rearview mirror.

"I'm not leaving you," I said. My heart was racing.

"Coach, now isn't the time. I am not about to chance letting anything happen to you." Pops bent the corner doing damn near fifty, he slammed on the brakes and came to a violent stop. "Go! Go!" he yelled.

"I don't want to," I said refusing to get out of the car.

"Coach, get the fuck out of the car now!" he yelled. Pops reached over to open my door and pushed me out of the car. I landed on my side and by this time the old Chrysler and black van were bending the corner.

"Run Coach!" yelled Pops.

I hesitated because I didn't want to leave my father. Although there wasn't much I could do besides die with him, I was willing to do that.

"Got damn it Coach, run!" Pops yelled while looking back. I reluctantly got up, turned and started running. It was too late, the Chrysler had boxed Pops in and the gunmen in the van were out, guns drawn. I stopped at the corner and hid behind some bushes as I watched the men snatch Pops out of the car and drag him to the van at gun point. They threw him in the back, then sped off with the Chrysler in tow.

That was the last time I saw my father alive. And I have to live with the fact that I cost him his life by hesitating. If I had followed his instructions and just ran he would have had enough time to get away as well.

*****

"You peon muthafuckas think ya'll gone get away with snatchin' me. Do you know who the fuck I am?"

"Yeah, a dead man," one of the masked gunmen jokingly said.

"Muthafucka, I'm King David!"

"Yeah, and I'm King Tut. Why don't you just shut the fuck up and accept the fact that yo' ass 'bouts to die."

The black van pulled into the driveway of an abandoned two- family flat on the east side of Detroit. The van stopped at the side door of the house and one of the gunmen slid the door open on the van.

"Ya'll ready for this bitch?" he asked.

"Yeah, bring his ass down in the basement," a man standing in the doorway demanded.

"Come on bitch, show time."

Two gunmen snatched King David up and escorted him into the house and down into the basement. It was pitch dark down there the only light was the sun rays peeking through the dusty windows. It smelled like death down there. Needles, empty beer cans, dirty soiled mattresses, clothes, etc. cluttered the basement, giving it a musty smell. The gunmen escorted King David to a wooden chair and pushed him down in it.

"Tie his ass up," one man ordered.

Two masked men immediately began wrapping rope around KD's skinny frame.

"You lollypop ass nuccas really think ya'll gone get away with this. As soon as my man finds out I'm missin', the city will be shut down," KD snapped confidently.

"And who is your man?" asked one of the masked men.

"I'm certain you've heard of him, Dump."

"Dump? You hear this old clown nucca. He thinks Dump is going to save him." Everyone started laughing.

"So you think Dump is going to save you, huh?" asked the masked man, as he peeled off his mask, which had been muffling his voice.

King David's eyes damn near popped out his head at the sight standing before him. His entire body was filled with rage and disbelief. He couldn't believe what he was seeing. It was his right hand man, Dump. The very man he thought was going to save his life.

"Why Dump?" asked King David.

"Question is, why not?" Your time is over, been over but your bitch ass refused to pass the torch so, I'm taking it."

"What do you want" asked King David.

"What I have always wanted for you to see me as the king. I could have just had them kill you but I needed for you to know who dethroned you."

"So, what's next, Dump?"

"For you to call me King."

"I will never call you King. You are a snake and I fault myself for not seeing this coming."

"Oh, you will call me 'King Dump' one way or another. We're going to start with your fingers, one by one we're going to chop 'em off. And then we'll work on the toes and so forth. But you will honor me before you die. Grab that saw and bring it over here," ordered Dump.

One of his flunkies quickly retrieved the power saw and handed it over to Dump. The saw made a violent screeching sound as it came to life.

"You hear that?" Dump asked while squeezing the saw's trigger. "Now tell me, what's my name?" he asked while lowering the saw to King David's right foot.

"Clown," King David answered.

"Wrong answer," Dump said, then pressed the spinning blade against the bone of King David's big toe. Blood shot everywhere as Dump forced the blade through.

"Ahh…" screamed King David in agony. His big toe now sat in front of him, the bone could be seen where it was disconnected, and blood continued to spurt in all directions.

"Just think, only nine more to go," Dump taunted.

"Now let's try again. What' my name?"

"Coward!" yelled King David, as he spit in Dump's face.

"Pull his pants down," ordered Dump. "Pull 'em all the way down, his boxers too."

"What you gone do now, suck my dick!" snapped King David as he sat there exposed for all to see.

"Nah, bitch. Keith, grab his dick and hold it up."

"What?" Keith asked in disbelief, not wanting to touch another man's dick.

"Just do what the fuck I said," yelled Dump. He was getting frustrated. All he wanted was the respect of the streets. He had managed to turn Keith and a few other workers under him against King David. Keith reluctantly grabbed a hold of King David's manhood and tried not to make eye contact with him.

"That's right, Keith, do as you're told. I knew you were a spineless-snake-coward-bitch nucca. I should have killed…"

        The sound of the saw and sudden pain cut King David's sentence short. I mean literally cut it short. He was in so much pain that all he could do is hope for death. Dump held King David's dick in his hand, which was now detached. He held it up in the air, and then said, "You are no longer a man. You are a bitch to the highest power," he said, then burst out into a sinister laugh.

Dump slapped King David hard across the face with his own dick. "You may never call me King, but your son lil' Coach, I will definitely be his King. Finish this bitch off," Dump ordered as he handed the saw to Keith.

Just like that, Dump crowned himself the new King. He had waited long enough for his opportunity to take over and today was that day. He exited the basement as King Dump, while his best friend and boss screamed in severe agony as

Keith and the gang finished torturing him. They cut all his toes and fingers off, and severed his head, arms and legs. Dump left orders to box up King David's body parts and have them delivered to the streets in broad daylight. Dump wanted to send a clear message that he was the new King.

Chapter Two

I ran full speed back up to 7 Mile and Conant to Church's Chicken on the corner. I picked up the pay phone and tried calling home but the phone just rang and rang. "Come on, pick up," I said as the voicemail picked up for the fifth time. I slammed the phone down, angry with tears in my eyes from not knowing what to do. I took a deep breath and pulled myself together, now was not the time to be folding, King David needed me. I scanned the parking lot and spotted a Checker cab, startling the Arab driver as I banged on the driver side window. He cracked the window just enough to speak, "Yes, can I help you?"

"Can you take me to Caldwell Street?" I asked.

"Do you have money?" the cab driver asked.

I pulled out two crispy twenties and watched as the driver's eyes lit up. He turned the key to start the cab. "Get in. Get in, I drive you."

We lived about twenty miles from Church's Chicken and the cab driver was trying to run up the meter driving slow as shit. We must've gotten caught by every light on 7 Mile. As we pulled onto my street, I could see a lot of cars down near my house and the street was blocked off making it impossible for us to get down the street. I gave the driver both twenties and then jumped out, "Thanks." I ran full speed non-stop, all the way to my house. Police cars and yellow tape from the crime unit had my house blocked off. I tried crossing the tape when a young officer grabbed my arm. "Where do you think you're going, young man?"

"I live here. That's my house," I said trying to move past the officer, but he had a firm grip.

"Just calm down and let me try and locate the owner, but you cannot pass this tape, it's a crime scene."

I could see a large brown box with blood stains sitting in our front lawn but I didn't pay it much attention 'cause I was desperately trying to locate my mother, so I could let her know about my dad. A few moments later, I saw my mother being escorted to a squad car by a female officer. My mom was hysterical. She was screaming and crying at the top of her lungs.

"Ma!" I yelled out.

The officer took his eyes off me for a brief second, which was all I needed. I bolted towards my mom full speed. She turned to face me then met me half way with open arms.

"Corey, baby, are you okay?" she asked a bit relieved after examining me from head to toe. My dad and I had just left the house. We left together, so Ma was concerned.

"Ma, they took dad," I said softly.

"I know baby," she said crying then pulled me close to her.

"I know," she sobbed.

"Is he okay, where is he Ma?" I asked.

"No. Why?" Mom screamed. She went back into a trance. I thought she was having a nervous breakdown out there. She fell to both knees and kept banging on the ground cursing God, asking "Why?"

A female officer helped mom up to her feet and carefully escorted her to an awaiting squad car. I felt absolutely helpless as I watched my mom breakdown. I had never seen her cry a day before in my life.

My mom was the most beautiful woman you'd ever meet. I mean inside and out. Moms was a petite red bone with short black wavy hair, who stayed laced in nothing but the best, courtesy of Pops, King David. She was in her early 30's and had this I'm young forever attitude. She wouldn't let me call her Ma too often; she said it made her feel old. We were on some first name basis shit. She made me and all my friends call her by her government, Tina. But Ma Dukes was my dawg, she always had my back and treated me like a brother rather than a son.

When I was 10, she started letting me hit the weed with her. She said she'd rather I smoke with her at home than to be out getting high doing some bullshit. We just had that relationship most nuccas wish they had with their Moms. Moms was a rider too. She bust her gun and was a natural born hustla, which is why King David nabbed her in the first place. It was Ma Dukes who introduced King David to his coke and heroin connect in Cali, which is where Ma Dukes is originally from. Pops was out in Cali looking for some work back in the 70's when he met Ma Dukes at a strip club. Ma Dukes used to strip back in the day and I guess she put that pussy on Pops just right 'cause, when he left Cali, he took Moms back to Detroit with him, her and two bricks of work. They've been on some Bonnie and Clyde shit ever since. They had me a few years later, I'm the only child.

*****

I was standing there in our front lawn watching all the movement, when I saw a crime unit open that brown box and started taking pictures from different angles. I saw what appeared to be an arm, and my stomach touched my ass as I feared the worst. I looked closer and swallowed hard, not wanting to accept what my eyes were seeing. It was an arm, that of my father. I knew it was him by the distinct tattoo he had on his forearm, which read 'King David' with two arrows on each end, one facing up and the other one down. The arrows symbolized the game. King David said that 'the same nuccas you see at the top will be the same nuccas you see at the bottom.' Each time I thought about that metaphor, it meant something different every time.

This can't be, I told myself. My daddy, was a warrior, he didn't go out that easy. But there was no denying it I knew that tattoo from anywhere and the light brown skin of King David's, which was identical to mine. I couldn't hold my stomach from the sight, my knees buckled as I threw up everything that I had eaten in the past two days. My best friend Rocko slid past the tape and rushed to my side. "Coach man, get up," he said trying to pull me to my feet, but I was still throwing up my guts. "Come on Coach, I got you man." Rocko was my dawg for real. We had been best friends since birth. We were the same age and our birthdays were only two days apart, mine on the 26th of February and his on the 28th. Growing up, we always celebrated our birthdays together. All the girls in school thought we were brothers because we somewhat favored both standing at 5'10" and weighed about 160 pounds soak and wet. Rocko was a little darker than me though, but other than that we could definitely pass for brothers. We both wore our hair in low fades with the pencil waves courtesy of 'Murray's' grease.

King David and Rocko's dad, Dump, were stick-men. They had the same relationship Rocko and I had.

When you saw one, the other one wasn't too far away, which is why I couldn't understand how something like this could happen and to my dad, he was King David. They had just snatched him not even two hours ago, and yet he beat me home in a box. "Where was everybody when all this was going on?" I asked myself.

     We lived dead center on the block in a ridiculously renovated house with about ten additions and four extra garages. King David owned the entire street both sides of the block and four houses were fenced in together with ours in the middle. A Pit-bull kennel was out back with at least thirty dogs. We had modern security surveillance cameras posted throughout the block and our house, not to mention all the workers on the block who were holding heat. Then on the opposite side of the street, Dump had a similar setup with his house sitting directly across from ours. So I couldn't understand how nuccas would feel comfortable enough to hit the block and leave a box with King David in it. I could hear the husky voice of Dump nearing as I sat on my knees still puking.

"Let me through, this is my brother's house!" Dump demanded.

"Dad, over here!" yelled Rocko.

"They killed KD, dad. Somebody pulled up and sat this box on the grass, and peeled off," Rocko said giving Dump a brief run down.

"I know son," Dump softly said. He kneeled down and picked me up and pulled me close to his large frame. He hugged me tight and rubbed my head as if I were his very own son. "I swear to you, Coach, I'm going to find who did this, that, I promise you. You know unck has never lied to you, right?" Dump asked now crying his heart out.

"They killed my daddy." I sobbed into Dump's chest.

"It's gone be alright. Unck, is going to handle everything. Come on, let's go across the street."

We walked across the street to Dump's crib where everybody was gathered. I couldn't help but think, where were all you nosy muthafuckas when those nuccas threw my daddy's body out here.

"It's gone be alright Coach, baby. Auntie is here for you," Kathy said while rocking me back and forth in her arms on the sofa. We were all seated in the front room, nobody saying much with the exception of Dump. He paced back and forth barking orders into the cordless phone he held. "I want every nucca on the block suited and fuckin' booted in ten minutes!" he said, then slammed the phone down on the glass coffee table. "Kathy, take Coach in the back and wash him up," Dump ordered.

Kathy was Dump's latest broad he was fuckin' and sponsoring. She was at least twenty years younger than him and the only reason she was dealing with Dump was on the strength of his money. Kathy was a bad little bitch; chocolate skin, long black silky hair, tight stomach, fat ass, big titties and a pretty face. She was your typical bad hood bitch who had fallen on hard times and was looking for the highest bidder to take care of her ass.

Dump stood 6'8" and weighed every bit of 350 pounds. He was not at all in shape, his stomach protruded over his pants, he had rolls on his back and neck, and his hygiene was never on point. Dump was black as they came and ugly as hell. God must have been in a bad mood when he made Dump, cause his ass was not a sight you'd want to see. Rocko really lucked out not receiving Dump's genes. I guess he took after his Moms, but I never met Rocko's old bird, she supposedly died in a car accident when we were babies. Dump got his name from killin' nuccas and dumping their bodies in the river over the Belle Isle Bridge. He was King David's right hand and under boss. They grew up in the very houses that they lived in and been friends like Rocko and I since day one.

"Come on Coach, let me run your bath," Kathy said pulling me up from the sofa.

I was like a zombie. I didn't care nothing about taking no bath, but I was too drained to argue, so I reluctantly followed Kathy into the back and into the bathroom. Kathy closed the door behind me and locked it, then started running the water. She began removing my clothes starting with my shirt and then pants. "Don't be shy now, Coach, take off your drawers, the water is almost ready," she said.

I was only twelve at the time but I knew all about pussy. King David used to pay strippers to suck my dick and to fuck me. I was too young to bust a nut, but I was gettin' it in and my lil' dick would rock up in a minute. I had my eye on Kathy's little ass since Dump started fuckin' with her and she would always playfully flirt with me and Rocko, telling us we were scared of pussy.

"I'm gone get in with you," she said dropping her silk house robe to the floor. She was ass naked and smelled like a fresh rose. She seductively climbed into the whirlpool style tub and dipped her entire body into the water, then stood up covered in soap suds. "You comin' Coach, Dump told me to wash you up," she said softly. "Why you shy? I'll turn my head," she said, then turned and started messing with the radio. Keith Sweat's crying ass came pouring out of the speakers. I quickly pulled down my boxer shorts and stepped out of them, as I lifted my head Kathy was staring right at my shit. "Hmm. How old are you, Coach?" she asked jokingly.

I wasn't at all ashamed of my blessing 'cause for my age I was well developed. I climbed in the tub a little tensed, as Kathy noticed.

"Relax Coach," she said pulling me towards her, then turning me around. I sat between her legs while she softly scrubbed my back with a sponge, then reached around and washed my chest.

I'm lying there with my back against her chest with my eyes closed head to the ceiling, thinking about all that has happened. Kathy wrapped her thick legs around my waist and rubbed her soft fingers across my face. She whispered in my ear sincerely "You're the next King, Coach."

Chapter Three

"Run!" My father's voice echoed in my head, as the event played back in my mind for the thousandth time. "No... No..."

"Coach, man wake up," Rocko shook me, trying to wake me.

I jumped up, eyes bucked like I'd just seen death.

"Calm down, my nucca. You was just having a bad dream. Get yourself together, my dad wants to see you, he's waiting outside," said Rocko.

"A'ight, give me a minute," I said breathing hard as if I were really running. I was hoping Rocko was right about me only having a bad dream and that none of this was really true. All that hope died as I walked out the front door and saw the yellow crime tape, which still surrounded my house. It was morning though, I must have slept the night through after Kathy gave me that hot bath.

"Come on Coach!" Dump yelled through the car window after hitting his horn, which broke my trance.

Dump never talked, he was always yelling. I guess that was his way of communicating and it worked 'cause when his big musty ass yelled, nuccas straighten up and paid close attention. I climbed in the passenger side of Dump's 1500 Suburban which was triple black. All he drove was trucks 'cause he was too big for anything else. He left all the sports cars to King David.

"How ya doing?" Dump asked almost empathetically. I just blew out some air in frustration while shaking my head.

"Didn't I tell you that Unck was going to find out who did this and take care of it?"

I was all ears as I turned to face Dump.

"Well, I got 'em," Dump said.

"Who?" I asked desperately.

"Let's take a ride," Dump said before turning the key and pulling away from the curb.

Within minutes, we were pulling in front of this large abandoned two family flat on Charest Street just a few blocks over from where King David was kidnapped. A bunch of late model cars lined the street. I recognized nearly all of them. Keith's black El Dog was parked next door, Cane's black Volvo was behind Nate's black Jeep. All my dad's crew drove black cars with nothing extra. The side door of the house swung open as Dump and I walked up the driveway. It was Keith standing with the door ajar.

"What's he doing here?" Keith asked Dump looking down at me.

"Revenge!" Dump answered brushing past Keith and down into the basement of the house.

"You coming?" asked Keith, as I stood there. Without answering I followed Dump downstairs to see all the owners of the late model cars out front. They were all chit-chatting amongst each other but ceased at the sight of me.

"Coach?" Cane said as if it were a question. I was now standing in the center of the basement with all eyes focused on me. I was just as much surprised as to why I was there as them.

"Turn that light on," Dumped ordered.

As the light came on, I saw a man sitting in a chair tied up at the waist and around the ankles. His head was covered with a bloody white pillow case.

"Now that we're all here. Let us proceed with why I called this meeting. First as we know, King David is dead. Now is not the time to grieve nor whimper, but to avenge KD in the best fashion I know how, murder," Dump said as he then snatched the pillow case from the man's head.

I couldn't believe my eyes, it was Craig; the very man who practically raised me. King David brought Craig home into our family when my mom gave birth to me. Craig was an all-around nanny so to speak. He cooked, cleaned, helped me with school work, drove me to school, even taught me how to shoot ball.   He was like my big brother. All Craig cared about as compensation was crack. King David kept him with plenty of it to tend to the family and Pit-bull farm. He even built Craig a guest house out back next to our in-ground pool. 'What was Craig doing here, and why was he beaten up and gagged?' I asked myself before trying to rush over to him. "Craig!" I yelled with tears now in my eyes. I don't think Craig could hear me 'cause he had been beaten pretty bad, his head was all swollen and he looked dazed. Dump grabbed me by the shoulder and pulled me back. "Coach," he said holding me close to him. He knew how much I loved Craig. "You hear me, Coach?   This is the man who killed your Pops ..." Dump said. I blanked out as he continued to talk into my ear almost hypnotizing me, but I refused to believe it. Craig would never do anything to hurt King David. Why would he?

"This is the man who killed your father, Coach. Look at him the very man who lived under the same roof and ate off the same plate as blood. But we're going to make it right," Dump said pulling a chrome 45 from his pants. He reached around leaning down over me and put the gun in my hand. With his hand still on mine, he raised the gun and pointed it at Craig's head.

My heart was beating a million miles a second, tears running down my face with fear, hate, and confusion in my heart. "This is the man who killed your daddy, Coach. So you're going to kill him," Dump whispered in my ear infuriating me further. Craig appeared to be coming to his senses after Keith doused him with a bucket of cold water. His mouth was duck taped shut, but he began tryna' mumble his last words, as if to try and tell me something. His eyes delivered his message.

"All you gotta do is squeeze the trigger, Coach, and he's dead. Make your father proud Coach.

I closed my eyes to block having to see Craig, then squeezed the trigger. "Boom!" The blast from the gun shot was the only thing I heard. I didn't open my eyes to see if in fact I had killed Craig, I just turned and walked toward the steps and out of the basement.

"That's right young Coach!" Nate hollered out as I exited the house.

Dump was still inside.

⁎ ⁎ ⁎ ⁎ ⁎ ⁎

"Dump man, what were you thinking bringing Coach down here and to have him do that? Don't you think he's going to tell?" Keith asked.

"Yeah, for real Dump, he's only a kid," said Cane.

"Listen to you scared nuccas. Coach ain't gone tell shit. Tell who? Ya'll some slow muthafuckas. Ya'll still don't get it, do you? I had Coach kill Craig for two reasons. One, Craig was in the way and he would have never crossed King David in a million years. Two, Coach will now love me. I found the nucca who killed his father. Not to mention settling any suspicion nuccas might have had. We just killed two birds with one stone. Or should I say bullet. You hear that, you bird ass nucca!" Dump said laughing while looking down on Craig's dead body. The impact from the blast knocked him back on the floor. The top part of his head was now missing. Keith and Cane joined in on the laughter.

"Man, ya'll clean this shit up. I'ma go make sure our lil' man is okay," Dump ordered, leaving Keith, Cane and Nate to clean up the dirty work.

"Yeah, just remind me to stay in good grace with yo' treacherous ass," Nate joked, as Dump walked up the stairs. That was music to Dump's ears. He loved the newfound power and the fact that his plan was coming all the way together.

*****

"Don't sweat it, Coach, I did the same thing too after I killed my first mothafucka," Dump advised. He was standing over me as I threw up my lungs. "Come on, we gotta get going," Dump said. I pulled myself together as best I could, then followed Dump to the truck.

For a while, we just rode in silence. Dump kept looking over at me, though, asking if I was cool. "Yeah, I'm good," I lied.

"Listen Coach, your dad would be proud of you. Today you became a man, you hear me?"

I didn't know how killing somebody made you a man, but I wasn't about to interrupt Dump's speech either. "That slimy mothafuckin' crackhead, Craig, killed your dad over some peanuts. He was tryna' run off with ya'll money and cover his tracks. I never did trust his ass. I tried warning David, but he insisted that Craig was loyal. Shit, ain't no crackhead loyal to nothin' except his pipe. And you remember that shit Coach. Had your dad listened to me, he would still be here with us today. God knows, blood couldn't make us any closer, but it was KD's way or no way. But Coach you're not like your dad in that respect. You have always had your own mind which is why your dad nicknamed you Coach, 'cause you would always call the play."

I started day-dreaming after hearing that, because it brought me back to when I was a litlle fella. One day I asked my dad why he didn't make me his Jr. I thought maybe he had another son or something, but Pops told me I was nobody's follower, not even his. He told me I was bred to lead, so he dubbed me Coach. He would always let me make decisions on whatever we were doing, whether it was business or not. He would say, "Coach, call the play." I guess that was his way of molding my judgment and letting me be my own man.

"You hear me talkin' to you Coach?" Dump asked. "What do you want to eat?" We were sitting at the drive-thru window of Coney Island.

"Huh… get me chili fries and a Coke," I said snapping out of my trance.

"That's all you want? You gots to start eating, Coach, or you're going to be little as hell just like your old man," Dump joked, then ordered our food. We rode around for hours while Dump told story after story about he and my father coming up in the game. He got so emotional that he started crying. I couldn't believe my eyes, I had never seen Dump show compassion for no one, not even Rocko. Dump always showed one face, his killer grill and an occasional smile, which was still a bit intimidating. When Dump laughed, even if the shit wasn't funny, nuccas around would laugh too, not wanting to challenge Dump in any way.

"I love you like a son, Coach," Dump said reaching over putting his arm around me, then pulling me close to him. He kissed me on the forehead and just held me. "Unck is going to take care of everything, so don't you worry," he said.

I hadn't felt that safe since the last time I saw my father alive, and I believed him.

Chapter Four

I had never seen so many Caddys before in my life, there must have been a mile long of assorted Lacs of all flavors. Players from all over the city and mid-west had come to lay King David to rest in the highest fashion. Today was the funeral, but it seemed more like a fashion show than anything. Nuccas were hopping out in full length minks, three-piece suits, black gators, Dobs and enough jewelry to open a pawn shop. The majority of these funny dressin' ass nuccas I had never seen before, but I guess King David knew them.

The funeral was held by King David's request, at Belle Isle, which is an island off downtown Jefferson Ave. that everybody goes to hang out at in the summer to cruise, show off their whip and pick up chicks. Apparently, King David told my mom about his wishes a long time ago 'cause he never mentioned it to me. It made sense though because King David never went to church and didn't allow my mom to take me. He thought church was one big concert. You pay to get in and for your money they put on a show and sell you hope. So, I could hear Pops now, 'I wasn't born in no church, so I damn sure ain't leaving in one.' Pops was funny as hell, Moms called him Kool Silly. The thought put a smile on my face as I sat there in my chair eyes closed head to the sky. The sun was beaming down as it was a beautiful day in July. The slight breeze coming off the river made the sun bearable.

My mom and I were seated directly in front of King David's solid gold casket with the letters 'King David' engraved in black old English letters. Dump, Keith, Cane, Nate and Rocko were also seated in the front row. This was the only real family King David knew. His parents had passed long before I was even thought of and like me, he was an only child. He used to always tell me from time to time, we'd be riding and smoking joints and he'd just feel the need to school me. One of his key principles was family. He believed that just because a person is born into your family doesn't mean ya'll will remain family. He'd look over high and cool, then say "Coach, sometimes in life a man has to make his own family."

I tried to keep from looking at his casket because it brought me back to seeing his arm sticking out of that box. It was a closed casket, so I couldn't help but wonder how they had arranged his parts or did they even bother. My mom had her arm wrapped around my shoulder, while rocking back and forth. Since there was no viewing of the body, Dump had life sized portraits blown up, depicting King David's life in the game and as a family man. There were eight pictures posted, four on each side of King David's casket. There was this one picture that I had never seen before of my father holding me in his arms in the hospital after Moms gave birth to me. The smile on King David's face was that of a man who had just struck the lotto. Man, I missed him. I was lost going back down memory lane thinking about all the good times we had. My dad was the absolute best; there were no bad times because he saw to it that first Moms and I were taken care of. Not just money or material things, but making time for the family. He was true to his principles about family. I don't ever recall him and Moms having no big arguments. King David had everything under control, so there was never anything to argue about, that's why he was King.

I had heard just about every story there was on how my dad was a real playa, solid stand up man, friend, comrade, and yes, King. Nuccas were now sharing stories reflecting on how they came to know King David. A lot of them nuccas were lying just for the sake of wanting to be seen and heard. 'I never heard my father make mention of none of these peons,' I thought to myself. My mom declined to speak, as did I because what I had to say was for my dad only. I wasn't making a speech to a bunch of strangers, but the moment everyone else had been waiting on had arrived. Dump took to the podium and began his long heartfelt eulogy.

I paid close attention to Dump's every word because for a minute my Pops was living again. I knew what Dump was saying was true and accurate as he went back down memory lane. He told the story of how he and my father robbed Pick and Save Grocery Market back in the day. Dump also told how Pops shot the old Arab owner in the ass as they fled with a bag of cash, and they were chased by an undercover off duty cop who caught King David while Dump got away. King David took the wrap on the chin and did a five year bid as a result. Dump laughed as he explained what he thought to be a bag full of money, was actually a dummy bag because the owner was smart enough to make up a bunch of fake stacks of hundred dollar bills with white paper between each stack. The real money was in the freezer, he later found out. I had heard that story a million times from both Dump and King David, and it was still as live as the first time I heard it. Together they dubbed that move 'Dummy mission', and since then nuccas would say, "Don't have us on no damn dummy mission." Dump kept it together, not wanting to show that side of compassion he had shown me days earlier. Whenever his voice quivered, he'd take a sip of water, clear his throat, and then finish speaking.

King David must've thought about death a lot cause it seemed as though he had his planned out. He left strict instructions to Moms and Dump not to bury him in no damn cemetery. He said that he didn't want to be buried next to some nucca he didn't know. "Send me out in style."

What he had in mind was how King used to do it back in the day, but first, it was the reception. King David told Moms that the reception came before the burial. What he meant was if there was going to be a party, he didn't want to miss it. Dump went all out for the reception, he flew King David's favorite band in to perform live 'Frankie Beverly and Mayes.' They were set up right next to King David's casket, as they played hit after hit, starting with the very song we had been listening to while sitting at the light right before King David was kidnapped. *'We Are One,'* they sang, sounding just like the original cut. Then 'Joy and Pain, it's like sunshine ….and rain.' I could hear King David's light voice singing along and ballroom dancing with a cool smile on his face.

My mom escorted me to the dance floor so we could step to the music. She would always throw on some classic oldies but goodies and start steppin' right there in our living room. She'd have her brown liquor, a joint and Newports –

couldn't tell her nothin'. I'd come in from playing and she'd grab me, then we'd start steppin'. She taught me how to ballroom dance when I was five years old. I hadn't seen much of my mom in the past week. She had been locked in her room grieving hard. I felt so helpless not being able to do anything to help her. So, I did what was best, which was to allow her time and space to grieve. Moms almost looked her normal self as she gave me the golden smile with a wink. That made me feel so much better, just knowing that she was going to be alright. That's what her wink meant, that 'I'm alright, baby.'

"You're so handsome, Corey," she said smiling. Only Moms called me Corey. "You look just like your daddy twenty years ago when we first met," she said leading our steps.

"Ma, what do you think dad's doing right now?"

"Knowing your daddy, he's somewhere on this dance floor ballroomin'," Ma said, then closed her eyes.

Nuccas partied til the sun began to set, which was the scheduled time to send King David out in style like the true King he was. Everybody gathered around the shoreline of the river facing Canada, while we waited on King David's casket to be carried over. Dump, Keith, Cane, Nate, Trey and Skip were the pallbearers. They carried King David's casket over to the shoreline and placed him on a wooden raft, like you'd see in Africa on the Discovery channel. There were flowers and pictures which covered the raft, and people were placing single roses on top of the casket as King David set out on the river.

Dump did a final toast, not a drinking toast but a playa's toast, "We lived a fast pace life with no regrets;

poppin' tags and cashin' checks, full length minks, gator boots, hoppin' out of Lacs spendin' hoe money, and talkin' shit. From Detroit to the moon, baby, you the best. We did it all, everything except death. That's why we're gathered here today, to send a playa' out in style. So may you rest."

They lowered King David all the way into the water, then lit a fire around the four corners of the raft. The sun had set beautifully giving off an orange beam of rays, which reflected off the river. Dump did the honors of pushing King David out into the river. We all watched as King David coasted into the setting of the sun. My mom and I stood there until we could no longer see King David's raft. The fire was set, so that the raft would dismantle and the weight of the casket would cause it to sink. King David wanted to be buried in the water cause he believed that there was life in water.

"You a'ight, my nucca?" Rocko asked comin' up from behind.

People had started to leave, so Moms was being courteous by thanking everyone for coming out. She left me standing at the river.

"I'm good," I said turning to face Rocko.

"Just checkin' on you. You know I got your back for life, right?"

"No doubt," I said hitting rocks with Rocko.

"So, when you gone come hang with the crew? We ain't seen you since all this happened. You see , Rome and Dirty Black on deck. Nuccas missin' you, dawg."

Rome, and Dirty Black were standing nearby waiting on Rocko to call them over. We were all crew, but it was understood that my stickman was Rocko. And the rest of the crew wanted to make sure everything was straight before they holla'd, so they sent Rocko to holla' first. He waved them over. "What up dough, my nucca," Rome said giving me dap. Rome was the pretty boy of the crew. He was high yellow with green eyes and had good hair. He was on his Chico Debarge shit, always in the mirror changing clothes like he was a professional model working the runway. Whenever we hit the mall and saw some pretty girls, we'd send Rome's pretty ass to holla' first. And if the girls were on some not feeling us shit, we'd sick lil' Pimp on their ass. This nucca swore up and down he had the blood of a pimp. But the funny thing is, nobody in his family was a pimp. He had studied enough pimp flicks such as 'The Mack and 'Dolemite' to where he had that pimp talk down to a science. If the girls weren't feeling us, he'd go into pimp mode snapping on the girls' clothing, shoes, hair, whatever wasn't up to par, he was cracking on it. He was the youngest in the crew and the shortest. He wore his hair permed and always had on some dressy shit. We'd tease his ass on the daily about wearing his church clothes on the block and to school. "Pimpin'," he said with rhythm.

And then there was Dirty Black. Black got his full alias because growing up he was a dirty mothafucka. He wore the same clothes damn near every day, and his house was filthy. The crew never made fun of him, though, since he was our nucca, plus his ass could scrap. I have seen Black get into fights with grown men and held his own and sometimes even won. I wasn't sure exactly how old Black's ass was, I just know he was at least five years older than Rocko and me. He had been left back so many times, he was in the seventh grade when I was in the second and

Rocko and I caught up to his ass. It didn't matter though, Black was our man and if you tried one, you had to see all of us. We would all pitch in me, Rocko, Rome, and Lil' Pimp to buy Black clothes and shoes whenever we hit the mall, so when we went out we'd all be fresh. We hung out so much together that people in the hood and at school started calling us them 'Zone Nuccas'. That was the name of our hood 'The Zone.'

"What up with ya'll nuccas over there acting all shy and shit. I ain't seen not one of ya'll get on none of these young hot and ready," I said laughing, trying to lighten up the mood and to let the crew know the boy was good.

"You know Pimpin' got some numbers. A hoe ain't gone do but one or two thangs," Lil' Pimp said.

"Oh yeah, and what's that?" I asked, waiting 'cause I knew he had something slick to say.

"Bitch gone choose or lose," said Lil' Pimp

We all bust out laughing with the exception of Lil' Pimp. He was dead serious with his pimpin'.

"This nucca lying, he got no number and the bitch was retarded and ugly," Black said.

"It is seven digits in a number, you simple muthafucka, and baby girl recognized the presence of a pimp and couldn't help herself. Shit, long as she pay like she weigh, she on the team," snapped Rome, while shaking his head, making his perm bounce.

"That's right Pimp, talk that shit," I laughed.

It felt good to have my nuccas around me. They were my family.

Chapter Five

With King David gone, the house just seemed empty and dead. He was the life of everyone. Every morning before he hit the streets, King David would fix us breakfast. I'd know it was morning by the aroma coming from the kitchen; grilled onions and bell pepper going into cheese omelets, with Bob Evans beef sausage patties, toast, fruit, and orange juice was how King David laid us out every morning. Today was no different; I was going to keep the tradition of us eating breakfast together going. I watched and sometimes helped King David in the kitchen, so fixing everything was not a problem. I put on his signature white chef coat and went to work. By the time I finished setting the table, Moms came walking into the kitchen. I rushed over to pull her chair back, and then gave her a kiss. "Good morning, baby," she said smiling. "What are you doing up so early?" she asked while digging into her omelet.

"Cooking us breakfast! You want some coffee?" I asked while pouring two cups. There was a knock at the door. "I wonder who the hell is up this damn early besides us two," Ma said joking as she tried to get up.

"I'll get it, finish your food," I said as I set the two cups of coffee on the table, then headed for the front door. "Who is it?"

"Uncle Dump, open the door."

"What's up Unck?" I asked after opening the door.

"Just checkin' on you. You a'ight?" he asked, stepping into the house.

"Yeah."

"What's that burning, yo' mom back there cooking? " Dump asked walking toward the kitchen.

I followed him into the back, "Nah, that's my work. Sit down while I fix you a plate."

"Tina, how are you this morning?" Dump asked, as he leaned over to kiss Moms on the forehead.

"Better" Moms answered.

I turned around with Dump's plate in my hand and stopped in my tracks. He was sitting in King David's chair at the head of the table, and for some reason, it angered me.

"Cory, what's wrong?" Moms asked me seeing the look on my face.

Dump turned to face me to see what was going on. I shook my head as if I were shaking off a sudden dizziness. "Nah, I'm okay. Just a little light headed."

"Have you been to sleep since… yesterday?" asked Dump.

"Probably not. I woke up to him in here cookin' us breakfast. You know his daddy used to cook every morning," Moms said.

"I wanted you to take a ride with me Coach, but maybe you should get some rest," Dump said.

"Yeah baby, go take a nap so you don't exhaust yourself. I'll clean up the dishes."

I wasn't in much of a mood to sit out there anyway seeing as though Dump was sitting in King David's chair, and the fact I didn't have the nuts to tell him to get up. "Yeah, I think I'ma go lay down for a while. I'll see you later on, Unck."

"A'ight, baby boy."

I took off King David's chef coat, then hung it up on the rack. I left Moms and Dump to talk while I headed to the movie room. I climbed into my plush leather recliner, which sat right next to King David's identical recliner. I turned on the 54" TV using the remote and pushed play. '*Scarface*', King David's favorite movie was in mid-play at the scene when Tony had Frank killed. King /David and I had been watching the movie for the millionth time, when he got a call. He told me to take a ride with him and paused the movie. That was over a week ago...

*****

"You know I found out who did that to David, right?" Dump said as if it were a question. He and Tina were still having breakfast.

"Who?" Tina asked almost choking on her coffee.

"It's going to hurt you when I tell you. It sure hit me hard when I found out."

"Who, Dump?" demanded Tina.

"Craig."

"Craig, my Craig?" Tina asked in disbelief. She didn't buy it for one minute, but she had been wondering where Craig had disappeared to. And where is he?" asked Tina.

"Well, let's just say that Craig is no longer with us."

Tina just shook her head. She knew her role as a woman and knew never to question a man about his business in detail. But the shit didn't sit right with her. Craig was family, and he had no reason to kill King David, nor the means. Craig was no killer.

"What are you thinking about?" Dump asked grabbing Tina's hand, then began rubbing it softly."

"This is just too much for me right now."

"I know Tina and I'm here for you. If there's anything I can do, I mean anything, don't you hesitate to ask."

"Okay," Tina said shaking her head.

"How are you on money?" asked Dump. He was trying to see if she had found King David's stash or if she already knew where it was.

"I guess I'm alright, but I don't know for how long. I checked David's safe last night and it only had a few thousand in there. I know he's got some money around here somewhere. Do you have any ideas as to where he might've put it?"

"Your guess is as good as mine. You know David as well as I did, and that money could be anywhere. I know he didn't see nothing like this happening, which was probably why he only had some loose change in the safe, and didn't think to tell you where the stash was. And trust me, I know David was holding!" Dump assured. He was jumping for joy on the inside that Tina hadn't found King David's stash because it meant two things, that he stood the chance of finding it, and that eventually Tina would need his help to survive and that would be the day he had his way with her.

Dump had a thing for Tina since the first time he laid eyes on her back when he and King David met her at the strip club in Cali. Dump didn't have the balls to step to Tina 'cause he knew his ass was sincerely ugly. "Look at Red, coming our way," Dump told King David the evening they met Tina.

Tina approached Dump and King David at their V.I.P. table and asked if she could have a dance. Her attention was totally focused on King David. It was always like that, all the women would flock to King David while shunning Dump. But no more…

"I'ma tear this house up later on and see what I turn up," Tina said.

*****

I woke up a few hours later to the sound of NWA blastin' outside in someone's trunk. I could never watch the entire movie '*Scarface*' without falling asleep. King David would get on my case, saying that "This is not a movie, but a lesson." He was always in there studying so he called it, watching '*Godfather*, *Scarface*' and documentaries on old mobsters. The screen was blue cause the movie had ended. I hit the stop button on the DVD, then turned the TV off. I peeked out the window to see all my nuccas and a few hoodrat's. This one girl, Amanda, was out there among the rats, but this girl was no rat. She was the baddest chick I had ever laid eyes on and if she'd just give a nucca the time of day she'd be the baddest chick I ever laid hands on. But she wasn't feelin' the boy like that, I guess 'cause she was three years older than me. She was always coming around there ridin' this nigga Deal$' dick.

"Tina, what are you doing?" I asked Moms. She was in the basement going through a bunch of boxes and rubbing her hands against the smooth walls. "I'm trying to find where yo' daddy put the money. Do you know where it is?" she stopped and asked.

"What money?"

That slight bit of hope Tina had on her face suddenly disappeared. I didn't know where no damn money was. I never had to worry about money. King David gave me plenty every morning. He told me to never go anywhere broke, not even to your grave.

"Don't worry about it, baby," Moms said.

I could tell that something was bothering her, but she didn't want to worry me. "Are you alright?" I asked sincerely.

"Yeah, it'll be alright," Ma said flashing that golden smile that always assured me that she was good.

"A'ight, well I'ma 'bout to step out. I just wanted to let you know before I left. Do you need me to do anything before I go?"

"Nah, but you be careful."

"A'ight," I said kneeling down to kiss Moms on the cheek. By the time I made it outside, Amanda had disappeared. I scanned the crowd of hoodrat's but thre was no sign of Amanda.

"Who you lookin' for, Amanda?" teased Rome. He knew me like a book and he knew how much I liked baby girl.

"Nah, nucca I was lookin' for yo' mommy." I snapped.

"Nucca stop lying, you know yo' ass was lookin' for Amanda. If you hurry you can catch her up on 7 Mile ridin' shotgun with Deal$' lame ass," said Rocko.

I hated the sound of that nucca Deal$' name. The only reason I didn't like the nucca was cause he had my hoe. He didn't pose no real threat, though. He was one of Dump's flunkies. They called him Deal$ cause he always had some type of deal on something and had all kinds of connects.

"Anyway, what up dough?" I said hoping to change the subject.

"Ain't shit," answered Rocko.

"So, why is all these nuccas and hoodrat's on the block?" I asked pointing to all the people.

"Something 'bout a meeting," Rocko said.

"A meeting. What kind of meeting?" I asked.

"Dump's crazy ass called a hood meeting and said for everyone to be out here," advised Rome.

"Yeah, yo' daddy sho' is crazy pullin' me away from my hoes. Don't you know pimpin' is a full time job," said Pimp.

"Nucca the only hoes you got is the ones in yo' socks," snapped Rocko.

We all bust out laughing. Everybody on the block had started moving towards the front porch of Dump's crib. He was standing there with Keith at his right and Cane at his left. The nucca raised his hand as to silence the crowd.

After everyone quieted down, Dump began his speech. "I have called this meeting because as we all know last week we lost King David. He will forever be missed, but as he would have wanted it, the show must go on. So, I am your new King. From now on, you are to address me as King Dump. We will…"

Dump's speech was interrupted by dozens of conversations, whispers and the outburst of Danny. "What you mean, call you King Dump? David is my King. Danny was one of King David's loyalists. He was on King David's payroll as chief of security over the block. Danny's outburst sparked several others to challenge Dump's self appointment as King.

"Who the hell are you to just crown yo' self King? The street gotta crown its own King, just like it did with King David," Barbara snapped. She was an old head hustla' from King David's and Dump's era. She stood almost 6" and weighed about 250 solid. Barb, as we called her, wasn't going for nothin'. "King Dump, ha!" mocked Barb. "I wish I would…" She turned and left and many of her followers did just the same. They followed Barb, leaving Dump on the porch to finish his speech.

Dump had gotten so frustrated by the lack of respect, nuccas waving they hand like 'fuck you', as they left. Dump cut his speech short and walked into his house with Keith and Cane in tow. No sooner than the door shut, Dump was laying down the law. "Ya'll know what to do, so let's get it done!" he ordered.

Chapter Six

I couldn't stop thinking about Dump's speech, nucca had the balls to call himself 'King Dump'. My Pops ain't been dead a good two weeks and Dump was already trying to erase his legacy, that's how I felt hearing Dump's speech. The whole King thing is something that started in the Zone and only existed in the Zone. No one else in Detroit was on no King shit, in every other hood it was the Wild West, every man for himself.

Back when King David and them were coming up, the dudes from that era crowned Pops King 'cause he was the only one making noise in the Zone as far as making some real money. He had organized the Zone into blocks, putting dope houses and hoe houses on each block. It was Pops who gave everybody a roll to play so that they could eat too. Out of respect, nuccas started calling Pops, King David. He was the representative for the Zone. If there was beef with other hoods, it was King David's call to either go to war or play ambassador. And since day one, Dump wanted to be the king.

It was morning and I was in the kitchen doing what I do, putting breakfast together for Moms and me, when the door bell rang. It was Rocko and Black. "What up, dough? What the fuck ya'll doing up so early?" I asked.
"Shit, we came to see what was good with you. But what's that smell, yo' Moms cookin'?" asked Rocko.
"Yeah, that shit smell good as E-mothafucka," Black said rubbing his stomach. My nucca was like a monk or some

shit, he only spoke when it was time to put in some work and time to eat.

Rocko brushed past me with Black on his heels heading straight into the kitchen. They were family, so they were not at all ashamed.

"Hey Tina, how're you this morning?" Rocko asked Moms as he washed his hand, then grabbed a plate. Black did the same.

"Hey Rocko, hey Black," Moms said picking up her coffee cup and standing to her feet.

"Where you going, Tina?" You ain't gotta leave cause of these two bums" I said joking.

"Yeah, for real we ain't nobody, just two hungry souls," laughed Rocko and Black as they chowed down on the scrambled eggs and sausage links.

"Nah, I have to get ready to go. But thanks for breakfast, baby. It was delicious," Moms said giving me a kiss on the cheek before excusing herself.

"So what's up man? I ain't never seen you two nuccas up this early, especially yo' ass, Black."

"This nucca woke me up," Black mumbled with his mouth full.

"I wanted to let you know that we got the green light," Rocko said in between bites.

"Green light to do what?" I asked.

"To hustle," Rocko whispered not wanting Tina to hear him.

"What the fuck is this nucca talkin' 'bout Black?"

Black shrugged his shoulders like 'I don't know.'

"Remember how King David wouldn't let us hold the block down and get our own money?"

"Yeah," I said.

"Well, that shit is over with. Dump gave all the young nuccas in the Zone the green light to hustle."

The sound of Dump's name made my blood boil. "He still on that King Dump shit?" I asked.

"I know, he's tripping with that right? But look at it this way, Coach, we can finally step out of them nuccas shadows."

Everything Rocko was saying was hittin' home cause for the longest, Rocko and I would fantasize about when it would be our time to shine. King David didn't let us hug the block and get money cause he felt like even though we may very well grow up to be hustlers, we still needed to grow up. He often said to youngins on the block who he suspected of part time hustlin', "A'ight now, when that van pull up ya' ass betta be 21 and not twelve and tell."

But now Dump was on some new Zone order shit. And it was killin' me inside, because truth be told, I wanted in. But under no circumstances was I going to call him King Dump.

"So, what you think, you in?" asked Rocko.

"We 'bout to get this paper…" I said rhyming.

"That's what I'm talkin' about. I knew you wouldn't let ya' man down," Rocko said excited.

"What ya'll so geeked up about?" Tina said as she stepped into the kitchen.

"Ain't nothing,'" I said.

"Hmm. Hm. Well, don't let nothin' get ya'll into no shit. I gotta make a run, Corey. If you need anything page me 911," Tina said.

"Where you going with that?" I asked noticing that she was carrying King David's burgundy Cartier jewelry box.

"I'm taking it to get cleaned, then appraised."

"A'ight, see you later on," I said.

 Soon as Moms left, Rocko picked up the cordless phone.
"Time to call some hoes and see what's up for the day," he
said.

"Call Felicia and them," I said.

"You mean Amanda," Rocko joked then began talking into
the phone.

        Felicia was the head hoodrat in the Zone. She was
Barb's oldest daughter and could pass for her twin. Amanda
was Felicia's little cousin and they always hung out, so if
Felicia was coming through, nine times out of ten Amanda
would be in the pack. Rocko hung up the phone and said,
"They on their way through."

"Who?" I asked.

"Felicia and them. We gotta get some new hoes 'cause I'm
tired of fuckin' these same beat down bitches," Rocko said.

"For real," Black added. His ass was the last one who
needed to be complaining. The hoes were only fuckin' with
his ass on the strength of us, that and all the liquor they
could drink.

"But see all that fenna change once we start getting this
money," Rocko said rubbing his hands together. "So let this
be our last time fuckin' with these dusty booty bitches,"
Rocko said raising his glass as to propose a toast.

"Here's to new pussy," he said. We all clicked glasses of
orange juice then repeated after Rocko "New pussy."

We took sips from our glasses, then bust out laughing.

"Let me go get ready," I said excusing myself. I had to
jump fresh if Amanda was gonna be in the spot. I
rummaged through my closet looking for a fresh outfit and

grabbed this brand new royal blue Polo shirt with the white horse. I had copped it a few weeks ago and was supposed to rock it to this party the night King David got snatched. The shirt made me think about Pops for a minute. I pulled out some crispy white Polo shorts to match the top and some white and blue trimmed Gucci gym shoes. I took a quick shower, than borrowed some of King David's cologne and got dressed. I had to be the freshest nucca on deck anytime we stepped out. Rocko was always fresh too, but I think I had him by just a bit 'cause he borrowed some of my swagger.

I stepped in front of the mirror on my bedroom wall to check my situation one last time. Satisfied that everything was on point, I winked my eye as King David used to do before stepping out.

"Look at Coach pretty ass," Rocko said nudging Black, as I walked out the back patio door. Nuccas and bitches were everywhere. All we had to do in the Zone was call one person and tell them a party was going down at such and such spot, and the entire hood would be on deck in ten minutes. It was summer and that's all we did on the daily, party! Felicia and her pack was on deck. All of 'em were wearing bathing suits and were sitting on the edge of the pool with their feet in the water.

"Hey Coach!" Rocko hollered waving me over. He and Black were behind the bar serving up concoctions of all kinds of liquor.

"What up, dough?" I said joining them at the bar, but still scanning the pool in search of Amanda.

"Where the meat and shit at for the grill?" asked Rocko.

"Yeah man, I'm hungry?" Black said.

"Go look in the deep freezer inside the guest house," I answered, as Black stepped off.

"Don't worry, my nucca, she's here. She just stepped inside to freshen' up," Rocko said, as he was talking about Amanda. "Matter of fact, there she go right there," Rocko said nodding in Amanda's direction.

"Damn..." I said taking in all her beauty. She was wearing a two piece white bathing suit that covered up very little. I watched her every step like a cougar as she walked over to join Felicia at the pool. Her ass was moving from side to side and titties going up and down. It was just something about baby girl that made my blood boil. She was so fine that whenever we were within ten feet of each other, I'd get the bubble guts. And when she looked at me... kind of how she's looking at me right now. I can't stand eye contact with her.

"Why don't you let me work the bar, while you and Black work the grill," I said.

"Nucca, you can't run forever. If you want the bitch you gonna have to step up and say somethin' you know like, how you doin'? Can I take you out? Bitch don't even know you exist," Rocko said coming from behind the bar.

"You think you know me, huh?" I said.

"Like E-mothafucka'," Rocko said before leaving.

He was right, though. I needed to say something to her, but what?

"Pimpin'," Rome said, as he approached the bar breaking my train of thought.

"What up dough."

"Ah, it ain't nothin' going on but big city pimpin'. I wanted to introduce you to my latest hoes," Lil Pimp said, speaking

of the two butt ugly hood rat's he had on each arm. "This is
Betty and this here is Nancy. Ya'll hoes say hi," he said
pushing them forward.

"Hi…" Betty and Nancy said in unison.

"A'ight, now excuse ya'll selves while I conduct this
pimpin'," Lil Pimp directed.

"Man yo' ass is burnt out. Where you find them two bitches
at?" I asked.

"See, I keep tellin' you I's a full blooded pimp. I ain't find
them, they found me on the track doing what I do best, hoe
handling. They say the needed some guidance on this here
pimpin' and so I baptized 'em. They are now official Road
Runners."

I couldn't do shit but laugh 'cause some how this nucca
convinced these two bucket head hoes that he was indeed a
real pimp.

"But let me ask you one thing, Lil' Pimp," I said still
laughing.

"Shoot baby."

"It's 90° out in this bitch. What the fuck you doing wearing
that hot ass wool suit.. I know yo' ass is sweating," I said
laughing.

"Nucca, pimps don't sweat. Suckas and simps is the only
ones that sweat. I could be sittin' on the sun itself, dressed
in a three piece suit with gator boots and still be the coolest
mothafucka' you know," Lil' Pimp said shaking his perm
while going straight pimp mode.

"A'ight, well since you know so much my nucca, tell me
this, how do I get her to feel me and stop shunning a
playa'? I asked looking directly at Amanda.

Lil' Pimp turned and leaned against the bar, so that he too faced Amanda. "Oh, you talkin' 'bout baby girl. See, where you fuck up at is you sweatin' the bitch…"

"How is that when I never said really one word to her?" I said.

"If you'd let a pimp finish you might learn something. Now as I was saying, you sweatin' the bitch. You sweatin' her with yo' eyes. Trust me a bitch knows when you sweatin' them. That's why in the pimp game it's best to let a hoe choose her poison. You gotta have that 'it' factor to the point where now she sweatin' you. You gotta seem like your out of her league and she's guaranteed to start wanting you.

"Why you think she's on that lame Deal$ dick so hard? Cause the lame knows how to work what he's got. Once you master the art of not sweatin' bitches', they'll flock to you. You's a fly nucca, you just need the confidence now."

Maybe Lil' Pimp was right, I had to get my weight up. And now that the crew was about to start getting money, I could build my own identity and pull any bitch I wanted. I took Lil' Pimp's advice and didn't sweat Amanda's fine ass no more that day, although it was hard not to. I even decided to holla at a few hoodrats just to see if Amanda was taking note. And sure enough she and Felicia made their way over to the bar to interrupt a conversation I was having with Tameka and Toni, two little hot and readys that had a reputation for fuckin'. All they needed was a joint, couple shots of 'Bubby face' and they were hot and ready.

"Huh… excuse us," Felicia said throwing her weight around. She knew Tameka and Toni didn't want no drama, so they excused themselves.

"Why you blockin' Felicia?" I asked laughing.

"Hell no! I know you got better taste than that," Felicia said with her nose frowned up.

"I was just entertaining."

"Hmm. . Anyway, can a bitch get something to drank?" Felicia asked.

"Here," I said handing Felicia a whole bottle of Henny.

"What you say, me, you and that bottle take the party inside?" I said fake flirting with her.

"Coach please. You wouldn't know what to do with all this pussy," Felicia said rubbing her wide frame. She was probably right, but I was only trying to make Amanda jealous. She had been standing there the entire time and I hadn't as much as looked her way. I could see her watching me though, just waiting for me to acknowledge her, but I didn't.

"I'm keeping this bottle though," Felicia informed as she walked off with Amanda in tow.

I watched Amanda's back side as she threw that ass side to side. It was just a matter of time…

Chapter Seven

The next day the crew all met up at Rocko's crib to talk to Dump about putting us on. To our surprise though, we weren't the only ones there looking for work. Lil' Pookie, Joe, Dre and Cee from Bloom Street were on deck. We didn't have no beef with them nuccas 'cause they were all from the Zone, but we didn't really fuck with them like that either.

Dump had reevaluated his thirst for King. He understood that us youngins were the future of the Zone, and it was us who'd crown him King. Fuck what Danny and Bark was talking about. Dump was on some competition shit amongst the youngins, our crew versus Bloom Street in terms of hustlin.' "Just so everybody knows, that here is grown man business, understand," Dump said holding up a large bag of crack packaged into individual dime packs. "You take my shit, you're responsible for it. Not yo' daddy, not yo' momma, sister, brother, cat or dog; nobody but you. I gave it to you and that's who I'll be collecting my money from. So, please don't take my shit if you're not going to have my money, cause again and I want ya'll to say it with me all together now, 'this is Grown man…shit,'" We all said it in unison

Dump handed everybody in the room one large zip lock size bag full of rocks and explained that there were fifty rocks in total, which was $500. He told us to keep $200 and bring him back the rest. He lay down the law on hustling as far as the police, Dump told us to never keep nothing physically on us in case of a raid. He then broke down the consequences of snitchin'. He informed us that there would be no exception to the rule because snitchin' was unforgiveable in the eyes of the streets. We all knew what that meant, death. He then gave us advice on dealing with slick talkin' crack heads. "These muthafuckas will sell they own momma a dream. They'll say anything to get what they want. You're going to hear every story ever told, but don't go for it. No credit, cause on due day, I don't want to hear, 'oh I'm waiting on Charlie Brown to cash his check.' 'Cause ole Charlie done ran that same story on Bill up around the corner and cross town," Dump said lacing us with the game.We must have sat there for hours listening to Dump drill us on the do's and don't of the game. , but not one second of his spill was boring. All us youngins had longed for this day when an old head would really just give us the game. I had gotten most of it from King David, but he wouldn't let me play it…

After Dump's lesson on Game we all filed out the crib, sacks in hand. As we exited the door, Cane handed each of us black brand new .38 special. Dump knew that the older nuccas in the Zone who were still up under King David's order would oppose to the youngin's on the block. He told us to shoot first and figure shit out later. We broke off into our perspective groups, Caldwell nuccas and Bloom nuccas. Rocko and I were team leaders as Dump called it for Caldwell and Drew the team leader for Bloom. The blocks were already doing numbers, so we didn't have to worry about soliciting customers or custos, as we called them. Dump just wanted to bring everybody under his new rule and the only way he could do so was through the youth.

Under Dump's ruling there would be no more spots. They were crackhead houses King David used as operation points for cracksheads to cop from? Dump felt like the spots were sitting ducks just waiting to be raided. But by us being mobile and not carrying any drugs on we stood a better chance of not getting caught. And another reason Dump decided to fuck with us youngin's is because even if we did get caught, we wouldn't face time under the juvenile act. If one of us went to juvy, Dump promised to have somebody other than our parents to pick us up. He even gave us phony last names to use. I must admit what Dump was doing was in fact genius. My only concern with not being in a spot was Tina seeing me out on the block pitching. She had never treated me like a baby and always let me make my own decisions, but I wasn't sure how she'd take me hustling, especially since she knew how King David felt about me out there on the block.

Being the young boss that I was, I passed off my $500 bundles to my main man Black to dump for me. I told him we would split the $200 down the middle and to make up for the loss I convinced Dump to double my packs to a $1,000 sack. We pumped in eight hour shifts for sixteen hours a day, starting at eight o'clock in the morning. We shut down shop at midnight, so every night between eleven and twelve we had what we called 'The Rush'. Cars of custos would be lined up bumper to bumper copping all they could before the shop closed. I loved the traffic, it just brought so much excitement. I hated the fact that I wasn't in the midst of it all. I would watch the block from Dump's Chevy Suburban. Nucca' working under me and Rocko would turn in their sales for me to hold. In case of a raid, the police wouldn't get any money off nobody. Dump had a stash box in the side door panel where I kept the money and my .38 special.

I envied my nucca Rocko as I watched him maneuver the block, directing traffic and calling shots like a seasoned vet. I wasn't envious of him per say, I just wished I was out there with him. No one knew other than Rocko why I had chosen the position of securing the money. Black, Rome and even Lil' Pimp were on the block making moves. Lil' Pimp saw how much money we were counting up every night and all that pimp shit took a back seat. Well almost, he had his two hoodrats out there on the block running up the cars making sells and tryna sell some pussy on the side.

Together we had Caldwell on lock. We were doing every bit of $10,000 a day Monday through Saturday, and about $5,000 on the Lord's day. Every night after 'the Rush,' we'd meet up at my crib in the guest house. We'd count our bread for the day and I'd take Dump's cut which would be personally delivered every morning in separate envelopes marking who the money came from. In exchange, I would be handed fresh sacks to pass out to our team for the coming shift. After we counted up the money and broke bread, we'd order either pizza or hit the Coney Island.

Money was coming in so fast and so much of it that I didn't know what to do with it. I remember King David sitting in the same chair I did every morning while counting up his last night's bread. Only difference was that there was a lot more money on the table. "In due time," I told myself.

For the past two weeks I had done my best to keep my affairs from Tina. I hadn't changed up my schedule, every morning I was still cookin' us breakfast and even started helping clean up around the house. With Craig gone, somebody had to do it. While I was fixing Tina's plate, she caught me by surprise when she said, "You make sure you be careful out there." The statement took me for a whirl, I almost dropped Tina's food. "What, you didn't think I knew what you were up to?" she asked. My eyes were wide from anticipation of what was coming. I didn't try to deny what I had been doing, but rather see how much exactly Tina knew. We had this thing where we never lied to each other. However, if there was a don't ask, don't tell type of situation, that was a different story.

"You don't think I know you've been sitting in Dump's truck for the past two weeks holding money and watching for the cops. I am your mother and better yet, I am not stupid. Don't you know by now that you can never get one over on me?" Tina asked calmly.

I was looking into her eyes to see if she was pissed, but I couldn't tell. She had that coolness about her just like King David, which made it hard to read her. "So, I take it you want me to stop hustlin'?" I asked coming clean.

I didn't say that, what I said was, you make sure you're careful out there. You're all I got now and I am not trying to lose you no time soon. Do you hear me, Corey?"

"Yes," I answered. Inside, I was jumping for joy. "I figured ain't no sense in me tellin' you not to hustle when I know damn well you're gonna do it behind my back anyway."

I really didn't know what to say, so I just listened...I was waiting on the next shift to start, so I could go hand to hand with all those custos right beside Rocko. There was no way I was going to let him out hustle me. "I know your happy ass can't wait to go outside, but before you go out, give yo' momma some money," Tina said.

She didn't have to ask twice. I dug in my pocket and handed Tina the entire bank roll, which had to be about $1,500.00 "keep it," I said. I wanted to make sure she didn't have no second thoughts about me hustlin'. I watched Tina as she folded the money, then tucked it in her bra. "Got her!" I thought.

*****

I was the first one on the block that day. It was only 7 o'clock and the birds were still chirping, but I wanted to get a headstart on the rest of the team. I wanted to be already working the block when Rocko finally got up. Dump wasn't too happy about me waking him up early, but I figured he'd get over it. The quicker he gave me my sack, the faster his fat ass could climb back in bed.

Around 7:30 a.m. custos started lining up for the morning rush. I directed traffic like a vet standing in the middle of the street taking orders and sending them on their way. "Cop and go. Got them boulders bigger than yo' shoulders. Cop and go." I popped as I handled the morning rush single handedly. I must have served about thirty cars and was almost out of my first sack, when this white minivan pulled up with two white dudes in it. "Got them bolders bigger than yo'...." My words were cut short as I realized the possibility of these two crackers being the law.

The driver rolled his window down and attempted to hand me a twenty dollar bill that was rolled up, but I hesitated and didn't serve him right away. "What's this for?" I asked.

"Come on, I ain't got all fuckin' day here. Are you going to serve me or not?" the driver asked.

"That depends. Are you five – O.?" " Huh, do I look like it?" he answered. Going against my better judgment, I took the twenty dollar bill, then handed the man two dime rocks. No sooner than the exchange was made, the driver and passenger were out the van and all on me like a cheap suit.

"Get your fuckin' ass against the van." The driver ordered. 'And yes, I am five –O. Next time, don't accept a question for an answer."

The passenger shook me down and found eight dime rocks, and $900 cash, and my .38 special. I was so geeked to be out on the block that I had forgotten the number one rule Dump had taught us, never keep nothing on you. And here it was, I got caught with everything, money, dope, and a gun. By that time, everybody was showing for today's shift and to witness me getting hauled off in the back of the white minivan. I could see Rocko amongst the crew. He was throwing up his hands as to say 'what happened?' I could only shake my head and watch as the block became a distant blur, as the two undercover copss pulled off with me in the van.

Chapter Eight

King David had always told me about that 'jail was for dummies.' And that's exactly how I felt sitting inside Frank Murphy's Hall of Justice Juvenile Center. The two undercover cops dropped me off as if it were routine, just another day on the job, so to speak. I was escorted into a musty bullpen which reeked of piss and shit. There were blood stains and burgers all smeared on the walls, and wads of soiled toilet paper that decorated the holding tank.

I guess the boys in blue had been quite busy that morning 'cause the tank was packed wall to wall with young men. I tried to appear normal and blend in with the rest of the bunch, so I found an opening on the wall nearest the door and put my back up against the wall. I listened to the several conversations taking place, which were all about the same thing, getting out! Shit, I felt that. I watched as dudes came in and out of the tank. They were going to see a referee, which was basically a juvenile judge. He was setting bail, giving court dates, or remanding that ass to the custody of Frank Murphy, pending the outcome of charges.

I had seen both ends, but the majority of the dudes were being released. They were just waiting on their parent or guardian to come sign them out. After hours of waiting, my name was finally called by the deputy. I had given the bogus name Rich Fulton as Dump told me to. The deputy, who was a fat older white woman, escorted me to the fingerprint station where she stuck my fingers onto an ink pad, then rolled them on a photo card. I was then escorted to another bullpen to wait. This bullpen only had a few dudes in it, and no one was talking. I paced the floor back and forth until I couldn't take the silence anymore. I stopped abruptly in front of this one dude who was just staring off into space.

"Hey, my man, what's up with this here tank? Why ain't nobody moving like the other tank?" I asked. "Cause ain't nobody in this tank going home," the dude said, and then put his face down in his hands. "Yeah. This is the upstairs tank," a young boy added, as if he'd been there before.

My ass sunk into a corner like all the rest of them in the tank. "This can't be right. Dump said we'd be immediately released to our parents under the juvenile act," I told myself. 'This gotta be a mistake. "Yes!" I thought. "Come on, everybody line up here against the wall. Ya'll getting ready to go upstairs." The deputy said, while standing with the door ajar.

I reluctantly got up and followed the rest of the dudes out into the hallway. We lined up against the wall as the deputy did a quick head count, then buzzed us through these brown double doors. We were shuffled onto an awaiting elevator, which sounded like the cable cord was going to snap as the shaft slowly rose to the third floor. Once off the elevator, we were handed bed rolls and brown jumpsuits by the deputy working our unit, which was 5-South. It was an intake unit for new commitments. We were stripped searched and told to put on our jumpers, along with a pair of thong Bob Barber shower shoes. We were then assigned a room and given a handbook with all the jail's rules. I sat my bed roll on my bunk then I headed back out to the common area. Nuccas were playing spades, while some watched TV and a crowd was over by the ping pong table watching these two nuccas go at it.

Everybody just seemed to not have a worry in the world, but I was focused on one thing, getting the hell out of there, and soon. I walked over to the deputy and asked about a phone call. "Ms. Weaver's your counselor and she's already gone for the day. You'll have to catch her on Monday," the deputy said. I had to catch myself before I spat in that pig's face. I turned on my heels and headed back to my room. 'Where the hell is Tina?' I thought. I closed the door to my room behind me and turned off the light. I was hoping none of those dudes would come trying to introduce themselves 'cause I wasn't looking to make any friends. I spread my sheet across my bed enough to cover the mattress, kicked off my flip flops and laid back in my bunk. I tried reading the handbook they had given us during intake, but I threw it up against the wall after reading the introduction. I figured that I wouldn't be there that long to need to know the rules.

King David said the fastest way to get something over and done with is to face it head on. I was trying to figure out how that applied to this situation when I yawned. I guess that was Pops giving me a hint, sleep.

   I dozed off and slept through the entire day and night. I was awakened to doors opening. I could hear the deputy's key as he turned the lock on my cell. "Breakfast," she said. I was slow getting up, so the female deputy turned on my light and repeated herself. "Young man, did you hear me? I said breakfast." "I'm coming." I said rolling out of bed. I guess yesterday wasn't just another bad dream, I told myself as I stumbled to the sink to splash some cold water on my face. "Last call! Last call for breakfast!" My stomach was touching my back, I hadn't eaten since yesterday's breakfast. There was no way I was about to miss this meal. I raced out of my room and to the end of the line, which only had two dudes remaining. We were handed two cinnamon rolls, two box cereals, two cartons of milk, and a carton of orange juice. I punished that shit and was still hungry. Seeing as though there was no more food, I went back to my room and crashed out. That had become my routine for the next two days, eat and sleep. I hadn't slept that much in my life, but running those streets will have you burnt out and in need of some two day rest.

Monday morning Ms. Weaver, 5-South unit's counselor, was at my door bright and early. "Rich Fulton," she said. I was still asleep, but could vaguely hear someone talking. "Rich Fulton," she said shaking my leg. I snapped out of my deep sleep, and then I sat up to gather my senses. "How are you? I'm your counselor, Ms. Weaver. I understand you came in over the weekend." "Yeah, when can I call home?" I asked eagerly.

"Well, I have received several messages from a Ms. Tina Townsend, your aunt. And I phoned her back letting her know that you're scheduled for court this morning. She said she'll be here." "And what time is that?" "You're scheduled to see Referee Perkins at 9:30 a.m." "What do you think's going to happen? Do you think I'll go home today?"

"That will be up to the Referee. But I don't see why not. You better get ready, it's almost that time." Ms. Weaver said before leaving.

I jumped out of bed and grabbed my towel from my bed roll. I hadn't washed my ass since Friday and was a little tart. I had heard the stories about shower rapes, and don't drop the soap shit. I wasn't scared, but I didn't see the need to be making unnecessary stops in the shower. The only reason I was taking one today was because I didn't want to be in court musty.

As I walked toward the shower room with my shower slides on and a towel dapped over my shoulder, all the nuccas in the common area gave me a round of applause, as if they too had noted that I had been ducking the water. I couldn't help but laugh once inside the shower room. I took the large trash can, which sat against the wall and pushed it in front of the door, so if anyone tried to enter I'd hear them and have enough time to get dressed. Satisfied that I had secured the door, I quickly got undressed, then tiptoed into the shower trying to avoid stepping into the various dirty puddles of water on the floor. I showered almost standing still, I didn't want to brush up against anything. That place was everything I had heard about, in fact I think there was some stuff left out 'cause that place was filthy.

I lathered once and rinsed just enough to knock the funk off me, then dried off and got dressed. I rushed back to my room to hit my grill with that state toothpaste and slapped some gel deodorant on before heading out to the common area.

It was exactly 9:20 a.m. and Ms. Weaver was at the front door calling off names for those scheduled to go to court. "Fulton," she said as she kept reading from her clipboard. I took my place in line and waited to be escorted out of 5-South unit. I looked around one last time in hopes that would be the last time I saw any of those faces. We boarded the dilapidated elevator all squeezing in, and Ms. Weaver hit the ground floor button. By the time we made it through the brown double doors a deputy was calling my name for court "Rich Fulton." I was escorted into a tiny court room by Ms. Weaver and the deputy. I could see Tina sitting in the back with Rocko and Black. I smiled at the sight of them all.

"All rise. Court is now in session. The Honorable Referee Perkins, presiding. Court is hearing case# 1020 State vs. Rich Fulton," the clerk advised the record. "You all may be seated." said Referee Perkins. He was a middle aged black guy who appeared to be a hard-nose. He took his time shuffling through the pages before him, grunting to himself from at the content. "Okay, very well. I have read enough here. Is counsel present?" he asked. Yes, your honor. Mr. Davidson is here on behalf of the defendant." My lawyer stood. Tina had retained him to represent me. He was also King David's lawyer, had been since the 70's.

"And how would your client like to plead to, let's see three counts... No excuse me two counts, one for drug possession/distribution and the other for firearms violation?" asked Referee Perkins. "Not guilty at this time, your honor." "Okay, I am setting preliminary exam for two weeks. And I am setting bail at $5,000 with ten percent. If there's nothing else, court is adjourned," Referee Perkins said before hitting his gavel. "All rise."

Ms. Weaver had informed me that Tina was already out front posting my bail and that I had to be back in court in two weeks. "You stay out of trouble until then." Ms. Weaver said with a smile as she escorted me to the discharge bullpen. "I will," I assured her, as well as myself.

I never wanted to see the inside of that place again. I paced the floor until the deputy opened the bullpen then escorted me to the front door. Tina rushed over to give me a hug first, then Rocko and Black. "What's up, jail-bird?" Rocko joked. "Shit," let's get away from here before they change their mind and lock my ass back up." I said, as we all laughed...

As Tina drove us back to the Zone, I could tell that she was a little disappointed. I had to be the man around the house now, and I couldn't do that while sitting in someone's jail cell.

'I gotta step my game up,' I told myself, as I reached over and grabbed Tina's hand. I just wanted to let her know that I loved her and that I was going to do better. From her wink, I could tell that she got my message.

Chapter Nine

Back on the block, Rocko, Black and me posted up in front of my crib. I could see the curtains at Rocko's crib slightly moving and seconds later, the front door swung opened. Dump was standing there in his boxers looking like an old washed up wrestler. His beady eyes focused in on me as he yelled "Coach! Get yo' ass in here." Rocko and Black were clowning me 'cause they knew Dump was about to chew my ass. I shook my head and let out a deep sigh, as I reluctantly crossed the street. Dump slammed the front door behind me. "Sit yo' ass down," he ordered, pointing to the sofa. I walked over and took a seat next to Kathy who was pretending to be watching the news. She cut her eye at me and smiled, as if to mock Dump while he went into his spill. "What the fuck were you doin' out there all by yourself?" Dump snapped. I knew him too well, and he wasn't looking for an excuse, so I just let him finish venting. "You tryin' to do too much. There's a reason ya'll were sectioned off into teams. Everybody has a role to play. And here it is you take it upon yourself to go against the grain. You got caught with all the work, money and pistol. How stupid is that? I expected more from you, Coach. Like I told you before, this is grown man business. So, you're going to pay for everything you lost by working it off. And until you do, you are back in the truck on look-out status. I'm done with you for now. Come see me later on to pick up your sack," Dump said, as if to dismiss me from his presence.

I felt real small getting up from the sofa heading out the door like a little child who had just been chastised by his father. I didn't like that feeling, and the fact that Dump had called me out in front of Kathy irked me…. 'But when you're on some flunky shit, what can you expect?" I asked myself as I headed toward my house. "What happened? What he say?" Rocko called out, but I kept walking past him and Black. I knew just how to fix this… "Oh, you ain't fuckin' with us now?" laughed Rocko and Black.

Once inside the crib, I went straight to my stash. As I pulled the shoebox down from the top shelf in my closet, I could tell that someone had been in it from the way it was positioned. Sure enough, as I counted my knots I discovered that it was light $1,700. I only had four G's left and I owed Dump $600 off that sack. I found Tina in the attic rummaging through the insulation on the walls. "What are you doing?" I asked, as Tina pulled her hand from behind the insulation and turned to face me. She was sweating bullets and looked really distraught. "Did you take some money from my box?" I asked lightly. It wasn't a big deal if she had. I just wanted to make sure that it was Tina and not some thief creepin' through the crib while we were gone.

"Yeah! I had to bail you out with $500 and I had to take care of some things," Tina answered, as she wiped her forehead of sweat.

"It's cool, but what are you up here doing? You don't look so well," I said.

"Come here Corey," Tina said as she escorted me by the hand over to a wooden chest, where we both took a seat. "Momma has something she needs to tell you," Tina said looking me in the eyes. I knew something wasn't right because the only time Tina called herself Momma was when she was concerned. "Corey, your father's money, I can't find it nowhere. I tore this house up from top to bottom looking for it and I can't find it. Do you know where he might've put it?"

"Nah, I don't," I answered shaking my head no. "Damn!" Tina shouted, and then put her face down in her lap. "How much money do you have now?" I asked.

"Baby," Tina said sitting up to look at me. We're broke..."

'Broke? How were we broke? I didn't know what broke was...I know King David didn't leave us twisted like that.' I thought to myself. That money had to be around here somewhere. But right now I had to be the man. I didn't have time to be on no damn treasure hunt. Moms needed me and I couldn't let her down. I dug in my pocket and counted out two G's, then handed it to Tina. "Here!" I said while wiping the tears from Tina's pretty face.

"What's this for?" she asked looking at the money.

"I need for you to cop me some work, as much as you can for them two stacks. Holla at whoever you gotta holla at, but I need the work. I gotta go handle something right quick, but I'll meet you back here in about an hour... And Ma, don't worry. I got us," I said, and then gave Tina a kiss on the forehead.

Tina didn't say anything; she just tucked the money in her bra. I knew she had someone who would sell her the work, being King David's wife and all. Nobody would probably fuck with me since I was so young, but through King David, I knew all the major players.

*****

With only two grand left to my name, I counted out half of it and put the rest back in my stash box. I went into King David's library and pulled down an old book called *The Art of War* by Sun Tzu. King David had often read the book, but that wasn't my reason for removing the book from the shelf. Behind that particular book was a lever, which accessed King David's hidden artillery. I flipped the switch and watched as the book case did a 180° turn. Gun s were everywhere. Everything from handguns to assault rifles filled the wall on individual hooks with fully loaded clips on each gun. I settled on a chrome .45 semi-automatic with a pearl white handle and the letters KD engraved on both sides in black. That was Pops favorite gun. He didn't carry it outside the house though; it was more of a collector's item. I tucked the gun into my belt, pulling my hoody over the handle, and then hit the switch to turn the arsenal back into a book shelf. I replaced *The Art of War* on the shelf, and then hit the door.

The morning rush was just about over as I crossed the street headed straight for Dump's crib. Rocko and Black were leaning against Rocko's new four-wheeler watching me as I knocked on the door. Kathy's sexy ass opened the door without asking who it was. She moved to the side to let me in, and then closed the door behind me. I walked over to the coffee table where Dump, Cane, and Keith were seated and tossed the stack of money on the table in front of Dump. It was in a white envelope sealed shut.

"What's this?" Dump asked picking up the envelope.

"Yo' money for the sack I lost. And a little something extra for the .38 they took."

"That's what I'm talking about," Dump said with a smile while looking at Cane and Keith. They were all treating their nose and were all glassy eyed. The Dump I had just seen earlier was in the best mood of his life. I had no idea Dump was getting high, when Pops was alive he never showed one sign of it. King David hated any hard core drugs, whether it was powder, hard, heroin, pills, all that shit was a man's demise, he would often tell me. I looked down at the powdered lines on the glass table, then back up at Dump in total disgust.

"When you owe a man, you pay 'em," Dump said finishing his statement. "How much is it?" Dump asked.

"A grand. That ought to cover it, right?"

"Sure, that's more than enough. I guess you're ready to get back to work then?"

"Absolutely," I said as I turned and headed for the door.

"Hold on, Coach. Aren't you forgetting something?" Dump said holding up a large sack of rocks.

"Not at all," I said keeping my step right out the front door. Kathy winked at me to say 'Good job' before closing the door behind me.

"What the fuck he mean, not at all?" Dump asked while looking at Cane.

*****

"Coach, what's up nucca. Why you actin' all brand new on us. You straight?" asked Rocko as I headed back across the street to my crib.

"Yeah, I'm on something right now," I said not stopping.

I waited eagerly by the front door for Tina to get back. Every car door that shut sent me flying to the window to peek out the curtains. She had been gone for hours and I was starting to worry, 'where is she' I thought, as I began pacing the floor of the living room. I heard the sound of Tina's horn to her gold colored Cadillac Seville, she was blowing for a custo to move out of the middle of the street. I raced to the front door and snatched it open and rushed outside to help Tina from her car. "Did you get it?" I asked excited. "Boy, be cool. Wait til we get in the house," Tina said sounding cool as a fan. I followed her back into the house and into the kitchen where she pulled two Ziploc bags of hard powder from her crotch area. She set the bags on the kitchen counter and said, "Don't touch nothin' I'll be right back." Tina disappeared into the pantry, a few moments later, she returned carrying a small black digital scale, a large Pyrex glass pot, sandwich baggies, Arm and Hammer baking soda, and a bottle of some white powder labeled Miami Ice. She sat all the stuff on the counter, then said, "Now, pay close attention, 'cause I'm only going to show you this once."

I was like a geek in science class. I paid extra close attention and asked questions along the way, as Tina began cheffin' up the coke. Tina got the work from ole' Clint on the flip side of 7 Mile. Clint was an old comrade of King David's and would do anything to see his people straight. Clint gave Tina the playa's price on the coke, giving her 4 ½ ounces of fish scale, or as we call 'em in the Zone 'big eight'. I watched as Tina emptied both packages of coke into the Pyrex. She then measured out two ounces of cut 'Miami Ice' 56 grams to be exact and dumped it inside the Pyrex.

"What's that for?" I quizzed. "It's to stretch the coke. Anytime you're cooking 4 ½ or better you can stretch it to half of that weight. But the work has to be A-1, or it won't come back." "What do you mean come back?" " It will fall apart. Let's just say that you'll lose all your money and the work, you might as well flush it." I guess I got it, almost. I watched as Tina weighed a half ounce of baking soda, 14 grams, then tossed it into the Pyrex. "And what's that for?" "The baking soda will bring the cut and coke back together to rock form once I cook it," Tina said as she carried the Pyrex over to the sink and ran some warm water into the jar, only covering the top of the mixture. She then took a spoon and began stirring the mixture in fast swirls. She took the plug to the sink and stuck it down in its hole to block it up. She then grabbed an ice tray from the freezer and sat it on the sink. "What's the ice for?" I asked. "You'll see in just a minute," Tina answered while carrying the Pyrex over to the microwave and putting it on 1:30.

I raced over to the microwave and stood beside Tina as we watched the contents inside the jar begin to simmer. Tina pulled the jar out about halfway through the set time and swirled the jar in a circular motion maybe ten times before placing it back in the microwave. She let the time run out, then walked the Pyrex carefully over to the sink and began to swirl it again in a circular motion. "You see this," she said holding the jar down to where I could see inside. "Once everything is together in a complete gel, you know it's ready." She said as she dumped two ice cubes in the pot. I could hear a clink sound and watched as the once gel turned into a hard cookie and then rose to the top of the jar. Tina pulled the cookie from the jar, then sat it on an awaiting paper towel to air dry. "And that my friend is how you cook crack. That game right there cost your father ten grand to learn, so guard it. Don't share it with no one under any circumstances. You hear me?" Tina asked firmly. "Yeah!" I answered shaking my head. I was still amazed that my mom had so much game. I had seen King David cook up before, but never really paid attention to detail. Tina had just given me the blueprint and I was only twelve years old. There were a few things I still needed to grasp, like how to tell if powder was good work, but I was content for right now. I'd let Tina handle the end. After the cookie finished air drying, Tina put it on the scale to show me the profits. "See that?" She said. "You just turned 4 ½ ounces into 6 ½ ." I started doing the math on how much I'd made altogether. In the Zone we were cutting $1,500 out each ounce, so off just two ounces I would have more than doubled my money.

"A'ight, I can take it from here," I told Tina grabbing the coke off the scale and headed out back to the pool house.

Chapter Ten

I couldn't let Tina down again, and I knew King David was looking over my shoulder, so I damn sure wasn't about to fuck up again by going back to jail. I had to come up with a way I could sell my work and not be hand to hand. 'Think, think' I told myself, as I paced the floor while constantly looking at the work sitting on the coffee table. "Cop and flip, baby," I could hear King David's voice in my head, 'just cop and flip.' Bingo! I thought racing over to the sofa in front of the coffee table. Pops never went hand to hand. He was always coppin' and flippin' as he called it, which meant buy and sell as quick as possible. It all made sense now, nuccas who used to buy work from Pops that weren't from the Zone did so because King David had that butta and it was always at a playas' price.

I came up with cop and flip strategy of my own after playing with the numbers a bit. I was going to start selling double-ups. Whatever you spend, I'd double it in work. So if a nucca gave me $50.00 I would give him ten dime rocks for his money. I decided that the double-up would only be sold to non-smokers, nuccas on the block getting' money, 'cause I wasn't tryin' to mess up the game and create no new enemies. By selling double-up's I would at least double my money as well and it should be a quick flip. I just had to convince nuccas to fuck with me. Just as I finished chopping up the work and putting the rocks in hun'd dollar sacks, the door bell to the pool house rang. It was Black. I scanned the backyard before letting him in.

"What up, dough, my nucca?" I said shutting the door behind him.

"Shit, just coming to check on you. You been on some real secret squirrel shit since we picked yo' ass up from juvy. What's up?" asked Black.

I think I had my first customer in Black. "Sit down, my nucca," I said motioning him toward a comfy recliner. "I was just about to fry up some wings and fries. Are you hungry?" I asked.

"Hell yeah," Black answered rubbing his stomach.

"Here," I said tossing Black the remote to the TV and the controller to the Nintendo. I knew Black like the back of my hand, and if I were to win him over, it would have to be through his stomach.

I dropped thirty wings into the deep fryer and two baskets of curly fries. I quickly made some Kool-Aid while the wings and fries browned and rose to the top of the grease. I dumped the wings and fries into a bowl with a paper towel, so that they could dry and cool, then grabbed a bottle of Frank's original hot sauce. I sat the wings and fries on a tray in front of Black on the coffee table. He paused the game and dug in like I knew he would. As we ate, I casually brought up the conversation about hustling, just to see where he was at.

"Man, I'm through pushing for Dump," I said.

"What you mean?" Black asked between bites.

"That nucca he talkin' to us like we his flunkies and shit. He don't ever talk to you like that?

"Yeah, that nucca do be tryin' to front on a nucca. Only reason I ain't said nothin' is 'cause on the strength of Rocko."

"That's what I'm saying, but I ain't going for nothin' dawg. My daddy ain't even talk to me the way dude be hollering and shit."

"So, what you gon' do? How you gon' eat?"

"King David used to always say, "There comes a time in every man's life when he's got to hold his own nuts."

"True dat. But what are you going to do?" asked Black.

"I already got me figured out and I'm done holding another nuccas' nuts. Question is, what are you gonna do?" I said tossing black a hun'd dollar sack.

"What's this?" Black asked.

"It's a double-up. Ten fat ass dimes for the playa's price of fifty dollars.

"For fifty?" Black repeated while eyeing the sack.

"Yeah, you can make a few extra dollars on the side. While you pushin' for Dump, you can slide one or two of these boys in a day and make your own bread. Dump will never know, as long as you don't try to overdo it."

I was just free styling, but I could tell by the look on Black's face that he was buying into my spill. I figured if I kept talking and didn't allow him time to really think it over, he was sold. "Just think my nucca, you out there all day sixteen hours a day selling for another nucca. The least you can do is scrape up a couple hun'd for yourself. Just think by the time school starts back, we'll be the freshest nuccas ever."

"Let me get two double-ups," Black said digging in his pocket and handing me a hun'd dollar bill.

"Look, you know Rocko is our man, but we gotta keep this between us 'cause his loyalty is to Dump first. You feel me?"

"I got you," Black said.

"Well, look, I gotta shoot a few moves, but we gone get up later and kick it. Hit the mall or something," I said standing to my feet.

"A'ight. That's a bet," Black said giving me dap.

"Hell yeah!" I shouted after closing the door behind Black. I knew Black could hold water and was good with money, so that was one custo on lock. I tucked about five double-ups into my drawers and underneath my jock strap. I was about to hit the streets and I had learned my lesson about lancing. The only way five-0 was going to get the work off me was if they strip-searched me and that wasn't going down. I patted myself, content that I couldn't feel a bulge, I grabbed the rest of the work and stashed it before hitting the door. I hopped the privacy fence, which separated our crib and King David's pit bull farm. It had been weeks since I had messed around with the dogs. They were all game fighting bloodline pitbulls, some Kobi, tiger striped, red nose, etc. They were all wagging their tails excited to see me. I brushed past them all, rubbing each across the face as I headed towards ole' Bruno. Bruno was the oldest pit on the yard and just like Pops, he was the king. He was definitely King David's favorite dog on the yard. Bruno was a legend in the city and the circuit of dog fighting listed as a grand champ, undefeated. But those days were long behind ole Bruno, he was retired. His only job now was to mate and hold the yard down.

"Come here, Bruno" I said kneeling down to rub the old champ. "Come on let's take a walk." I said as I put his leather leach around his collar. 'Up Bruno, come on baby, you still got it. Up Bruno," I encouraged as Bruno leaped the back gate into the alley with me. I wanted to take the alley up to the side street because I didn't want anybody on the block to see me as I made a detour, turning down Bloom Street. My target and reason for coming down the street was just yards in front of me. "Slow down, Bruno," I whispered. Bruno's old fat ass was nearly dragging me.

"What's up, Coach?" Lil' Pookie said recognizing me.

"Ain't shit. What's up with you?" I asked coming to a stop where Pookie was posted.

They were all out there taking turns serving custos and getting money. Their set up was almost identical to that of Caldwell's, everything focused at the center of the block.

"What you come around here to spy on us?" Lil Pookie said breaking my train of thought.

I was just taking in all the movement and seeing who was doing what. "Nah, I actually came to holla at you on some business," I said.

"What's up with it?" asked Lil' Pookie.

"Let's take a walk," I said leading the way. Once we were down the block and out of anyone's hearing, I went into my spill just as I did with Black. I showed Lil' Pookie one of the double-up sacks and he was sold off that alone. He didn't have any real loyalty to Dump. He bought all five packs and said he'd be hollering at me soon as the shit was gone. By the time we did a full lap around the block, we were hitting rocks. "And remember, keep this shit on the low," I told Lil' Pookie as I bent the corner headed for Caldwell.

I hit the block to see Lil' Pimp and Rome out there pitching to custos. Rocko was nowhere in sight. 'Good' I thought because I wanted to pull Pimp and Rome aside so I could holla' at them real quick. "What up dough play boy?" I said, approaching Lil' Pimp. I tried to give him dap, but he back stepped while looking down at Bruno. "Ah, don't tell me Pimpin' scared of ole Bruno," I teased.

"Not at all, I just don't want that filthy beast jumpin' on my pimp attire," Lil' Pimp shot while brushing off his suit jacket as if it had dirt on it.

"Anyway, my nucca, I need to holla' at you and Rome," I waived Rome over. He had just finished serving a custo.

"What up dough Coach?" Rome said giving me dap.

"Bruno," he said kneeling down to play with the ole champ.

"Ain't shit. I need to holla' at ya'll about some B.I."

"What's up my nucca?" asked Rome standing to his feet now.

I nodded toward Lil' Pimp's two hoes, which he promptly made them excuse themselves.

"Man, I got some work and it's for the low."

"What you talking 'bout Coach?" asked Rome.

"I got them double-ups. You give me fifty dollars and I give you double in work. I know ya'll nuccas tired of pushin' all day for Dump's ass."

"True. True," Rome said nodding his head.

"You can think Pimpin' been out here getting pimped if you want to. I been had my own shit, but not at the price you talkin', tell me more," Lil' Pimp said.

"Come on, follow me," I said leading them across the street and back into the pool house.

I went to my stash and pulled out four double-ups and tossed two to Rome and the other two to Lil' Pimp. "The rocks are the same size as the ones ya'll pushin' now, if not bigger. And the work is butta" I said as they examined the sacks.

"So, you gone give us these for fifty bones? asked Rome.

"Yeah, fifty each. Look, all you gotta do is mix it in with your sales for the day. Just don't try to overdo it and Dump will never know you're out here double hustlin'."

"Shit, let me get both of these," Lil' Pimp said handing me five twenties.

"What about you Rome, you cool?" I asked.

"Yeah, let me get these,"   Rome said handing me two fifties.

"Now look, Rocko is our man but Dump is his daddy, so don't tell Rocko about our lil' venture," I said looking at them both.

"We got you pimpin','" Lil' Pimp said.

"A'ight, holla' at me when ya'll ready to re-up," I said letting them out.

Chapter Eleven

The word had spread like wild fire that I was on with that butta work and was giving out double-ups. Nuccas was stopping by the crib at all hours of the day trying to get on, nuccas from Bloom St. and even off the flip side of 7 Mile. I hadn't put the work out there like that, so who the fuck was running their mouth? I knew it would just be a matter of time before Dump got wind. In the mean time I had work to flip.

The past three weeks I had been on straight grind mode. I had run through ten big eight's and was now copping a half brick at once. I had mastered the art of cooking up, it only took me that one time Trina had shown me and I had it down to a science. There was so much traffic coming through the crib that Tina said something to me about it. "You don't shit where you lay your head at," she told me. In other words, that meant find someplace else to set up shop.

I was feeling that because I wasn't trying to disrespect the crib and bring no heat on us. I bought a sky pager and told nuccas to page me when they needed some work. I hired Felicia to drive me around for $100 a day. Tina let us use one of King David's work cars, an old clean black Buick Regal, which King David dubbed 'Do Dirt' 'cause the only time he drove that car was when he was doing dirt. The car still had that new car smell to it, every morning Felicia and I would hit the car wash, then Coney

Island before making my rounds dropping work on nuccas
on Bloom St. and the flip side of 7 Mile.

Felicia and I had been hanging tough like we were
stick-men. After we finished making our rounds, we'd
cruise the hood with the sounds banging. Felicia's loud ass
would be hangin' out the window flossin' on the haters.
Nuccas knew better than to try her 'cause she could scrap
like E-mothafucka, which was one reason I chose her to
drive me around, that and the fact that I was too young to be
seen behind the wheel by five-0. And the fact that I'd be
seeing more of Amanda didn't hurt neither. My plan had
come together. Nuccas were copping double-ups left and
right all day and I was establishing my own rep in the streets
as Coach, and not Lil' KD as some nuccas saw that black
Regal bend the block, they knew a young boss was on deck.

With all the attention sure enough came trouble, or as
known in the streets, tests. One day Felicia and I were at the
park at Atkinson Elementary School, just chillin' by the
whip taking in the scene. Nuccas were playing basketball,
while all the hustlas gathered in a circle shooting dice.
Rocko was on the dice and was breakin' them fools while
talkin' cash money shit. "Nucca, bet that money any part of
it," he popped, referring to the pile of money in front of him.
"What I can't get a fader?"
Nuccas were all backing down not wanting to call any bets.
"Pass the dice, nucca. You see ain't nobody tryna' fade yo'
ass," Lil' Pookie said.
"Nucca, the only thing I'ma pass is a natural on my come
out," Rocko said shaking the dice high above his head. I
stepped up and threw three hun'd dollar bills in the center.
"Let 'em roll," I said. I wasn't gambler. King David told

me the only nuccas that gambled were the ones tryin' to come up and go down. I was already up in the game and three lil' hun'd wasn't going to hurt me, I just wanted to keep the festivities going. "That's what I'm talkin' bout, Coach. Show these broke ass nuccas how Caldwell nuccas get down," Rocko said then rolled the dice, catching nine as his point. 'I'm taking all bets around the board starting with you lil' nucca," Rocko said talkin' to Lil' Pookie.

"Nucca, bet a stack you don't straight make it," Lil' Pookie said throwing down his bet.

"Nucca, bet I buck this bitch the same way I caught it. If it don't come four nickel, I don't want it," Rocko said "Who else?"

No one said anything. 'Scared ass nuccas," Rocko said spinning the dice out his hand quickly. Four, five the dice landed on. "And point made," Rocko said reaching down to pick up his money. He had shot the turn on us, I wasn't trippin' but Lil' Pookie was pissed.

"Nucca you cheatin!" he yelled.

"Nucca, if I'm cheatin', then bust me in my mouth," Rocko said tucking the money in his pocket.

Just like that the entire park turned into one big riot, Caldwell vs. Bloom, as Lil' Pookie stole on Rocko. I fired on Dre and Felicia cracked Dee over the head with a bottle of Remy Martin. We was all out there going toe to toe throwing hay makers, when gunshots rang out.

Nuccas knew the drill, it was time to go. I pulled out my .45 from my waist and let off two shots in the air to give Felicia and Rocko enough time to get in the car. We all jumped in the Regal and skirted off laughing. It was all good, we had fought them nuccas a million times growing

up, but there was never beef because we was all Zone.
Nuccas were just drunk, that's all.

"You see how I flatlined that nucca?" Rocko asked from the
back seat.

"Yeah," I said laughing. But you should've seen Felicia
over there putting in work," I said still laughing.

"Shit, I looked up and nuccas was swinging, so I started
dropping muthafuckas," Felicia said.

"Yeah, nucca yo' ass was cheatin' though," I laughed.

"I call it hustling," Rocko said.

"True. True."

"I know one thing, that shit blew my high. Let's get a bag,"
Felicia said.

"Here, roll this up." Rocko passed Felicia a bag of ganja.

"I gotta stop and get some papers," she said. We pulled into
the Sunoco gas station on 7 Mile and Syracuse and Felicia
got out to go get some paper.

"But on some real shit, my nucca, you need to be careful out
here with what you doing," Rocko said out of nowhere.

"Fuck you talkin' about?"

"You gon' try and play stupid like I don't know what you
out here doing. Like I don't know you sellin' work, the
whole hood knows."

"Yeah, so what's up?" I asked turning to face Rocko.

"I'm just saying be careful 'cause nuccas is talkin'."

"Talkin' like what, like they gone try me?"

"You know I'm in the middle of this shit. Dump talkin' like
since you sellin' yo' own shit, that you gotta be man enough
to keep the wolves off you."

I pulled my .45 out and held it up. "Man, I wish a nucca
would. That'll be their last time tryin' Tina's son."

"Calm down, Charles Bronson. I know you can handle your own, I'm just putting you on point 'cause now that nuccas know you ain't under Dump's protection, they may try you. I got your back, though my nucca," Rocko said, reaching forward hitting rocks with me.

"Hold on, freeze the game," I said as Felicia climbed back into the car.

"Roll up," Rocko said as Felicia pulled away from the pump.

Chapter Twelve

"He wants to act like a man, then I'm gone to treat his little ass like a man. Can't have him out here selling his own work without consequences. Pretty soon it'll be an epidemic, nuccas be on some 'fuck Dump' shit on the block," Dump said while bending the corner in his Suburban. He had been circling the Zone all night clocking everybody's moves to see if the word was true about nuccas pushing extra work. "You see that," he said pointing to a long line of custos on Bloom St. "Ain't no way mothfuckas can try and tell me that the shit is slow. And it's after hours."

"Yeah, but what we gone do about it?" Keith asked from the passenger seat.

"What I should've done to begin with."

*****

I woke up late the next day for some season, I think I might've smoked one too many joints with Rocko and Felicia last night. I rolled off the sofa in the pool house where I fell asleep and looked at the clock on the wall, it was almost eleven. "Shit," I said as I rushed out and into the back patio door to the main house. I forgot to cook breakfast. I had told myself that no matter how much money I got, I would still keep the tradition. King David said, "When a man can no longer keep his routine, he's changing, whether it'd be for good or bad." I wasn't trying to change.

"Damn," I said closing the door behind me. I could smell eggs and sausage in the air. Tina was at the stove doing what she do, cheffin' up everything. "Hey Ma," I said kissing her from behind.

"Good morning, baby. I see you finally got up. What I tell you about burning yo' self out?"

"I know," I said taking a seat.

Tina was setting my plate down in front of me when a breaking story on the news flashed across the mounted television above the table.

"Turn that up," I said.

It was Felicia's house. I could see Lil' Pimp, Rome, Black, Rocko, Lil' Pookie, Dre, Felicia, Amanda, and a host of other people in the background as the cameraman zoomed in on two medical examiners walking a stretcher to a white van. There was a body on the stretcher and I could tell the person it was dead because they had a white sheet covering the body from head to toe.

"Oh, my God," Tina said holding her face as a photo of the victim flashed across the screen. It was Barb, Felicia's mom. The anchor said that the victim, Barbara Gaines, had been shot to death after what police are calling a home invasion. They weren't sure as of yet the motive and there were no witnesses. The victim's daughter, Felicia Gaines, discovered the body this morning.

"Where you going?" Tina asked with a bit of concern.

"I gotta go check on Felicia," I said pushing my chair in.

"You be more than careful," Tina said giving me a kiss while rubbing my back.

"Okay," I said as I headed for the door.

Felicia, stayed the next street over on Buffalo, which separated Caldwell and Bloom St. I jumped the back gate into the alley and came up through a vacant lot and walked down a few houses where everybody was posted.

"What up dough?" I said hitting rocks with the crew.

"Man they killed Barb," Rocko informed me as if he knew who did it.

"Who?" I asked.

"Shit, I don't know," Rocko said shrugging his shoulders.

"I walked Felicia home this morning after leaving yo' crib, and I was halfway down the block when I heard her screaming, so I ran back to the house to see what was up," Rocko said getting choked up.

"Rome, who they say did it?" I asked.

Rome shrugged his shoulders, "I don't know."

"So, you mean to tell me that don't nobody know nothing?" I yelled while looking in all directions. "All you nosy muthafuckas out here, and don't nobody know nothing?" I yelled.

"Coach, calm down," Kathy put her arm around my shoulder. "'Come on, let me take you home," she said, as she escorted me to her car. "What is wrong with you out there screaming like you done lost your damn mind," Kathy fired up a joint, and then started the car.

"You know, I just find it hard to believe that out of all them nuccas standing out there, that ain't nobody see nothing," I said taking the joint from Kathy.

"Coach, but you know the rules to the street. Even if somebody did see something, they ain't gone say nothing. It's just how it is."

"Nah, you ain't feeling me," I said passing the joint back to Kathy.

"I'm tryna feel you."

"Look, when them nuccas dumped my daddy's body on the block in a fuckin' box, ain't nobody see shit. And he was the king! Shit just ain't adding up around this muthafucka," I said hitting the dashboard.

Barb's murder brought me back to King David's murder. Seeing Felicia out there helplessly crying her heart out made me remember how not too long ago I was doing the same thing. Kathy, I could tell had become a little uncomfortable with the conversation for some reason.

"I know there's a code in the street. But I ain't talkin' about go and tell the cops, I'm talkin' bout the Zone handling Zone B.I," I said breaking the silence.

"But Coach, you act like Dump and 'em didn't find out who killed King David. Craig killed him, am I right?" Kathy asked.

"Fuck nuh, Craig didn't kill my daddy. But somebody had to take the blame."

Kathy's eyes got big as I made the statement.

"You know well as I do, Craig wasn't no killer." Our conversation had become too tense and there was an uncomfortable long silence, so I had Kathy drop me off back at the crib. I didn't want her to think my gripe was with her, so before I got out I tried to relax and ease the tension, "And what you think you're my guardian angel or something?"

"Why you say that?" Kathy asked blushing.

"Cause this yo' second time calling yo' self saving me."

"I guess you could say that," she smiled, still blushing from ear to ear.

I winked my eye at her to let her know it was all good, then closed the door.

*****

"That's a good start," Dump said while looking at the news with Cane, Keith, and Nate. "These muthafuckas want to do their own thing, we'll let 'em. But just like I told all they ass comin' in, this here is grown man business. Ya'll catch a mothafucka out there sellin' after hours, lay they ass down. Shit, we got enough money to sit back and shut shit down for a while, so if we must, we'll get on some Wild West shit," Dump said.

Chapter Thirteen

It was after midnight and the entire crew was posted on Caldwell in front of Dump's crib, drinking and paying homage to ole Barb. Nuccas were taking turns telling stories about how Barb used to hold the block down, and how she was a soldier. After we finished telling our story, we'd pour out a little liquor, then pass the bottle to whoever was next. The bottle of Henny was like the mic. Dump's old ass was out there with all us youngins, the bottle was on him. Even though he and Barb hadn't been seeing eye to eye since King David's passing, she was still family. Everybody loved Barb because she held no punches and was funny as E-mothafucka. Dump hit the Henny hard, he kicked off into his many stories about Barb. He was recalling their story of how back in the 70's Barb did fed time for bank robbery. She had been hitting all the MBD branches in the city, and was dubbed 'the briefcase bandit' because she'd walk into the bank suited and booted carrying a briefcase. She'd walk to the teller counter as if she was on real business, pop open the case and hand the teller a note informing them it was a robbery. Barb would leave the bank after getting the money as if nothing happened. No one in the bank besides the teller would know that they had just been held up. Dump's rendition was cut short by gunshots. Everyone stopped and looked at each other. The shots sounded close, but there was nothing happening on our block. Seconds later, more shots rang out, then tires screeching as motors roared.

"What the fuck was that?" asked Lil' Pimp.

"Sounded like it was coming from Bloom," Rome said.

"Yeah, it did sound close, huh?" Rocko said.

"Come on, let's go make sure them nuccas is straight around there," I said leading the way.

We all piled in Dump's truck with heat on lap. We just had a scrap with those fools, but now wasn't the time to be holding onto no bullshit. By the time we made it around there, the smoke had cleared and people were now coming out of their house. There was a crowd gathering in the middle of the block in front of Dre's crib near the curb. We all jumped out the truck, tools on display and joined the crowd.

"What happened?" Dump asked pushing his way through the crowd to where Lil' Pookie laid bleeding badly.

"We was out here chillin' when this van pulled up. Lil' Pookie went over to see what they wanted and they just opened up on him. I ran in the street and bust back, but they got away," Dre informed us. He was shaking like a leaf, with his gun still in his hand.

"Pookie, don't die on me, youngin'," Dump said as he kneeled down clutching Pookie's small body in his arms.

He didn't look good. "Keep yo' eyes open, Pook. You gotta keep yo' eyes open. Help is on the way," Dump said rocking Pookie in his arms.

Police sirens and ambulance chirps could be heard in the nearing distance, which meant it was time to go cause we was riding dirty. Dump gave Rocko the keys and told us to go wait for him at his house. There wasn't much we could do there to help. We all just kind of mope as we drove back around to Dump's crib. We sat in the living room, no one saying anything. We were waiting on word about Lil' Pookie.

About ten minutes later, Dump came walking through the door with his white T-shirt now   soaked in thick blood. Everyone's attention focused in on him as we awaited the news.

"Is he alright dad?" Rocko asked.

"No, son. He died before the ambulance could get there," Dump said dropping his head.

That was a blow to all of us. Seeing Lil' Pookie die made us realize that any one of us could be next. Pookie's death really hit home because in the Zone the murder rate prior to King David was zero, now Barb and Lil' Pookie too. We'd hear about other nuccas dying, but death was foreign to us.

The front door flew open startling everybody. "The police just found Danny's body in the trunk of a car on Keystone." Keith said while looking at Dump.

"What?" Rome asked in disbelief. "This shit is getting crazy," Rome said.

"Take me around there," Dump said standing. "Rocko, I want all ya'll asses to stay in the house til I can figure this thang out. You hear me. Coach, Rome, Lil' Pimp, all ya'll, stay off the block," Dump said as he hit the door.

"Man, this shit is wild as fuck. Who ya'll think doing all this shit?" Rome asked, with fear in his eyes and voice.

"What, you think it's the same person?" asked Lil' Pimp.

"I would hope so. That way we only gotta kill one muthafucka," said Rocko.

We all shared our different theories on what, who, and why. But none of it was making any sense.

*****

"Did you see the look on their little faces?" Dump asked.

"Yeah, scared straight," answered Keith as he and Dump drove around nowhere in particular. They weren't going to see Danny's body, they knew where he was. Hell, they had put him there.

"See, that's how it's supposed to be. Their young asses in the house scared to death. Now they'll be too scared to be out after hours tryna' double hustle. We just got one more thing to handle, and things should be back to normal," Dump said as if he had it all figured out.

*****

The current events had made it impossible to sleep. I had pulled an all nighter with the crew and was still going. Black came through the crib to cop some work 'cause the rush was about to start.

"What up dough?" I said giving him some love.

"Where the fuck you was at all yesterday, nuccas was worried something might've happened to you."

"I had to help my Grams move. But why would nuccas think something happened to me?"

"You didn't hear what happened to Lil' Pookie, Barb, and Danny?"

"Nah, what?"

"Come on, let's sit down on the porch," I said as Black and I took a seat in the two lawn chairs, and I filled him in.

"You bullshitting!" Black said not wanting to believe his ears.

"I wish I was, my nucca. But shit is real. Somebody is around here bringing the pain, and nobody knows who or why."

While Black and I was kicking it, Deal$ pulled up in his brand new Grand National and parked in front of my crib.

"What the fuck this nucca park his shit in front of my crib for," I said talking to Black. "That nucca know I don't fuck with him like that."

"He got yo' girl in the car with him," Black said talking about Amanda.

"Fuck that bitch."

Deal$ rolled the passenger window down and leaned over Amanda and said, "Lil' Coach, let me holla' at you."

Black was laughing, "That nucca tryna' stunt on you, my nucca. He called you Lil' Coach," Black said, still laughing.

"You think that shit funny, huh?" I said looking over at Black.

"I mean we can mop the nucca if you want to. You know I don't like his ass either."

"Coach," Deal$ called again waving his hand through the tee top.

"Let me go see what the fuck this nucca want," I said getting up. I walked around the front of the car and stopped at the driver's door. With my murder mask on, I asked "Nucca, what's up?"

"Whoa, Lil' Coach. Man, I just wanted to holla at you on some business. Ain't no need to get all hostile."

"Well nucca, get out the car and holla," I said, still with my murder mask on. Deal$ climbed out of the car, and we stood in the middle of the street, "So, what's up? What business do we have?"

"I'm tryna' get my hands on some good work and I hear you got it."

"Well, you heard wrong. I ain't got no work for sale."

"Come on Coach, you know I'm up on game. You actin' like my money don't spend."

"It don't. Not with me." I started to walk pass Deal$, but he grabbed me by the arm.

"What you think lil' nucca, I'm 'posed to kiss yo' ass. I was tryna' shop with you, but since you on some bullshit, I'ma just take that shit. Nucca, what you got in your pocket?" Deal$ said while trying to go in my pocket.

I snatched away from that nucca and all in one motion I pulled my .45 from my pants and started dumping on Deal$' ass. The first shot knocked him off his feet. He landed on his back looking up at me with bitch in his eyes, I stood over him and let my clip ride. I emptied out on that nucca, he was leaking like E-mothafucka with his chest steaming.

"You bitch ass nucca. Don't you ever put your hands on me!" I shouted. My adrenaline was pumping and I had zoned out for a moment. My zone was broken by the screams of Amanda. She was screaming at the top of her lungs. I turned just in time to stop Black.

"Black, no!" I shouted as I ran around the car to where Black was standing, gun drawn and aimed directly at Amanda's head.

"No, Black," I said lowering his gun.

"But the bitch might tell," Black said still wanting to off her.

"You ain't gone say shit, are you Amanda?" I asked.

"No..." she cried.

"A'ight then, get yo' ass out and run. And remember you ain't seen shit." I said opening Amanda's door. She ran as if she was running for her life.

"I'm tellin' you my nucca, you should let me kill that bitch," Black said.

I walked back around the car to see my work. Deal$ was out of there. His eyes said it all, he had that blank stare dead people always have when they first die.

"Corey! Get yo' ass in here, now!" Tina ordered.

Chapter Fourteen

"Corey, what were you thinkin', killin' that boy?" Tina asked nervously, as she paced the living room floor, while constantly peeking out the curtains.

"He was tryna' take my money," I said from the sofa.

"Do you know what this means?" Tina asked, but I was unable to answer because we were interrupted by a pounding at the front door.

Tina creeped to the front door and then looked out the peep hole as somebody pounded the door once more. She quickly unlocked the bolts and opened the door letting Dump in. Police sirens could be heard in the nearing distance.

Dump walked over to me. "What the hell has gotten into you? You're out here gun hoe. Don't you know that nucca is laying out there dead. And the police is on their way with their little note pads. Somebody's gone say something. So what are you gon' do?" Dump asked.

Not knowing what I was going to do, I shrugged my shoulders and put my head down.

"Nah, nucca. I told yo' ass this was grown man business. You gone have to face the music on this all by yourself," Dump said heading for the door.

Tina called out to him, pleading for his assistance. Dump, "please don't let them take Corey. You know he's all I got, please," she begged.

That was exactly what Dump anticipated to happen. All he wanted was for Tina to break down, and now that she did she was vulnerable. She was like clay in Dump's hand, which was vital to his next move if his plan was going to work. "A'ight, but you listen to me," Dump said holding Tina by the shoulder, looking her dead in the eyes. "We're going to have to hide Coach somewhere for a while, just til this thing blows over. Can he go stay with your brother in Cali for a while?"

"Yes," Tina cried while reaching for the phone. They were making plans for me like I wasn't even sitting there. I jumped up and said, "I'm not going to Cali. Matter of fact, I'm not going nowhere."

"See. See what I'm talkin' about, Tina? Ever since KD passed, I ain't been able to tell him nothing," Dump said.

"Corey, sit yo' ass down and be the fuck quiet."

"Hello," Tina said crying into the phone.

"Ya' ass gone be in jail you stay around here too much longer," Dump said.

The word jail hit me like a brick. Lord knows I wasn't trying to spend no more time parked there, and for a body, there wasn't no telling how long I'd be sitting. I tried to rationalize the shit though. "Who gone testify against me?" I asked Dump, out the blue.

"Probably that pretty lil' girl you let get away."

"Amanda ain't gone snitch. She's from the Zone, she knows what's up."

"She might be from the Zone, but she's not in the game, so that makes her a citizen. If she were to testify on you that wouldn't make her a snitch 'cause she's not in the streets. And my hands are tied as far as doing something to her. You can't bank on the notion of hope that she won't testify.

There's too much at risk right now," Dump said, now talking in a much calmer tone.

"Soon as the street clears, you're going" Tina said hanging up the phone. I'ma go pack his shit right now."

Dump sat me down on the sofa, then walked over to the window and pulled the curtain back so I could see. "You see that, he said pointing to all the police and news crew. "This shit is real life. You only get one of 'em to live, so don't be in no rush to throw it all away. Give me some time to work things out, and I'ma send for you. Trust me, all this shit gone be right here when you get back."

*****

I felt like a little kid who had absolutely no control over my life, as I sat near the window at the back of the plane. I could see Tina and Dump waving me good-bye from the tarmac at the Detroit City Airport on Connors and Gratiot Avenue. Tina had tears flowing down her face as she continued to wave. Dump had a smile on his face which read victory. For some reason, I just felt like he wanted to send me away. He could have done something to stop all this, his hand was too strong. I was beyond pissed at him and Tina. I didn't even bother waving back, I just watched as their heads grew smaller, as the 747 inched down the runway and sat for takeoff. I had never been on a plane before, but I was cool. I was too busy fumin' to be worried about flyer's fright. Out of all the things King David and I did together, we never took a flight. I don't know if it was because King David was trafficking drugs the majority of the time, or if he just didn't like planes. But we did a lot of traveling. The last place we went to was Cedar Point, an amusement park with roller coasters and assorted rides. It's in Sandusky, Ohio. Pops rented an RV. He and Dump, they took me, Rocko, Black, Rome, and Lil' Pimp. It was just the fellas. "Damn, I miss you," I said to myself closing my eyes as the plane blasted into the sky.

*****

The impact from the plane's tires screeching against the asphalt woke me up as we landed at LAX airport in Los Angeles, California. It had been a long flight straight through and I had slept the majority of the time away, but I was still tired. The plane did a few laps around the tarmac while waiting on an open gate. We finally pulled in and passengers began unloading the plane. I grabbed my two bags from the overhead bin and fell in line as we inched one by one off the plane.

It was hot as hell stepping out of the terminal into the cursing sun. There was not a cloud in the sky to try and hide from that sun, which was beaming down. I started sweating just from standing there. I put my hand to my forehead as if it were a visor, then scanned the pedestrians standing at the curb with signs in their hands. I saw my name, Corey Townsend written in red marker on this white card. This light skinned, funny lookin' dude with Coke bottle glasses was the one holding the sign. He must have been Tina's brother, Robert. She told me once I got off the plane to look for a man with his description, he'd be holding a card with my name on it.

I shook my head and let out a breath of frustration, then walked over to the man.

"You must be Corey," the man said with a smile as I approached him.

"Yeah, but everybody calls me Coach," I promptly informed.

"Well, I am your uncle Robert. Come on, let me help you with those," Robert said, reaching down for one of my bags. We walked through the parking lot of the terminal stopping at the trunk of his ruby red drop top Benz. It was just like the one King David had, they were identical with the exception of the color. Robert popped the trunk using his key and tossed my bags in.

"You ever rode in a Mercedes before?" he asked popping the locks.

"Yeah, my dad had quite a few of 'em I said getting in.

"So Coach, what is it you like to do? Robert tried to make small talk as we drove.

"Just hang out and kick it with my friends. Stuff like that."

"You into sports?"

"Not really. I like to watch them, but I'm not big on playing them."

"What grade are you in?" You know school will be starting back in two weeks."

"Yeah, I know," I said thinking about the crew. I'm going to the eighth grade this year.

"I remember the eighth grade like it was yesterday," Robert said taking me back down memory lane.

   I wasn't trying to hear that shit for real, but I just let him talk. And boy could his ass talk. I don't know maybe he was just as nervous as I was. I didn't know him from Atom, and here I was riding shotgun with this nucca proclaiming to be my uncle. Shit, Tina never really spoke on her siblings or upbringing, and I had never met anyone until now from her side of the family. She'd show me pictures and say 'that's so and so,' but never a story. I just knew the story of how she met Pops and left, never to return. I know one thing, I was getting a headache from listening to this nucca run his shit. He spoke in a high pitch voice, and showed drastic emotion when speaking. The nucca kind of rubbed me as potentially being gay.

Gay or not, unck was living large! The nucca had a colonial style, five bedroom mansion built from the ground up sitting on two acres of private land out in some small town called Fresno, outside of L.A., a couple of hours away. I was in awe as we pulled into the gravel stone circular driveway, which was neatly decorated with a royal blue Porche, a yellow Corvette, and a black Jaguar. The house had a four car garage attached with an in-ground pool outback. Robert gave me a brief tour of the exterior of the house, then awed me even more as we stepped inside.

Fuck wall-to-wall carpet, or that 'itch' as Robert called it. He had wall-to-wall white marble floors. There was so much expensive shit hanging on the walls, I was scared to touch anything. I almost felt like I was walking through a museum. And the crazy part about it was that he lived in that big ole house all by himself. Robert took me up stairs and showed me my room. It was plush with throw rugs made of Italian silk. The bed was queen size with a wooden frame and thick pillars that rose nearly to the ceiling. I had my own entertainment system, and most of all, I had my own phone. I couldn't wait to call back to the crib. Here it was I'm standing in a two million dollar mansion in Cali, and the only thing I could think about was Detroit.

"I'm going to let you get settled in. I'll be downstairs if you need me. And call your mom to let her know that you made it alright," Robert said before leaving. He didn't have to tell me twice. I flopped down on the bed and picked up the phone. I was still fucked up with Tina for sending me off like that, so she'd have to be last. Plus I wanted to see what the word was. I called my nucca Rocko.

"Hello" answered Kathy.

"Put Rocko on the phone."

"Coach? Where you at?" asked Kathy recognizing my voice.

"What's understood need not be said," I shot.

"Boy, please. Anyways, are you a'ight?"

"Yeah, I'm good. But uh, is Rocko there?"

"Oh, you don't want to talk to me, huh?" Kathy said sucking her teeth.

"Baby doll, you know it ain't like that. You know you my peoples," I said.

"Hmm. Hm. Hold on, let me see if I see him," Kathy said placing the phone down.

(Few minutes later) "What up dough my nucca?" Rocko screamed into the phone.

His voice put a smile on my face. "Man, ain't shit. What's word, though?" I asked.

"Dawg, yo' name ringing like E-mothafucka in the streets."

I wasn't for sure if that was a good thing, or bad thing.

"What you mean, like nuccas or da' hook?"

"Both. Nuccas say you flat-lined that bitch nucca in broad daylight. The hook been to yo' house like four times, and the narcos keep circling the Zone showing people a picture of you."

My heart sank as Rocko informed me of the lastest details.

"You hear me, Coach?" Rocko said breaking my thoughts.

"Yeah, but how they know it was me?" I asked.

"Nucca, it was broad daylight outside. And plus you know nuccas talk like bitches."

"So, what's up with Amanda. Have you seen her?"

"Yeah, Black and I caught up with her at Felicia's crib. She know the deal."

"That's what's up. Good-lookin' my nucca," I said, feeling a little better knowing my nuccas were out there holding me down.

"So, how long you gone chill out?" asked Rocko.

"Man, if it were up to me, I'd be on the next thing smokin' back to the city. But Tina and Dump got the block on it."

"Well, my nucca maybe it's for the best. Just chill, and let shit die down. You ain't missin' shit."

"If one more person told me that I wasn't missin' nothin', I was going to nut the fuck up. I was missin' everything…"

"So, what's good other than that?"

"Shit, just out here on the block with the crew, me, Black Rome, Lil' Pimp and a few hot and ready's. Here, ya'll say what up to Coach," Rocko said passing the phone around.

"Coach, we love you," the hoodrats said in unison.

"What it do my nucca?" Rome asked snatching the phone.

"I'm good. What up with you?"

"Ah, man. Out here with the crew just chillin' you's a wild nucca. I heard you made a movie out this bitch," said Rome.

"Nah, where Black at?" I said cheezin'.

"Hold on my nucca," Rome said tossing the phone to Black.

"My nucca, where you at?" asked Black.

Some would think paradise. "I'm in hell right now," I said.

"Why you leave? Rocko and I holla'd at ole girl and she knows the business, although I still think you should let me stank the bitch," said Black.

"I's all good. I should be back soon," I said trying to assure Black as well as myself.

"A'ight my nucca, you stay up and holla at me whenever."

"A'ight, peace." we said at once.

I finished hollering at Rocko for a minute, then called Tina to let her know I had touched down. I had tried paging her and called the house phone about twenty times, but I kept getting our voice mail. "Oh, well" I thought. She probably stepped out the house, probably was tired of them funky ass hooks stopping by the crib. I unpacked my clothes, then took a long hot shower. My room had its own master bath attached with a king size tub which sat in the middle of the bathroom. There were three gold plated sinks lined in a row, with a self-flushing toilet. To top it all, off there was a built in stereo system inside the walk-in shower. I listened to DJ Quick; '*If it don't make dollars, it don't make sense.*" Those were the lyrics pumping from a local radio station. After I finished showering, I walked back into my room and picked up the phone. I tried calling Tina once more, but still no answer. It had been a long day and I was tired, so I crashed out.

A few hours later, I was awoken by the loud thumping of some techno music. I jumped up and had to gather my senses, 'cause I forgot for a second where I was. I rolled out of bed and walked out of my room, stopping at the stairs. People were everywhere.

'Who the hell is all these goofy muthafuckas?' I thought to myself, as I headed down the stairs in search of Robert. I spotted him doing the wop between two white chicks. He was wearing some skin-tight black pants with no pockets; in the 'D' we called 'em smooth booties. He had on a pair of purple Hush Puppies and a matching silk dress shirt, with his chest hairs showing. The only thing he was missing was a gold choke chain with the Cadillac symbol. But that getup he was wearing confirmed my suspicion of him being fruity. I walked over to where Robert was mixing it up, and tapped him on the arm. He spun around wildly, nearly putting my eye out. Obviously drunk, he slurred his words, "Coach, come on and join the party." He grabbed me and placed me between the two white chicks.

"I need to holla' at you!" I said trying to yell over the music.

"What?" Robert asked.

I moved my mouth slowly and pointed toward the kitchen. Robert excused himself from the two young white girls and followed me into the kitchen.

"What's up Coach, you like the party?" Robert asked while heading for the cooler to grab a beer.

"You want one?" he said holding up two MGD's.

"Nah, I'm cool. But I am hungry, which is why I came down."

"There's a large meat lover's pizza in the oven, it's yours. And if that don't fill you up, you're welcome to whatever. The pantry's over there."

"A'ight," I said heading for the oven.

"Who are all those white people?" I asked of the party going on.

"Oh, just some friends. We do this almost every night. What you thought your ole' uncle was a square, huh?"

"Nah," I said lying and laughing.

"Don't let the smooth taste fool you now. I throw some of the best damn shindigs in town. You'll see. But right now let me get back to my two young honey dips before they dip," Robert said, doing a gay ass shimmy out the kitchen.

I was starting to like unck already. When he picked me up from LAX wearing those thick ass glasses, I thought to myself that he was gonna be strict, but it turns out, he's a computer programmer geek by day, and a wild gay party host by night.

Chapter Fifteen

Two weeks later....

I had really gotten to know Uncle Robert, as I was now calling him. He was down to earth on a lot of things, and knew a lot. I was somewhat developing a liking for computers because of him. He showed me how to set up and format programs, we even created our own virtual video game. Robert told me, "it's not where you start, but where you finish." He answered all my questions regarding his childhood, and why Tina left for Detroit. He explained that it was eleven of them all together; some were spread out through the foster care system back in the day because their Mom was strung out on heroin. He said that he and Tina were the babies and had always been close, saying that they talked on the phone a lot. 'Now, I remembered Tina laughing and smiling into the phone saying, "Robby, you so crazy." She had been talking to her brother all this time. For the first time in my life I had really started thinking that I could do something other than sell drugs, and that's what Robert was trying to show me. He took me to his firm called Geeks, where they specialized in computer software, among other things. He was the man in that piece. Not to mention, half owner. "Robert!" was all you heard stepping inside the office, which was located in a high rise in downtown Fresno. His personal assistant, Gloria, this young hot Spanish chick, greeted him at the door with his morning paper and coffee.

"How are you today, sir?" She asked leading us into his plush office, and pulling out his gigantic leather chair for

him to be seated. "Who is the handsome young man?"
Gloria asked smiling my way.

"This is my nephew, Coach. He's staying with me for a while."

"Hello," I spoke, as I parked it on the sofa.

"Okay, Robert if you need me, I'll be right out front," Gloria said excusing herself, but Robert stopped her before she could shut the door.

"Yes," she said in a sexy accent.

"After your lunch break, I need you to take Coach here to the mall, and help him pick out some clothes for school. School starts tomorrow."

"Not a problem," Gloria said smiling before leaving. "All that talk about school made me home sick. Being in Cali and chillin' with my rich uncle was cool and all, but even after all the potential opportunities I could only think about the Zone. That's where my heart was.

I kicked it around the office until it was time for Gloria and me to set out. Robert dug into his wallet and handed Gloria a platinum Visa. He was on the phone, so he whispered, "Just get whatever he wants," tossing his car keys to Gloria. I had shown Robert our shake in the Zone, so we hit rocks as to say "I'm out." Gloria, was all smiles as she tucked the Visa into her bra.

"You ready?" she asked, leading the way.

Gloria was cool as hell. AS soon as we hit the elevator, she dropped that professional white girl voice. "I am so glad to get the fuck outta there, she said letting her hair down from its bun. She was flawless from head to toe, with an onion booty that could make any man cry. Gloria stood about 5'5" and weighed about 120 lbs. Her golden-brown skin made a nucca just wanna lick all over her body. I was in my zone undressing her with my eyes, when the elevator door opened letting us out on the ground floor.

I followed behind her purposely as every passing head turned, stunned by Gloria's beauty.

"Hey, Gloria," this goofy white boy working valet said.

"Hi." Gloria spoke dryly, as she handed him Robert's keys.

Moments later, Robert's yellow Corvette pulled up.

"Thank you." Gloria didn't give ole boy the time of day. She skirted out the parking lot as soon as my door shut.

"So, Coach where are you from?" Gloria asked after letting the top down. Her hair was blowing in the wind like she was a movie star.

"I'm from Detroit. How about you?"

"I'm from New Mexico."

"So, what are you doing way down here in a boring spot like Fresno?"

"I know that's right," Gloria said laughing. But no, I'm doing my internship right now. Your uncle was kind enough to let me do it here at Geeks."

"What you in college?"

"Finishing up, I am going to be a computer engineer soon. And I'll be making the big bucks like Robert and them."

"How old are you?" I asked.

"Don't you know never to ask a lady her age?" Gloria said smiling at me.

"The only reason people don't like telling their age is because they're not satisfied with where they are in life. But you don't seem to fit that description."

"Oh, my god. No you didn't just bust a philosophy on me," Gloria said laughing. "But nah, I like that. I'm 22. And how old are you?"

"Shit, in dog years I'd be 40."

"You are too crazy, Coach."

We continued to kick it as we drove. I couldn't help but wonder if she had a man. Then I wondered if ole unck had hit that on the late night while no one else was in the office. My thoughts were getting the best of me, so I had to try and think of something else.

Gloria took me through Beverly Hills. We did our shopping on Melrose at a bunch of little boutiques. I wasn't feeling a lot of the shit they had because most of it was tight fitting, and I wasn't about to be rockin' no smooth booties to school or nowhere else. I let Gloria pick out a few shirts, but for the most part I kept it gutta. I went Polo crazy. And I copped a bunch of Air Force Ones, which was against Gloria's advice. She said all them nuccas wore down there was Chuck Taylor's. I tried a pair of them shits on and it felt like I was barefoot. Those sneakers didn't have any arch support what-so-ever. I did take her up on her advice and copped a few flannels.

After we finished shopping, we hit Sizzlers to get something to eat, and to kill off the rest of the day. Gloria didn't want to get back to the office until it was time to punch out. I was good with it, cause that meant more time for me to lust off her beautiful self. I told myself when I got a lil' bit older that I was gone come back and fuck with her.

Chapter Sixteen

Lincoln Park Junior High, the sign mounted over the school's building read. Robert was talking me to enroll in school, today I began the 8th grade. My last year in middle school. Man, I missed the crew. I was supposed to be hittin' the halls of Farewell with Rocko, Black, Rome and Lil' Pimp. Instead, I was walking through the halls of an off brand hick town school with Robert by my side while a bunch of corny ass onlookers watched our every step.

"Man unck, is this the only school around here?" I asked as we stepped inside the main office. "I'm afraid so," Robert answered.

"Excuse me," Robert said in his gayest voice while mashing down on the silver bell which sat on the counter.

A healthy fat white woman appeared, and while looking over the rim of her glasses at Robert as if he'd lost his damn mind, she asked, "And how my I help you today?"

"Well, today...I would like to enroll my nephew in school. Yes, sometime today," Robert said sarcastically mocking the woman.

"And you are his legal guardian?" she asked.

"Yes."

"Okay, if you'd just fill these forms out. We can get this done in a jiffy."

Robert didn't know anything about me. He passed me the forms to quickly fill them out, then he signed them and raced back to the counter. "Miss..." he said laying on the bell. "Here you are."

The woman looked over the forms and said, "Very well. Sir you may leave. School lets out at 2:30 p.m."

I got my schedule and headed to homeroom, which was English class. Mr. Turner was written on my schedule as the teacher. Class was already underway when I opened the door. All eyes shifted on me as I handed Mr. Turner my schedule. He looked at me and then pointed to a set near the back. I was already not feeling that place because everyone just seemed goofy and country. The students were a mixture of Latinos, Blacks, Asians, and Caucasians. It felt like the United Nations in that piece. I took my seat next to this black kid who kept looking over at me out of the corner of his eye. He was a little skinny dude with a big ass cone head. It looked like his Moms forgot to shape his head as a baby. Finally, he turned in his seat and whispered. "I'm Louis."

I just gave him the nod, but he kept on talking like we were best friends. "Where you from?" he quizzed.

"Cut that talking out back there, Louis," ordered Mr. Turner. Mr. Turner was a middle-aged white man who looked more like a drill sergeant than a teacher. He had the high and tight crew cut, and muscular build of an ex-marine. I wasn't trying to make bad on my first day, so I paid attention for the rest of the hour.

As the bell rang, I looked at my schedule and I had economics.

"Let me see that," Louis said extending his hand for the schedule. We've got four classes together," he said handing me back the paper. "Come on, I'll show you where economics is."

"Who is this?" a black kid asked Louis as we headed up the stairs.

"What did you say your name was?" Louis asked.

"Coach," I answered.

The other dude was sizing me up. "Betta tell him bout wearing all the flame." He said, then rolled out.

"What the fuck is flame?" I asked puzzled.

"Don't sweat Jeremy. He's a wanna be Crip. He's talking about you having on red."

"So, what about it?" I asked.

"Crips feel like its disrespectful to wear red, or flame as they call it."

"Man, fuck that nucca- I'll beat his bitch ass."

"Don't worry about him. Come on, let's get to class before the bell rings."

*****

The rest of the day kind of dragged, I was in science class, which was my last class of the day. I watched the clock as it inched around striking 2:30 and the bell rang. I scrambled out of my desk with my lone notebook in hand, and headed for the door. Louis was at the door waiting for me, we had said earlier that we'd walk home together. Our houses weren't that far apart, and the school was only a few blocks over.

"You ready?" asked Louis, as I stepped out into the hallway.

"Yeah, let's get the fuck outta here," I said leading the way through the hall. As we passed the pack of whispering white girls, one of them pinched me on the ass. I turned around and stared them all down. I wasn't mad; I just wanted to know who had the balls to touch me. This one blonde girl with bit titties handed me a note and told me to read it later. All the girls snickered as Louis and I walked on.

"Who's that?" I asked of the pack.

"Holly and Jennifer, they're cheerleaders and the rest of them are nobodies," Louis informed.

"They fucking?" I asked

"What?" Louis repeated with a confused look.

"Never mind." I said, realizing who I was talking to. Louis probably had never seen a pussy, let alone gotten some.

As we exited the front of the school, I could see a large crowd standing across the street. Everybody was dressed in blue. I really didn't pay it no mind until the crowd started coming our way, meeting us in the middle of the street. Well, me anyway, I turned to my left where Louis was standing and he was gone. All I could see was the back of his head getting smaller, as he ran full speed in the opposite direction. As I turned around, I could see that nucca who was questioning my gear earlier in the hall. He was leading the pack and saying something to one of the lames with him. I knew it was some bullshit in the game, but I tried to keep on walking. The nucca stuck his hand out poking me in the chest, stopping me in my tracks. Like it was pre-planned, the rest of them lames formed a quick circle around us. I scanned the faces now with my murder mask on.

"Fool, what set you claimin?" asked ole boy standing in front of me. He was a couple of inches taller, but for the most part we were the same size.

"Set?" I asked confused. 'What the fuck was this clown talking about' I thought.'

"All the mothafuckin' flame you got on. You make me think you's a slob."

All this foreign shit dude was talking wasn't about nothin', but it still spelled danger in my eyes, so as he continued to pump himself up. I was digging in my pocket.

Before I knew it, the nucca had grabbed a hold of my shirt and was trying to tear it off my back. I wasn't going out like no bitch though, not in a million years was I about to let this nucca show me up.

" Mark buster- come out this shit," he said still pulling.

I pulled out my combination lock, which I had wrapped around my finger and cracked that nuccas shit to the white meat. The nucca was in a state of shock from the blow. He stood there with his eyes bucked, as thick blood started dripping from the deep cut between his eyes.

I wasn't about to let the rest of them nuccas geek themselves up to rush me, so I charged the nucca swinging wildly.

"That fool's crazy." I heard somebody say.

"Yeah," another agreed, as I continued to put that work in.

A passing parent jumped out of her car and rushed over pulling me off the boy. The nucca was beaten retarded. Blood was everywhere.

"What's your name?" the woman demanded, but I took off running…I got down to the corner, and as I turned left, this white kid who was standing with the door ajar to his house waved me over.

"Hurry up!" he said pointing to a car nearing behind me. Not wanting to get caught, I raced over to the boy's house, up the stairs and through the door. He shut the door just in time, as the nosy ass parent who'd pulled me off ole boy was scanning the block in hot pursuit.

"Good lookin' out, man," I said leaning over in the corner out of breath.

"No problem. I'd do almost anything to see that punk get mopped like that you gave his ass a pumpkin head deluxe."

I looked up at the white boy in amazement, he was using our lingo back in the 'D.'

"What you know about a pumpkin head?" I asked.

"That's what we call it where I'm from, when you beat somebody's ass real good."

"And where you from?" I quizzed.

"I'm from Detroit, born and raised."

"Stop bullshittin'," I said in disbelief.

"Seriously, look," he said turning around and lifting his shirt to reveal a mural of the city and downtown Detroit's skyline.

Still not convinced, I asked him a few questions. "What part of the city are you from, 'cause I'm from the 'D' too? " I'm off dat Eastside."

"Where at?"

"Woodward and 7 Mile. I lived in Sherwood Forest right across from Palmer Park."

"Who's the mayor?"

"Coleman Young, of course."

"What's the name of the island off Jefferson Ave. that everybody hang out at?"

"Belle Isle. Dawg, I am from the 'D,'" the white boy said heading for the fireplace mantle, showing me a picture of him standing in front of Tigers Stadium.

"So, what are you doing way out here in Cali?"

"I got kicked out of all public schools in Detroit, so my mom sent me to live with my father. How about you, what are you doing in a little town like Fresno?"

My mind flashed back to me standing over Deal$ emptying my clip on his ass. I didn't want to say, so I lied. "Yeah, me too. I got kicked out last year, so I'm living with my uncle for a while."

"Well, man, it's good meeting you. What you say your name was?" the boy said extending his hand.

"Coach."

"Nick. But everybody calls me white boy Nick."

"A'ight. That's what's up."

"I think the coast is clear," Nick said as he peeked out the curtain. If you want, you can chill here for a while, and then I can give you a ride home on my dirt bike."

"I appreciate it, man."

"A'ight, let me show you around."

Chapter Seventeen

Just like that, me and white boy Nick had hit it off. We were hanging tough every day. It felt good to be around somebody who was from the crib. The fact that Nick was white didn't bother me cause he had swagger, he wasn't corny by a long shot. He wore Air Forces and Polo shirts like nuccas in the city and sagged his pants too. Nick had a thick gold herringbone chain with an iced out cross with the bracelet to match. For real, I think Nick had more flavor than a lot of nuccas. And he was on his pretty boy shit; ole blonde hair, blue eyed cracker with a muscular build. The only thing though, Nick couldn't fight. He wasn't no punk and stood his ground, but he couldn't fight to save his life.

That nucca I split open with the lock had healed up and was trying to get some get back. His older brothers who were in high school had the school surrounded waiting on me to come out, so he could get his fade back. Nick tapped me on the shoulder to get my attention and let me know them nuccas were out there, but I was too busy walking and talking with Holly's fine ass. I was tryna' convince her to sneak over to my crib, so I could punish that pink pussy. Soon as we hit the double doors, all I saw was a blue blur of a bunch of nuccas.

The next thing I saw was a fist coming which connected with my jaw. Those nuccas ain't come to do no talking, it was on out there. I didn't have enough time to pull out my lock, because the sucka punch caught me off guard. I stumbled back dazed, but determined not to fall, 'cause I knew if I fell it was pretty much over. I swung wildly catching this fat black nucca on the bridge of his nose. I felt pain shoot down my back as somebody had hit me with a board. But I rolled with the punches and kept swinging.

Nick had popped off on ole boy who stole me, but that was the first and last punch he got off. They were on him like a cheap suit, and beating him like a cheap rug. The sound of the security guards bull horn made the crowd disperse. Those nuccas jumped in their cars and sped off. I had never been so happy before in my life to see a security guard. Lord only knows what would've happened to Nick and me if they hadn't shown up. I managed to escape the ordeal with only a busted lip and a small knot on my forehead. Nick though, had that pumpkin head deluxe. And by him being white, he bruised pretty bad. He took it like a champ though, and for that he was my nucca for life.

After that episode, we didn't have any more problems with those lames 'cause they knew we weren't soft and were going to fight. They even tried to induct us into their gang of Crips. But Nick and I weren't on no color shit. The only color we were on was green, money. Plus, Nick said those lames were false flaggin.' He said there weren't no real Crips in Fresno.

We just basically did us. Nick had some dirt bikes his father bought for him, and he had been showing me how to ride on the trails in back of our houses. We lived two blocks over from each other, but the land behind our houses connected. We'd ride for hours, often annoying the neighbors with the revving motors of the dirt bikes. We'd sometimes ride up to the main roads and wait on the police cruisers to wave us off. We'd flip 'em the bird, rev our engine and the chase would be on. Nick called it training. The shit was fun as hell, but I missed the excitement of the Zone.

My birthday was coming up and I wanted to spend it how I always did, with Rocko, us side by side, fresh to death and the center of attention. I had been trying to call the crew, but every time I'd call they weren't around. I felt like my nucca forgot about me. Even Tina, I had yet to talk to her. I thought maybe she was disappointed in me for killing Deal$. And she was just mad at me for a while. I missed everybody and just being in Detroit, period. Nick's father, come to find out was a pilot. He flew private planes for a concierge company. And he'd often let Nick ride shotgun with him on trips on weekends. Nick had told me that next weekend he was taking a trip to Detroit with his father on business. He knew how home sick I was and thought it would be a good idea if I came along.

"You sure your Pops won't mind?" I asked excited.

"Nah, it ain't no big deal. There won't be any passengers on the plane. We're just dropping off some boxes and switching planes. But we're going to stay for two days," Nick said.

"Hell yeah, I want to come."

"A'ight. It's a bet then."

*****

I knew uncle Robert was going to say no about me going with Nick to Detroit, which is exactly why I wasn't going to tell him. I wasn't about to blow my only ticket back to the city by opening my mouth. Unck had been more than good to me and I really liked him, but it was time to roll out. It was Friday, the weekend of the trip and we were to leave right after we got out of school. So, I told unck that I would be spending the weekend at Nick's, that way he wouldn't be expecting me home. I kind of felt bad for up and leaving like that, I knew unck would be worried and disappointed after he found out I went back to Detroit. He'll get over it, I told myself as I looked out of the window of the private jet. Nick's dad picked us up from school and drove straight to the airport, a small air field privately owned. We were riding high and in style. The jet was brand new and was custom fitted with wood grain tables, mirrors on the walls. It had two televisions, VCR, telephone and a bathroom. Nick told me when there were clients aboard the jet, that there would also be a stewardess, foreign bitches who didn't wear panties. I laughed at the thought. I felt bad about not telling Nick what I was up to either. I didn't want him to think that I had used him. He was my nucca for real, but I had had enough of Cali.

"Look," Nick said opening one of the brown boxes under his seat. He pulled a red taped color square from the box and tossed it to me. I read the words "Hell Angels." That was the stamp on the brick. I knew what it was. I had seen King David with a ton of them, but with different stamps. It was a key of coke. "Guess how much one of these cost?" Nick said grabbing the brick back.

"How much?" I quizzed.

"Ten thousand dollars."

"Ten stacks!" I repeated.

"Shh.." Nick said, then put the brick back inside the box. He didn't know that back home I used to be on the block. Nor did he know that I knew how much a key cost in

Detroit. I was already doing the math. A brick was going for $20,000-$22,000 depending on who you knew. And from listening to Nick I could tell that he had no idea how much a brick was going for in the 'D.' I was hoping he was a least right though on the price of them bricks up under the seat. There had to be at least ten boxes on the plane, which I helped load. And judging by the size of the boxes each box could fit twenty joints easily. I had a funny feeling when Nick introduced me to his dad, when he said that he was a pilot, I tucked my head back in disbelief. First, it was the name, he told me to call him Torch, and then it was his appearance. Torch looked like he was torched. His eyes were blood shot red, he smelled like a brewery, and he dressed like a biker wearing tight faded jeans and a black leather vest with the same Hell Angels patch on the back as the one stamped on the coke.

"Where are y'all taking it?"

"To Detroit with us. My dad just drops em' off, they've already been paid for. He gets $1,000 for every kilo he delivers."

I could only wonder who the hell was copping like that and to have pre-paid them. King David wasn't even doing it like that. That's the level I wanted to be on...

After stopping twice at two private air fields to re-up on gas, we were finally circling above the Detroit City Airport waiting on clearance to land. My stomach was filled with butterflies and anticipation as I watched the cars go up and down Gratiot Ave. It had been two months since I left for Cali, and it seemed like a lifetime. I took in a deep breath of that smog-filled Detroit air as I stepped off the plane. "Ah...Home."

Nick was busy helping his dad unload the coke from the plane into an awaiting U-Haul truck. I was going to wait until later to pull my disappearing act, but I thought 'what better time than now." "Hey Nick, I'm going to go use the bathroom," I said heading for the terminal."

" A'ight. We'll be in, just give us a few minutes."

I got to the entrance of the terminal and hauled ass across Connors Ave. heading into a small neighborhood across the street from the airport. I knew the eastside like the back of my hand. I cut down Sanford street and ran down to Gunston where I spotted a cab parked at the Amoco service station. I climbed in the back and handed the driver a crisp twenty.

"7 Mile and Caldwell, please." I said, as I sat low in my seat. I did it! I was back on deck with the free key of coke I clipped from one of the boxes while Nick was in the bathroom.

Chapter Eighteen

I told the cab driver to let me out at the corner of Caldwell and Hillsdale. I could see everyone out on the block running to and from cars serving custos. I wanted to just walk up out of thin air on nuccas and watch them look like they'd seen a ghost. I threw a towel over my head and proceeded down the block almost going unnoticed, I could hear a pack of hoodrats whispering, "Girl, who is that with that towel on their head," one of the girls said as I walked past them. I walked up behind Rocko and put my finger to the back of his head and said, "nucca, where that money at?"

Rocko was stuck for a minute, he put his hands slowly up in the air as if it were a real stick up. I bust out laughing and pulled the towel from my head.

"Coach," Rocko said excited as he turned around. "Hey yal'll, look, it's Coach." Rocko said rushing over to show me some love. When did you get back? Tina ain't say nothing about you coming back."

"I bet she didn't," I said, as the rest of the crew rushed over to show the boy some love.

"It's going down tonight fo'show, my nucca," Rome said.

"Yeah, we gone put something together for you," Lil' Pimp said.

I couldn't believe my eyes, he had finally cut that tired ass perm off. "What's up Pimpin', you ain't pimpin' no more?"

"Nah, baby. I'm a full blooded hustla now. I'm hustlin' the block and hustlin' hoes too," he said still with that pimp talk.

"Black, what's good my baby?"

"Ain't shit, man. You done got dark as shit out here soaken up that sun," he said, as he showed me some love.

"So, what ya'll been up to?" I asked.

"Just tryna' get this money and stay alive." Rome said.

"Yeah man, since you've been gone a lot of nuccas been coming up dead 'round this bitch. Dre, off Bloom got murked up at Pershing. Deon, off Buffalo got murked at the park on Syracuse, and nuccas been coming through bustin' at nuccas on the block every night damn near. Shit is crazy out here, so we got our bread during the day and shut down like we used to," said Rocko.

I could see the fear in all their eyes as Rocko recanted the latest events. It all brought me back to why I left. "So, what's the business with the hook, they still been through here asking 'bout me?" I asked.

"Nah, that shit died down 'bout a week or two later. It's been too much other shit going on 'round here," Rome assured.

That shit was like the weight of the world had lifted from my shoulders. That feeling was short-lived as Dump's musty ass appeared on the front porch.

"Coach, come here boy," he ordered, standing with his hands on his hips.

"Pss.." I said letting out some air, as I reluctantly headed for the porch. "I'ma holla at ya'll later on."

"In the house," Dump said holding the door open for me to go in. "What are you doing back in Detroit?" Dump asked as he closed the door.

That whole incident is done and over with," I said.

"Tina didn't say nothing to me about you coming back, so when did you get back?"

"Today. Look Dump, I can hold my own from now on. So, whatever I get myself into I'ma handle it. I'm not..."

"You're not what?" Dump interrupted.

"I'm not running no more, period."

"A'ight now, I want you to remember what you just said. Coach, you think you've got it all figured out, but you have no idea. I keep tellin' you this is."

"I know, grown man business," I said finishing Dump's sentence.

"Long as you know that. I'm going to start treating you like a man."

"That's all I ask," I said.

"So, what you didn't like Cali, or what?" Dump said changing the subject.

"It was alright, I guess."

Couldn't wait to get back here to nothin', huh? Well, alright, I ain't gone hold you up. I know your boys are waiting on you."

"Yeah, I'ma get going," I said heading for the door.

"Coach," Dump stopped me at the door, he was pointing to his head with his finger, and then said. "Remember."

I closed the door after nodding in agreement. ' Remember what?' I thought. "Nah, nucca you betta remember."

"Coach, where you going?" asked Rocko.

"I gotta put my shit up. I'ma get up with ya'll in a minute,"
I said, crossing the street heading for my house.

*****

"Tina!" I yelled as I walked through the house. Rick James
and Tina Marie was pumping through the crib, I knew she
was around here somewhere. "Tina!" I yelled as I walked
through the kitchen and out back to the patio. Tina was
sitting near the pool in a lawn chair with some dude beside
her. She looked like she had seen a ghost, me standing on
the patio deck. She whispered something to ole boy, then
jumped up trying to appear surprised.

"Corey," she said rushing towards me with open arms." We
embraced, then she stood back, so she could inspect me
from head to toe. I hadn't taken my eyes of that nucca
sitting by the pool with his shirt off lookin' like Sharlamar.

"Who is that?" I asked with an attitude.

"Oh, that's Ty, an old friend of mine," Tina said faking a
smile.

"What's he doing over here, and why he ain't got no shirt
on?"

"Excuse me, but I am grown. And I am still you mother."

"So, this is what you've been doing. This is why you ain't
bothered to return any of my calls."

"Come on in the house," Tina said grabbing my arm.

"Get the hell off of me," I said jerking away. Tina slapped
the cowboy shit out of me. My face was stinging like E-
muthatucka. If she wasn't my ole' bird, I would've
stomped her ass out.

"Get yo' ass in here!" demanded Tina, as she stood with the
door opened.

I mean mugged ole' boy one more time, then reluctantly followed Tina into the kitchen.

"Why you hit me?" I asked. Tina had never before put her hands on me.

"Let me tell you something. I don't owe yo' ass or nobody else for that matter a fuckin' explanation on who I'm seeing."

"So, you cheatin' on daddy?"

"Corey, your daddy is dead. And I am very much still alive. Furthermore, I am a young woman with needs."

"I ain't tryna' hear that shit," I snapped and walked off. I headed straight for my stash. I wasn't about to be sitting around here callin' another nucca daddy. Tina had lost her fuckin' mind.

"Where the fuck is my money at?" I yelled, as I held the empty shoe box in my hand. There was not a dime in there. I walked back out into the kitchen to find Tina and Ty. He appeared to be leaving as he kissed Tina on the forehead, kind of like King David used to do before he left out. I was steaming!

"Where is my money?" I demanded.

"I'll talk to you later," Tina said closing the patio door behind Ty. She spun around with her murder mask on, and said, "I spent it."

"You spent it? All of it?"

"Yes... something came up, and I had to pay for yo' daddy's plot."

"What about the work?"

"Gone."

"Yeah, just like me." I slammed the box to the floor, then stormed back into my room to grab my bag.

"What are you doing back?" Tina's words were cut short by the slamming of the front door.

Chapter Nineteen

I walked over to where Rocko and the rest of the crew were standing, stopping in front of Rocko with my murder mask on, "How come you ain't tell me Tina had that monkey ass nucca over here?"

"Come here," Rocko said pulling me away from everybody. "Let's take a walk." He walked around to the park on Syracuse and took a seat on the swings.

"Listen, my nucca, I didn't know how to tell you that shit. You know I felt like it was foul too, having ole' boy at the crib," Rocko said.

"How long has he been coming by the crib?"

"I been seeing the nuccas car out front a lot lately, and he been spendin' the night."

I couldn't even fathom the thought of this lame walking through the crib in his boxers, all up in the refrigerator.

"But that ain't all my nucca," Rocko said breaking my train of thought.

I turned and looked him square in the face as if to brace myself for the worst. "What else?"

"Dawg, word on the block and in the Zone is that Tina might be smoking."

"Smokin' what?"

"That ready. Crack…"

"Nucca, stop lying," I said jumping out of my swing.

"Coach, calm down. I'm just tellin' you what the word is. I hope that shit is wrong, you know I do."

I have never known Tina to fuck around with nothing except weed, but now that King David is gone who knows. Maybe she is, I told myself. "So, who told you this, that Tina's smokin'?"

"My nucca, everybody. They say she be coppin' from across 7 Mile, but ain't nobody around here in the Zone gone serve her, just on the strength of you and Kind David. Maybe she's just taking his death hard. Ain't like she's strung out or nothin'."

I couldn't help but think about all the money I had left in the stash that she spent, and all the work too. Something came up alright, I thought...

"I just wanted to put you on point, so you don't be through here not knowing what's good. But it's gone be a'ight, my nucca, a lot of our nuccas people fuck around. Shit, look at Black's momma and daddy, Lil' Pimp's momma and Rome's too. Hell, I ain't even got a momma. So, we all know that pain, and we all crew," Rocko put his arm around my neck, as we headed back to the block.

I appreciated the heartfelt speech from Rocko, but to be real, I wasn't trying to hear that shit. This was my momma here, and to be on crack was devastating. My initial intentions were to just leave the crib 'cause Tina was in violation by having Ty at the crib. But now my focus was to first find out who had turned her out on crack and murk they ass, it had to be Ty, I told myself as Rocko and I walked up the street. I was plotting my next move.

"What's in the bag my nucca? You been carrying that damn thing since you got back," Rocko said.

"Oh, clothes. Yeah, you right I'm tripping, let me go put this up and I'ma get up with you in a minute," I said hitting rocks with Rocko, then cut across to my crib. I walked around back and into the pool house, 'cause I didn't feel like dealing with Tina.

I locked the door behind me and closed the blinds on the two windows. I dumped a brick of cocaine onto the kitchen counter, and stabbed a steak knife into the center of it and pulled the wrapper off. I looked at the brick of cocaine as it glistened with oils and crystals, and told myself "Let's get it." I took the wrapper and soaked it in a Pyrex dish filled about halfway with water. I wanted to get any residue off the wrapper. I wasn't wasting shit. I cooked the entire brick 4 ½ ounces at a time, whipping each batch and stretching the 4 ½ to 6 ½ of butter. Then I sacked up 9 ounces worth of double-ups, and stashed the rest inside the motor of an old refrigerator we had out back. I was back, and back on my bullshit. I reluctantly went inside the house, so I could change into my block gear and grab a hammer out of King David's arsenal. As I tucked the brand new black .40 Cal Berretta into my pants, Tina stepped into the room.

"What are you doing now Corey?" she asked, knowing that I was up to something.

"Tryna' replace all the money you blew, or smoked up. Whatever you did with it." I said.

Tina's eyes lit up like she had hit a rock.

"What, you didn't think I'd find out?" I asked.

Tina went straight on the defense. "I done told you that I don't owe you or nobody else's ass no damn explanations. So, what if I've been treating myself. What? I am still your mother whether you like it or not."

"We'll see," I angrily said brushing past Tina through the door.

*****

"Got them double-ups. Copp and flip, baby is back in effect. Double yo' bread." I announced as I hit the block in straight grind mode.

"You back on?" Black asked excited.

"Butter pecan," I said pulling a fat hun'd dollar sack out of my hoddie pocket.

Nuccas were on them shit. I had sold 50 double-up's in a matter of two minutes.

I had another 50 double-up's to jump, and I knew just where to get 'em off.

"Coach, is that you?" Mario asked, as I walked up on the scene. "Nucca, where you been at?" he asked excited.

"Shit, man I had to lay low from that Deal$ situation. But it's all good. What's up? I see ya'll nuccas holding the fort down." I nodded to all the Bloom street nuccas.

"But what's up with you, you been a'ight?" asked Mario. He was posted on the hood of a car sipping on a fifth of Remy Martin. He tried to pass me the bottle.

"Nah, I'm straight, but good-looking. I got them double-up's back on deck." I showed Mario the work.

"Ah...so, you back out here. Hell yeah, let me get five of them shits," Mario said digging in his pocket.

"Got them double-ups!" I announced.

Nuccas were flocking and fighting over who was next. I had jumped all 50 packs and had orders for 20 more.

I was back at the pool house sitting at the coffee table counting the money I'd just made. It came out to about $7,000. That was a start, I told myself. I had to get another pager and find a steady connect though if I was going to get this money. I stashed the bread and grabbed some more double-ups to hit the block with. I set out on foot to see what was up with Felicia. It had been a while since I last saw her and I wanted to see if I could get my old driver back. I could see the pack of hoodrats sitting on Felicia's front porch as I turned the corner. I threw my hoodie on and walked up the block. Stopping in front of the pack of rats.

"Who dat?" Sussie asked, trying to peek under the hood.

"Never who dat," I said peeling back my hood.

"Oh my God, Coach!" They all went crazy and rushed down to show me some love. All of them with the exception of Amanda's fine ass. She was playing high-post as usual.

"What's all this damn noise?" Felicia's loud ass said coming to the screen. "Coach!" She yelled, then ran out to show me some love. "Boy, how come you ain't call me?" she asked, hitting me in the back of the head after we finished hugging.

"My bad. But I'm here now," I said.

"Thank God. 'Cause these nuccas 'round here is a bunch of fuckin' flunkies, and I know we 'bouts to get this money," Felicia said, more like a question.

"No doubt. That's why I came to holla' at you. You still down to be my driver?"

"We did that already. We gotta step our game up, Coach. Fuck them double-up's," Felicia said.

I knew Felicia had game, shit she was Barb's daughter, so I heard her out. "What you got in mind?" I asked.

Felicia pointed to an abandoned house directly across the street. "We can open up shop. Just how King David used to do it. Copp and go baby," Felicia said mocking ole' Pops.

"Where we gone get the custos from?"

"Come here," Felicia said pulling me to the side. "You act like all these fuckin' crackheads running around here got Dump's name on their forehead. His ass don't run shit 'round here, especially when I got mouths to feed. You let me worry about the custos. I just need you to have that butta ass work. Trust me, they gone come."

"Sounds like you had this on yo' mind for a minute."

"I'm just tired of scrambling, Coach. You feel me? Ain't no reason why we not 'pose to be rich. We know how to get money. Between yo' dad and my Moms they had the Zone on lock. I'm not 'bout to sit back and let a lame like Dump get all this money. But I need you with me."

"Let's do it," I said hitting rocks with Felicia.

"That's my baby. Damn I missed yo' fine ass. Come on and let's smoke somethin'," Felicia said as we headed up the stairs.

"Amanda, what's up? We ain't speaking?" I asked.

"Have we ever?" Amanda said rolling her eyes.

"Let me holla' at you for a minute," I said stopping in front of her.

"What?"

"Damn Shawty, it ain't like that. I just wanted to apologize for how things went down. I had been going through a lot, and Deal$ just caught me at a bad time. I know you had love for the nucca and I'm sorry. Can you accept my apology?" I asked sincerely.

"I just don't understand why you had to kill him," Amanda said getting all teary eyed.

"I ask myself that question everyday," I said lying. But I wanted to make sure you were alright, and I hope we don't have any harsh feelings. We cool?" I softly asked.

Amanda looked up at me with those pretty green eyes and wiped a lone tear from her gorgeous face. "We cool."

"Aw...That's so sweet. Now can you two sentimental muthafuckas come on, so we can blow these trees." Felicia tried to lighten the mood.

We kicked it all night at Felicia's. I was posted on the sofa with Amanda close to me, we chopped it up about everything. The girl that I thought was stuck up, was actually easy to talk to. I asked her why she never gave me the time of day.

"You never said one word to me, Coach," she said.

"True. True. But you always had this serious ass look on your face, like you are mean mugging somebody," I said mocking Amanda. She laughed and pushed me.

"Forget you. I don't be lookin' like that," she said still laughing.

"Nah, you know you're too pretty for that." I said.

"You like me, Coach?" Amanda turned and asked softly. We were looking into each other's eyes.

"That's what I been tryna' tell you, shawty," I said reaching for Amanda's hand.

"You making me blush."

"That's a good thing, right?" I said kissing the back of her hand. "Come on," I said standing up, still holding Amanda's hand.

"Where we going?"

"Back to my crib. You gone chill with me and keep me company? That's cool?"

"Yeah. Let me go tell Felicia and then we can leave."

*****

I couldn't believe it. I was alone with Amanda, the girl of my dreams. I had fantasized for so long about the day I'd hold her in my arms and kiss those pretty pink full lips of hers. And here I was, all alone with her. We were chilling on the sofa listening to *After Seven*. I had poured us a glass of champagne, and had the lights dimmed. I was trying to set the mood and hopefully I'd be swimming in some pussy in a minute. Amanda was looking amazing, and smelled even better. I scooted close to her and lifted her feet into my lap. "Take these off, and relax," I said, as I helped her take off her shoes.

I rubbed both her feet while Amanda looked over the rim of the champagne glass at me. The look she was giving me made my dick rock straight up, as she noticed and slid her right foot down to my stick. Not being able to withstand the tease, I pulled Amanda toward me. With our face inches apart and our hearts racing with lust in our eyes, I leaned in and kissed her soft lips. She tasted just as I had imagined, like heaven.

I slid my hand down the side of Amanda's face, and down to her arms. While still kissing, I lifted her halter top over her head revealing her perfect 32 D's with pink nipples were standing at attention. She tilted her head back and let out a deep sigh of satisfaction, as I inhaled one of her breasts. I worked out on both of them until I could feel the steam rising from Amanda's body.

I unfastened the button to her skin tight jeans and helped her peel out of them. She wasn't wearing any panties. I just wanted to savor the moment and take all her beauty in, so I stood her up and spun her around in front of me. She was blushing from ear to ear as I admired her every curve. My blood was boiling and my dick felt like it was going to explode. I quickly got undressed, then sat back on the sofa. I pulled Amanda to me and lifted her up, helping her mount the head of my dick.

"Oh…" Amanda sighed, as she slid down. She arched her back, giving it that C shape and gripped me like a seasoned vet, working her pussy muscles and throwing that soft yellow ass down against my pelvis. I reached around and palmed both ass cheeks to help guide Amanda up and down, but she reached back and moved my hands. She wanted to be in control, and I wasn't complaining because she had everything under control.

"Coach," she moaned as I kissed her softly on her chest.

"Yeah," I whispered. My voice was quivered, and I could feel pressure building up in my dick. It was a sensation that I had never before experienced.

"Coach…I'm coming…" Amanda said.

I could feel her wall contracting. She jerked violently, then continued throwing that ass on me while screaming, "Ah…Ah…Oh my God."

My stomach did a back flip as my dick exploded. "Ah.." I groaned from the unusual sensation. I had never bust a nut before. I had fucked plenty of times, and it felt good, but never once did I bust. I was out of breath, and so was Amanda. She leaned forward resting on my shoulder with my half limp dick still inside her. She began kissing me softly around my neck and rubbing her fingers up and down my chest. I couldn't believe it, but it was real. It wasn't long until we were going for round two.

Chapter Twenty

Two weeks later...

Everything Felicia said was gold. We turned the abandoned house across the street from her crib into a spot, and that bitch was doing numbers. We were doing 9 ounces in pieces on the daily. Instead of selling dimes like everyone else, we was pushing fat ass nickels. We had to be the first in the city to start nicks, as we named them

Felicia was pretty much running the spot, including from the spot workers, which were Felicia's hoodrats. She rotated them in and out in daily shifts, paying them $100 each. We had Phil, a local crackhead who was also the Zone's Mr. Fix it, he put iron bars on all the windows, and storm gates, and put T-boards on the front and side doors. The house was so secure to the point that if the police tried to raid, they'd have to wait until we let them in. We also had a serving hole. Money came in, and crack went out. No money, no crack. The only time those T-boards came down and those doors opened, was if Felicia or I was at the door.

My only job was to cook the crack. I couldn't trust nobody else with the recipe, so every morning I'd chef up 9 ounces of whip and wait for Felicia to come pick it up. We were doing good, Felicia bought her a new Jeep Wrangler and laced her crib with new furniture. Me, I was on stack mode. I had managed to put away $70,000, but for some reason it just wasn't enough. So, I didn't spend much with the exception of the money I'd been giving Amanda to hit the mall up with Felicia. Since that night she spent with me, we'd been together ever since. We had turned the pool house into our own little crib. Amanda moved all her clothes and stuff from around at Felicia's to the pool house. Ain't nobody sweat her moving in with me 'cause just like everybody else in the Zone, Amanda's people were strung out on crack. Felicia knew I was good people and would look after Amanda, so it was all love.

I hadn't been out the house much since Amanda moved in. We were too busy fucking, well she was fucking me...Besides all the sex, Amanda was capable as well. Living with her was like being married. She knew how to cook almost anything, and was no stranger to cleaning. In those two short weeks, somewhere along the line, we started calling each other boyfriend and girlfriend. And even though I was very much enjoying my baby's company, I was starting to miss the grind. Rocko came through the crib one morning while Amanda and I were having breakfast. Since coming home, I hadn't been really fucking with the crew like that 'cause I was on the grind, and laying up with Amanda.

"That's how you doin' it Amanda, you got my nucca on lock 'round this piece?" Rocko joked taking a seat.

"You already know," Amanda said, as she set Rocko's plate down in front of him, then leaned over and kissed me.

"So, when you gone come out and play?" Rocko teased.

"Nucca, fuck you." I laughed.

"But nah, seriously though. You know our birthdays are coming up, and you know we always do it big together," Rocko said.

"True. True."

"So, what we gon' do this year? We gotta do it real big for the haters, my nucca. And I know you holding too. Buffalo 'round there doing its numbers."

"Who told you that's me?"

"Oh, so you gon' try and lie to yo' manz? Nucca everybody knows that's yo' spot, and you just got Felicia runnin' it."

It wasn't like it was no big deal or nothing. I just didn't see the need to have nobody in my business.

"Yeah, but what about the party? What you got in mind?" I asked, changing the subject.

"I want to drop like ten stacks on this boy. We can go half and half. But I want to rent the State theatre and have Mc Breed do a show with Top Authority opening up. I already did the foot work and we can get both Breed and Top Authority for $7,000. And the State Theatre wants $1,500 for the booking. The rest will go to security and the cost for printing up flyers."

"Why would we spend ten g's to have some nuccas from Flint to perform at our party? I asked. "Breed and Top Authority will draw the crowd. On the flyer, it's going to have our pictures and name: Coach and Rocko's birthday bash. Come celebrate with two young Dons and enjoy live performances by Mc Breed and Top Authority. Cover charge $10.00 per head."

My eyes lit up at the sound of $10 per head. "So, who the $10.00 go to?" I asked.

"Us. This is a business move. We not only having our party, but it'll be basically free and we gon' make some g's doing it. The State Theatre holds about 2,000 something people, and with Breed, we gon' sell out, my nucca. So, you in?" Rocko asked.

"Yeah, we can do that. So, when is all this supposed to take place?"

"This weekend. I just gotta give them the deposit and we on."

I nodded to Amanda and she disappeared into the bedroom.

"You finally got that bitch," Rocko said smiling.

"You know how we do," I said hitting rocks with Rocko and laughing.

"What ya'll laughing at?" Amanda asked stepping back into the kitchen. She was carrying a brown paper bag in her hand.

"Ain't nothin'. Little inside thang, ain't nothin'." I took the money out of the bag and counted out five thousand, then handed it to Rocko for my half of the party.

"It's gonna be on!" Rocko said excited.

Chapter Twenty-One

Me and Rocko's party was the talk of the town.
Nuccas who were older than us was even showing us props
on getting Breed and Top Authority to do a show. And for
real, that's all Rocko and I wanted was for our names to
start ringing outside the Zone. We were already celebrities
in our hood, but we wanted to be known all over. We had
seen the response and the number of tickets we sold, and
decided we could do this every two weeks and get famous
doing it.

Amanda hit the mall up and got us fresh to death with
matching leather 8 ball coats and matching black Gucci gym
shoes. She, of course, accessorized with bamboo earrings,
herringbone necklace and anklet, Swiss Movado watch, and
Coach handbag. I splurged a little bit on a thick gold dookie
rope with a king tut medallion covered in crushed diamonds.
I had the black Karl Kani stone washed jeans with a white
Karl Kani T-shirt. And to cap it off I copped a pair of gold
frame Cazal's and had Louie at Customs inside of
Greenfield Plaza, lace em' up with some crushed ice around
the nose and arms.

Together, Amanda and I looked like something
straight out of *Word Up Magazine*. She had this thing about
showing up late to an event. I wanted to get there early
seeing as though I was part host. I wanted to meet and greet
all the playas and pushas as they hit the door, but my baby
wasn't having it. She felt like the world was waiting on her,
and she didn't want to disappoint them. In so many ways,

Amanda reminded me of Tina, they both were just so damn jazzy. Amanda insisted that we show up late and not only that, she wanted to do it in a limo. The way she was arranging thangs, one would think it was her party. But it was all good. My baby could do no wrong, and she knew to have her way all she had to do was bat those long eye lashes and talk in her little girl voice. That shit had been working on me since she first put it down.

Miles Limousine Service picked us up from the crib in a stretched out cocaine white box Lincoln town car. That boy was equipped with a phone, TV, VCR, full wet bar stocked with bubbly, and deep plush black leather seats. Amanda and I sunk down into the comfort of our seats and enjoyed the good life as we cruised down 7 Mile taking the longest possible route per orders of 'Captain Amanda.'

"Happy birthday, baby," she said, leaning over giving me a long passionate kiss. Then she presented me with a rectangle shaped jewelry box.

"What's this?" I asked smiling as I opened the box and pulled the 18 karat gold Rosary out.

"Put it on, Coach."

I hadn't told Amanda how I felt about God being just a myth. We had never had a conversation about religion, or a lot of other things for that matter. I didn't want to spoil the night, so I just put it on.

"You like it, baby?"

"Yeah, but what does it mean?"

"It'll protect you…" Amanda said, then she kissed me.

*****

There was a long line wrapped around the corner of the State Theatre, some people were even standing in the alley at the back entrance trying to buy last minute tickets. All heads turned toward the limousine, as the driver got out to open Amanda's door at the curb. We emerged like we were about to walk the red carpet. The attention was there, only thing that was missing were flashing lights. Two muscle back bouncers pushed through the crowd and then led Amanda and me inside. We could hear the on-lookers riding our jock

"They doing the mothafucka with them 8 ball jackets," one person said.

"Who is that young ass nucca?" I heard someone ask as we stepped inside.

The music was beating, Top Authority had already taken stage and was performing their latest hit *Black Superman*. Amanda and I both stopped and took our pose, so all the haters could see the moment they all had been waiting on had arrived, us. While flogging, we were also scanning the crowd in search of anyone from the Zone. The way Rocko had the shit laid out was crazy! There were row seats for your nobody ass nuccas who just wanted to see Breed and Top Authority, then there were tables with carded names, displaying all the playas and pushas, kind of like V.I.P., only not. Upstairs was where it was really going down. Someone upstairs hanging over the balcony was waving their hand at us.

"Baby, look!" I said turning Amanda around to see.

"That's Chanelle!" she said exited. 'Excuse me, how do we get up there?" Amanda asked one of the security guards.

"Follow me."

We were led up a series of spiral steps and onto the balcony where we found all our friends. Amanda split one way and I went the other.

"What up dough?" I said walking up on the crew. It was Rocko, Black, Pimp, Rome and some off brand brown skinned nucca. They all had bottles of Moet in their hands and plenty of weed in rotation.

"That's how you killin' 'em?" Rocko asked grabbing at the 8 ball leather jacket.

"Happy birthday, my nucca," Black and all the rest of the crew said hitting rocks one by one, and each handing me their gift.

"We gone open up the gifts later," Rocko said. "I want you to meet the man responsible for helping us turn out such a big crowd. Coach, this is Mc Breed." Breed and I hit rocks.

I'm looking at the nucca, and I'm looking at Rocko at the same time like, "You sure this corn-ball lookin' nucca is Breed?" But we were about to find out. Me and 2,000 other people. Top Authority had just finished their set, and Breed was up. He hit rocks with me and Rocko, then took a sip of Henny and escorted himself through the crowd straight to the stage.

An early version of 'Ain't no future in yo' frontin' came blasting through the woofers, and the crowd went crazy as Breed spit the lyrics. Yeah, he was no doubt, Mc Breed in the flesh.

Rocko reached behind the fully stocked bar and handed me a bottle of Moet. I popped the cork and hit bottles with the crew as if it were a toast. We were all leaning over the balcony rockin' to the sounds of Breed and yes, feeling ourselves. The night was perfect. Rocko and I were greeted by all kinds of playas and pushas from around the city, young and old. Nuccas wanted to meet us personally, some even exchanging phone numbers. I guess they figured that our young asses had to be doing something in the streets to have pulled a stunt like this off. That's how it was in Detroit. Once a nucca saw some potential in you, their interest was sparked. But you had to show something first, and Rocko and I were showing....

Breed took a break after doing eight songs, so it was time to hit the lower floor and stunt on all the haters. First, Amanda and I flicked it up, posing with Ten g's in all hundred dollar bills with the Detroit skyline as the background. Then Felicia and her squad did the damn thang, acting like the hoodrats they were. Then the crew flicked it up. Me, Rocko, Black, Pimp, and Rome. For some reason out of all the pictures we took, that was the only one I kept. Amanda cuffed the rest of them in her Coach handbag.

As everybody from the Zone headed through the crowd on our way back up to the balcony, a scuffle broke out. Rocko and I were at the back of the pack, all I could see were arms swinging. The music cut off, the commotion and instead of people going the opposite direction, they were joining the fight making it harder for me and the crew to get up there. Out of nowhere, some nucca stole the shit out of me in the side of my face breaking my Cazal's. Another dirty ass nucca tried snatching my chain off my neck, but it didn't break I caught him with a mean two piece sending him to the floor as Black and Rome put feet on him. I spun around in search of the first nucca who stole on me, Rocko was going toe to toe with him. I caught the nucca on the side of his head with my Moet bottle, shattering the bottle

into pieces and sending him to the floor. I pushed on
through the crowd in search of Amanda. In the distance, I
could see Felicia putting in that work on some yellow bone
broad. Felicia had the girl's hair wrapped around one of her
hands and was serving her with stiff upper cuts with the
other hand. "Boom! Boom!" Two shots rang out, sending
the crowd in every direction. As the crowd dispersed for the
exits, I could now see Amanda. She was kneeling down
over someone. I rushed over to her and she was holding Lil'
Pimp's body in her arms rocking back and forth. "What the
fuck?" I said, not wanting to believe my eyes. Lil' Pimp
was bleeding badly from his stomach and chest.

The rest of the crew gathered around Lil' Pimp as he laid
there bleeding out.

"I'm not gone make it," Lil' Pimp said, with that same look
of death I had seen in Craig and Deal$' eyes.

"Come on," I said grabbing Rocko and Black by the arm.

"Who did this?" Rome asked one of the girl's from the
Zone. She was crying her heart out, but managed to say "it
was them Six Mile nuccas."

Me, Rocko, and Black hit the exit in search of them Six
Mile bitch nuccas. Soon as we got to the curb, four raggedy
Chevys crept past with nuccas hanging out the window
throwing up the Six Mile signs and talking shit. I pulled my
9 mm Beretta from my waist and started firing into the
second car. I walked closer to the cars and fired non-stop
into the passing third and fourth car until my gun was
empty. One of the cars veered off and slammed into a
parked car. I was still squeezing the trigger as if I were still
shooting. I had zoned out.

I hadn't heard the man standing about twenty feet in front of me, when he yelled "Freeze!" Nor did I see the gun he had aimed dead on me. By the time I looked up, it was too late, I was hitting the ground. A single shot from the undercover cop's .38 special had knocked me off my feet. I was lying on my back looking up at the stars thinking, am I dead? My chest was numb and for a moment I couldn't move. In the distance, I could hear people screaming and cars speeding by. "Oh my God. Coach!" Amanda screamed as she raced over to me. "Baby, get up," she cried, as she tried to help me to my feet. But the undercover cop was all over me. He yelled for everyone to stand back with his gun drawn. He radioed for back-up while holding the crowd at bay.

Two more undercovers approached the scene, as sirens and lights filled the night.

"Miss, you have to step back. This is a police investigation," one of the plain clothes officers told Amanda.

"But that's my boyfriend," she cried.

"I understand, but you're going to have to step back."

"Sir, can you stand up?" an older cop asked leaning over me.

What the fuck he meant, he didn't see any holes or blood? I knew I had been hit.

"Come on, up to your feet." The old white officer pulled me up and slapped the cuffs on me.

"Have a medic take a quick look at 'em, then throw his ass in a squad car," ordered the sergeant.

Two young black female medics rushed over to me and did a quick assessment. "He's okay," One of them said. The officer who was holding me then escorted me to an awaiting police cruiser. As soon as I was in, the car sped off, with two other cars in tow. I could see Amanda standing at the curb with tears running down her face and both hands to her mouth. For some reason I knew that would be the last time I saw her for a long while.

Chapter Twenty-Two

They took me downtown to 1300 Beaubien Police Headquarters, and housed me on the 9th floor where they kept all the high profile criminals. Nuccas were up there for rape, carjacking, and murder. I had yet to be told exactly what I was being charged with. I knew they had me on gun possession at least, but to have me on the 9th floor was beyond me, so I thought. I took off my jacket and lifted my T-shirt above my head. I stood in front of the small foggy mirror mounted on the wall above the stainless steel pissy sink/toilet, and rubbed my chest where it still hurt. I had a big red bruise between my chest cavity, just above my stomach. I knew I had been hit, but by what? I looked down at the gold Rosary and lifted the cross to my face. It had a dent dead center in the cross, and the legs of Jesus had been blown off by what I guess was the slug that hit me. I thought about what Amanda told me earlier, then kissed the cross.

"Townsend, get dressed," a voice down the hall hollered, then my cell door lock opened. I put my shirt and coat back on, then stepped out into the dimly lit hallway. A deputy stood at the far end in the doorway. "Come on down. There's some people here to see you," the guard said.

An older cat who was two cells over from me, reached his hand through the bars, stopping me. He said, "Youngin', I don't know why you're in here, but I'm sure it's serious, otherwise you wouldn't be up here. Listen to me, don't say a word when you go in there. Tell 'em you want a lawyer…" I nodded in appreciation, and walked to where the deputy was standing.

"Right in there," the deputy said pointing to a conference room.

The door was open and I could hear two voices talking, "Come in and have a seat," one of the detectives said looking over the rim of his glasses as I stood in the doorway.

"Corey Townsend, is that it?" The detective asked, as I took a seat in front of him. His partner kept eyeing me while talking into the phone. I didn't acknowledge the detective's questions regarding my identity. "Is Corey Townsend your name, or isn't it?" The detective said angrily.

"I want a lawyer," I said.

The detective who had been on the phone, slammed down the receiver and stormed over to the table. "You hear this shit, Tom, the little fuck wants a lawyer," laughed Detective Jackson, which his name tag read.

"You're going to need ten lawyers to help you get out of all the trouble you're in," detective Tom barns said standing over me.

"First off, let me read you your rights. You have the right to remain silent. Blah, blah, Blah.." was all I heard, as the detective read me my Miranda rights. He had my full attention though when he started reading off my charges. "Carrying a concealed weapon, discharging a firearm in public, attempted murder, murder…."

"What you say, murder?" I interrupted the detective. My heart was beating a mile per second.

"Yes, murder on two counts. Possibly a third count. We're waiting to see if this girl pulls through or not, she's in ICU."

"That's what happens when you open fire into passing cars, people get killed" Detective Barns said while trying to look me in the eye.

I had to take a few deep breaths and calm it down. Maybe they're tryna' bluff me, I told myself. "I ain't killed nobody."

"No?" Detective Barns said walking over to a TV that was sitting on top of a long table. He turned the set on, and there it was, yellow crime tape blocked off the State Theatre, and news anchor recanted the tragic events. A picture of Lil' Pimp flashed across the screen. "Shot dead, at point blank range inside the State Theatre," one anchor said pointing to the scene behind her. "The victim has been identified as a only thirteen year old." The camera then flashed to the street where I had lit them Six Mile nuccas the fuck up. "Two more shot dead at close range, and another young woman is listed in critical condition. Police are calling this retaliation for the shooting and death of the thirteen year old, which occurred just minutes before inside the building. Police have a suspect in custody; his identity has not yet been released."

Detective Barns turned the TV off and looked at me. "Oh, it's very much real. And so will the sentence the judge is gonna give you. So, you need to start making some serious decisions if you want to save some of your life, cause we're charging you as an adult."

"Yeah, I feel you," I said teary eyed. But I was not about to let them see me fold. "And that's why I need a lawyer."

"Take his ass back to his cell. In twenty years, you'll still need a lawyer," detective Barns said, as he picked up the phone.

Within seconds, the deputy appeared at the door, and escorted me back to my cell.

I stood at the entrance of my cell and scanned the six by ten dimensions, thinking to myself, 'this is it' Reluctantly, I laid down on the wooden frame bunk equipped with a two inch thick mattress that reeked of bile and God knows what else. I balled up inside my jacket and zipped it shut like a sleeping bag. I wanted to muffle the sniffles and deep sobs of regret, for I thought my life was over. Two counts of murder were all I could think about. They gon' give me life, I told myself. I had worried myself tired and I drifted off to sleep.

*****

The next morning I was awoken by a deputy screaming at the top of her lungs at the other end of the hall. "Townsend, roll it up. Let's go, court!"

Court, I thought as I rolled out of bed and pulled my arms through my sleeves. I rushed over to the sink and splashed some cold water on my face. The lock on my cell popped and I stepped out into the hallway. "Stay strong youngin'," The old head two cells down said as I passed by. I couldn't help but wonder if he had heard me crying last night. Hopefully, I wouldn't be seeing him anymore, I told myself as I walked through the door where the deputy was waiting.

I was greeted by Detective Barns and Detective Jackson. "You sleep well last night?" Detective Barnes asked almost in a joking manner.

"I told ya'll I wanted to speak with my lawyer."

"Oh, I'm sure there will be one waiting over at the court house for you," Barns said placing handcuffs on me, then performing a quick pat search.

The two detectives signed me out at the front desk, then escorted me through the double doors leading to the streets. As soon as we hit the door, cameras were flashing from all angles, and two news reporters fired questions non-stop. "Did you commit the crimes last night?" one reporter yelled.

Detective Jackson pulled my jacket over my head and rushed me to their patrol car waiting at the curb. We peeled off and bent the corner heading north on Gratiot, 36th District Courthouse was just seconds from the station. Detective Barns pulled into the garage area where prisoners are received and honked his horn. A young black man working as a court officer stuck his head out the door, and waved us in.

I was escorted to a filthy bullpen and told that I was scheduled for an arraignment at 10:00 in front of Judge Drake. I was alone in the bullpen with the exception of the roaches, which decorated half of eaten food on the floor and bench. There was a phone mounted on the wall, my heart skipped a beat as I rushed over and snatched the receiver off the hook. There was no dial tone. I kept pushing buttons and hanging up the receiver, but to no avail. Damn, I thought. Where was my lawyer, Mr. Davidson? Had Tina even notified him? I found a semi-clean spot on the bench and parked it. I sat with my head down thinking of how I might come out of this. It didn't look good on the strength of the undercover cop who shot me, he had witnessed it all. I racked my brain for what seemed like an eternity, my thoughts were interrupted by the sound of a key inserted into the lock on the door. I sat up and watched as the door swung opened. It was my lawyer, Mr. Davidson. I was all smiles.

"How's it going kid?" He asked, as he extended his hand for a shake.

I let out a deep sigh of frustration, then said, "I guess I really messed up this time."

"Yeah, well the charges are a lot more serious than last time. But that's why I'm here. You let me do all the worrying. You just keep your mouth closed. Don't talk to anyone about the case. Not the police, or any of those jail-houserats."

"I got you."

"Right now, they're charging you with two counts of second degree murder. Don't worry about all the other charges because they'll run the time concurrent with the murders, that is if you're convicted. And depending on the amount of evidence, we may want to consider a plea bargain."

"How much time am I facing?"

"Right now 20 years to life. But trust me, they'll come with a plea. They're charging you as an adult right now, only because it's a high profile case. Once the media attention dies down, and we enter plea negotiations, I'm certain they'll be willing to try you as a juvy for a guilty plea. So, to answer your question, you're looking at about five years worst case scenario."

"Five years?" I repeated. That sounded like a death sentence. I'd be 18 in five years, I thought. "You can't do anything better than that?"

"We're going to try and beat this first, of course. I was just giving you the worst case scenario from my experience."

"Alright," I said reluctantly, as I dropped my head into my hands.

"It'll be alright," Mr. Davidson put his arm around me. 'Listen, I have to get upstairs and get ready for court. I'll see you up there."

I looked up from my hands, "Do you know if Tina's here?"

"Your mother?"

"Yeah."

"I notified her off your arraignment, I would think she'd be here. She was the one who retained me."

"Alright," I said, feeling a little better.

*****

The courtroom was packed to the max. Cameras started flashing again as the court officer walked me into the courtroom from the back door.

"Coach!" yelled Rocko. He was seated front and center behind the defense table next to Tina and Dump. I could see damn near the whole Zone on deck. I scanned the faces in search of my baby Amanda, but she wasn't in the building. Maybe she stepped out, I told myself as I took my seat at the defense table next to Mr. Davidson. I looked back at Tina who was stone faced. I don't know if she was just sick of me, or if she was high. Whatever it was, she didn't look good. I hadn't seen much of Tina since my return from Cali and found her poolside with that nucca Ty. I had really been keeping my distance to avoid them, when I saw his car out front I wouldn't go inside the main house. Tina looked bad, and I couldn't help but feel bad because deep down I missed her. I stared into my mother's eyes. I needed her now more than ever. We needed each other. She gave me that wink and cracked a golden smile I needed to know that everything was going to be alright. Just as I cracked a smile, I saw two older dudes rushing towards me from the other side of the courtroom. The first one leaped over the wooden rail and tackled me out of my chair. He was on top of me swinging wildly, and yelling "You killed my son. You killed my boy!" The man kept screaming, as police pulled him off me. He was still clawing at the thin air, screamed his lungs out, as the officers restrained him, then dragged him out of the courtroom.

As I stood up with a busted nose and lip, people in the back from the Zone and the victims' families had some words, then Felicia set it off. She stole on this older woman who looked old enough to be both our grandmother's. The old hag had called Felicia a bitch, and it was all she wrote. The courtroom was in mayhem. Police filled the room within seconds and had defused the situation, starting with Felicia. She went out the door swinging. Everyone, with the exception of Mr. Davidson and I, was asked to leave the courtroom. Tina winked at me, then put her hand to her ear, like call me. After the courtroom was cleared, the judge emerged from his chambers and quickly read off the charges, and Mr. Davidson entered a not guilty plea on each count. My next court date was scheduled for two weeks later, at which time it would be determined whether the State had enough evidence to go to trial.

"Preliminary hearing will be set for October 12th. I am denying any bond as of right know. The defendant is to remain in the custody of the Wayne County Sherriff's department. Where will he be housed?" asked the judge.

"At the juvenile detention center on maximum security, your honor," answered the prosecutor. He was a middle-aged Jewish dude, who looked like he wanted to give me a million years.

"Very well. Young man, you keep yourself out of trouble between now and your next hearing." I nodded in agreement. And with that, two court officers whisked me out of the courtroom and downstairs where Detectives Barns and Jackson stood waiting. They put me in the squad car and drove me over to juvy.

Chapter Twenty-Three

Six Months Later...

For the past 26 weeks I sat in juvy on maximum security with all the baby-gangstas, as the deputies called us. I had counted every day, and hoped that tomorrow would turn over something new. But 26 weeks and counting, I had started to lose all hope. I told myself that wouldn't be me, and yet here I was six months in. And to make matters even worse, Mr. Davidson had been out to see me three times in the past week, he wanted me to take a plea to a lesser charge and be sentenced as a juvenile. He was still talking the five year shit, and strongly advised that I take the deal, because he said he wouldn't be representing me if I went to trial. He said that Tina hadn't paid the rest of the retainer, and wasn't answering the phone. I knew he wasn't lying cause Tina wasn't picking up when I called the crib. My first court date was the last time I saw her. She hadn't been out to visit, nothing. The only person who came to see me was Mr. Davidson, and he was pressed for an answer. Trial was to commence in one week. "What would you do?" I asked King David, closing my eyes. Pops had been coming to me in my dreams lately, that's probably the only thing that was keeping me sane. Deep down, I knew that I had to do some time. But I was still holding onto that thread of hope that I just might get out. I couldn't let go of the streets, and it was pressing my time. If Tina and the crew were holding me down, it would be a lot easier. Amanda, I ain't heard from her either. The last time I saw her was from the back of the police car. I couldn't imagine doing five years all by myself.

Just like he said, Mr. Davidson didn't show up for court on the first day of trial. I wanted to hold out until the final moment to see if the prosecution would offer a lesser deal. They weren't budging, and were ready to begin trial in the event I turned down their final offer.

My new court appointed attorney, Mr. Lewis, stood over me at the defense table awaiting my decision. From the looks of it, I didn't stand a chance. Here it was trial day, and I'm dealing with a lawyer fresh out of law school who had never tried a case before, and didn't know what the hell he was doing. He wasn't even familiar with the specifics regarding my case.

"Mr. Lewis," the prosecutor said, as if she was annoyed while tapping his watch, and looking at my lawyer.

"They want an answer," Mr. Lewis said.

"Fuck it. Tell 'em I'll take the deal,"

I knew deep down it was the best decision. If I went to trial and lost, I'd be facing 20 to life and would be sentenced as an adult. There was no way I was going to beat the charges, the undercover cop was front and center ready to testify, as was a host of other people including Rome, Rocko, and the girl from the Zone who told us it was them Six Mile nuccas that killed Lil' Pimp. My lawyer, Mr. Davidson had sent me my motion of discovery a few days before trial was to start. He wanted to show me that the deck was stacked against me, and to go to trial would be a fool's move.

Rocko and Rome sat in the third row behind the prosecution's bench. They kept smiling and waving at me like I hadn't got their snitch paperwork. Both of them fools had identified me as the shooter. I just looked at them nuccas like they were dumb in the face.

Mr. Lewis rushed back over with the prosecutor on his heels, he was carrying a thick stack of paper. The prosecutor let the stack slam down in front of me, and said, "You've got ten minutes to look it over, and sign it." Mr. Lewis took a seat beside me and tried to thumb through the plea agreement. "Basically, this just means such and such." He tried to run the okie doke on me, trying to speed ball me, but I wasn't going for it. I wanted to read the part where it said I'd be tried as a juvenile, and do no more than five years in juvy. He showed me the stipulations, and I carefully read them twice to make sure I understood them correctly. I was satisfied that there wasn't no shit in the game, so I signed the plea. Mr. Lewis and the prosecutor hurried to the judge's chambers with the plea in hand. And about ten minutes later, they all emerged and court got underway.

Judge Drake shuffled some papers sitting in front of him for a brief moment, then cleared his throat. "I want to start by saying, that I am one hundred percent against the conditions of the plea agreement sitting before me. I believe that the sentence is far too lenient, and does not serve justice in the eyes of the victims' families and the community. The crime you committed and the lives you took show that you have no regard for the law, even at your young age, I believe you are beyond reform. But nonetheless, I have to accept the plea agreement as my hands are tied by the law. Does he understand the conditions set forth in the agreement?" Judge Drake asked Mr. Lewis.

"Yes, your honor. I have reviewed the documents with my client, and he's ready to accept the plea here today." Mr. Lewis answered.

"Very well then. Would the prosecution please lead the proceedings, and satisfy the elements to each count," Judge Drake said.

The prosecutor stood and took the podium. I also was asked to stand and raise my right hand to swear in under oath. There were two counts of second degree murder, but they were being dropped to aggravated manslaughter. I had to state in open court how I killed the two victims. The first was a 16 year old nucca who was riding shot gun in the second car. He had been shot twice; once in the shoulder and once in the right side of his temple. He died on the scene. The second was a 15 year old nucca who was seated in the back seat of the third car. He had been hit four times in the stomach and chest. He died in the ambulance on the way to the hospital. Both victims' families decorated the courtroom, and were furious at the deal the prosecution had struck me with. But like Mr. Davidson had told me, once the media stopped following the case, it would no longer be an attractive case to the State and they'd cut a deal.

About 20 police officers stood with their back to the judge facing the victim's families. In case something jumped off like last time, they'd be able to contain the situation more quickly.

"So, when you say you murdered Joseph Carrington, is that because you fired recklessly and purposely into the car where Mr. Carrington was seated?" asked the prosecutor.

"Yes."

"And, you were in fact trying to do exactly what?"

"I was just shooting. It wasn't at no one in particular. I knew that one of them had killed my friend, so I shot at all of them."

"So, your motive was retaliation to avenge your friend who had been killed inside the State Theatre?"

"Yeah."

"The prosecution is satisfied that the agreements have been met, your honor."

"Very well. And would the defendant like to address the court?" asked Judge Drake.

"This is your last chance to speak before you're sentenced," whispered Mr. Lewis. 'Would you like to say something?

"Nah, it is what it is," I said.

Mr. Lewis stood up, "No, your honor."

"Very well then. I am ready to impose sentencing at this time."

Judge Drake went into his spill about how I was a menace to society, and a nuisance to the black community. I wasn't hearing that shit, though. Fuck what he thought, he didn't know me and where I came from. So, how the fuck was he sitting up there telling me about myself, and passing judgement on me? I chalked it up to what he was really doing, which was venting on behalf of the victims' families. "I am sentencing you to the custody of Wayne County Juvenile System for five years, and a term of two years probation. You are hereby awarded to the State of Michigan until sentence is satisfied. Court is adjourned." Mr. Lewis slapped me on the back, as to say "we're done, and good luck." The court officers rushed over and escorted me out of the courtroom through the back door. I could hear people yelling and shouting angrily against my sentence. I looked back at Rocko and Rome for the last time, then headed out. It was all said and done. Now I had to figure out how I was going to do five year.

Chapter Twenty-Four

Green Oaks Maxi Center, read the sign mounted on a stone slab that resembled a headstone. The bus had pulled into the circular driveway of the juvenile maximum security center. It had been a long eight hour drive from Detroit to the Upper Peninsula of Michigan. The entire drive none of the 16 passengers, including myself, had spoken a single word. We were all shackled at the feet, and wearing belly-chains, which connected to a pair of iron handcuffs. I had stared out the window the entire drive, with knots in my stomach from the anticipation. I had heard every story ever told about Green Oaks. It was supposed to be the baby Jackson State Penitentiary; they called it Gladiator's school. If you were soft, you wouldn't make it.

So far from the looks of the place, every story seemed true. Barbwire lined the roof of the building, as did three rows of fences surrounding the place. And there was a gun tower which sat dead center of the parking lot.

As soon as the bus came to a complete stop, it was like boot camp. Guards dressed in all black army get-up were snatching us off the bus one by one. "Let's go you maggots!" one of the guards yelled from the front of the bus.

I was sitting there like, what the hell I done got myself into. They had us all lined up alongside the bus with our noses touching the freezing cold steel of the bus. It was a blizzard out that bitch, snow banks were as tall as me. We all were standing out there with no coats or hats on, and them slip and slides made by Bob Barker. I was so cold it felt like my feet, fingers, ears, and toes were going to fall off. Those racist Yankees left us standing out there for every bit of 45 minutes doing nothing.

Once inside, they lined us up against the wall, standing dick to booty while we got the shackles and chains removed. This cock strong drill sergeant looking mothafucka' was running down his laws, while stopping and spitting in people's faces through his tobacco chewing teeth. "Don't look at me, maggot," he snapped at this guy standing in front of me. He stopped, then did an about face and kept on into his speech. "Your asses are now wards of the State. And in case you're too stupid asses don't know what that means. It means that your ass now belongs to me."

We were led through a series of electronic sliding gates. Each gate we went through felt more like I was never going to see the light of day again. People were screaming at the top of their lungs from down long hallways as our group passed. They sounded like people who hadn't seen another human being in years. 'Where the fuck am I at?' I thought. Sergeant Slaughter led us into a locker room and ordered us all to strip down to our birthday suits. "Dick and balls, is all I want to see. Everything is to come off and place it in front of you. And do not snap or pop your clothing. We don't need no crabs floating around here." It smelled like a musty ass bum had died in that locker room. Those nuccas were funky as e-mothafucka, this one fool in front of me had a wad of shit caked in his drawers. And the guard was all over him, putting him on full blast. "Pick those up!" the guard ordered the young man standing in front of me. 'Now hold them up in the air. You all see this nasty muthafucker's drawers. This is not acceptable here at Green Oaks. You will wipe your ass after using the bathroom, and you will wash your ass at least once a day."

I was holding my breath trying not to inhale any of the funk, and I was damn near about to pass out that's how long the shit was taking. This yankee had us bending over at the waist, squatting and coughing, while he looked for contraband. After the humiliation, we were handed green jumpsuits, a bed roll, and hygiene pack, then lined up single file. I had already started not to like that place. I didn't know how I was going to make it there, and for five years.

*****

"Fresh meat!" someone yelled, as me and two other guys walked through the door.

We're all standing there shaking like a crap game, as we waited for the unit officer to assign us a room. We were in Alpha Unit, and it was said to be one of the wildest units because it only housed new commitments and fuck-ups. I could feel all the nuccas ice grilling me as I stood at the entrance with my head down. "Townsend, you're going to 215 lower," the officer said, taking my ID card they gave me in registry. I looked at the top tier and scanned the numbers on the cells. Damn, I thought as I stepped on 215, which was located all the way in the corner.

I reluctantly put one foot in front of the other and headed for the stairwell. There was about 15 cock strong lookin' nuccas posted on the steps, each mean-mugged me as I headed in their direction. I had already scanned the block, and that was the only staircase, so I had to walk past these fools to get to my room.

"Coach!" a voice called.

I stopped in my tracks and looked up to the top of the staircase.

"Eddie, what's good boy?" I said excitedly, more so because I knew someone there, and wouldn't have to deal with these clowns on the steps, hopefully.

"Man, ya'll nuccas move out the way and let my man up the stairs," Eddie ordered.

Them fools parted like the Red Sea. They went from mean muggin' me, to wondering who I was.

"Where they got you at?" asked Eddie after hitting rocks with me.

"Huh, 215."

"Oh, you're in there with the crazy nucca Dante. Come on, let me take you around there, so you can meet this fool. He one of them funny actin' west side nuccas. I had to put hands on him not too long ago." Eddie was from the flip side of 7 Mile off Gallager Street. We went to Farwell Middle school together. We had never really kicked it before, we were from two different hoods and thinking back, I think our hoods even got into it a few times back in the day. Eddie was in for killing this nucca named Dante up at Mason Elementary, that shit had happened about three years ago. I remembered it like it was yesterday though, 'cause just like me, they had Eddie all on the news and was charging him as an adult.

"Dante, let me holla' at you for a minute," Eddie said knocking on the room door, then stepping in. I was right behind Eddie. "Dante, this my man, Coach, from the city, They got him in here with you, so until we can find him somewhere else to be, this is where he is," Eddie said firmly.

The nucca Dante hadn't looked at me or Eddie. He was chopping up some onions and bell peppers on his locker. He was an ole' light-skinned pretty boy nucca with sandy brown hair, and about my size.

"Bitch nucca, you hear me talkin' to you?" Eddie snapped. He had put on some weight and was cut up like a bag of dope. He tightened his muscles up while standing over Dante.

"It's all good. I ain't got no beef with him," Dante said. His hand was trembling with fear, he was so scared that he dropped the plastic knife he'd been using to cut up the vegetables.

"*Wurppp...Wurppp.*"

"What the fuck is that?" I asked, turning to Eddie.'

"Them the deuces. Somebody's getting it in," answered Eddie as he peeped out the room. "Yep! One of them nuccas you came in with, they put him in with Kirk and Kirk is on his ass already."

"Lock down! Lock down! Everyone to their cell!"

"I'ma holla' at you when we come up off lock down," Eddie said hitting rocks with me, then rushing to his room.

That shit was crazy. I'm standing there looking through the small window of my door down at the situation. Ole' boy, Kirk had a long wooden knife that looked like a vampire steak. It was covered in blood, as was his shirt and hand. He was holding the guards at bay, while two medics scrambled to pull the guy who had came in with me to safety. He was leaking badly from the neck. He started choking out, so they laid him flat out and tried performing CPR, but dude checked out. His eyes locked on the ceiling, and I knew he was no longer with us.

"You gon' see a lot of that around here," Dante said looking over my shoulder, then went back to cutting up his vegetables.

Twenty-Five

Eddie had a reputation at Green Oaks, he had put that work in every nucca who thought they was like that. If a nucca was faking, Eddie was going to expose him. He'd walk right up to nucca and would be like, "Yo' I'm straight tryna see you in the room with the hands or the knife."
The nucca he approached would be like, "Yo' Eddie man, I thought we were cool, why you trippin'?"
Eddie would answer, "Nah, nucca, yo' name ringing too loud 'round this mothafucka, and I'm tryna' see if you really like that." If the fool didn't want to see Eddie in the room, he'd put the beats on him right there for everyone to see.

Everybody respected Eddie. From the prisoners all the way up to the warden. The nucca had so much clout, that he moved throughout the building like he owned it. Since my arrival, we had been hanging tough every day. Eddie laced me with two brand new pair of Nikes, some sweats, a couple of wife beaters, hygiene kit, radio, color TV, and enough commissaries to fill two lockers. The boy had the spot on smash and the suckas in check. Every week when we ordered our commissary, nuccas were just stopping by Eddie's room and handing him duffle bags full of shit. They didn't even owe him for anything.
Eddie said, "They owe me just because."

I wasn't tripping, shit we had to do something to survive in that bitch. I had been there three weeks and hadn't heard from a soul. I was stressing hard about the streets, and why the one's I thought was family had left me for dead. I would lay in my bed looking at the lone picture The best day of my life had turned out to be the worst night of my life. Instead of a birthday party, I guess it was more like a going-away party for me.

"Nucca, all you do is lay up in here and stress. Yo' ass starting to stress me out 'round this bitch," Eddie said walking into the room. The next day after I got there, Eddie beat his celly up in the middle of the night, and made him move out the cell, so I could move in.

"What I tell you about being in here slipping? Look at you. Got ya' shoes off, in here slipping." Eddie said, changing into his gym shorts. "All these nuccas around here ain't bitches now. And they might try you while I'm out at work or anything, so you gotta always be on point. When the doors roll in the morning, nucca, you see me up, boots laced, ready for war. I'm not 'bout to let no nucca bring me no move."

I knew he wasn't lying and was only trying to look out for me 'cause since I've been there, I saw about eight stabbings. And we had been on lock down damn near every other day. It was definitely going down. "Come on man, put ya' gear on and come shoot some ball with me." Eddie said, slapping my feet. "I'ma come chill with you, but I ain't gonna play. I'm still sore from that workout yesterday." I said rolling out of bed. Eddie had put me on his workout plan. Every other da y we'd hit the weights for two hours, and on our off days we'd do pushups and stomach. In the short time I'd been working out with Eddie, I was starting to see some results. I had to get my weight up around that bitch 'cause nuccas were walking around looking like grown ass men.

"Eddie!" nuccas yelled, as we hit the gym door. I was a few feet behind Eddie. No one was shouting me out, I hadn't earned my own name around there yet.

"E-Double," one dude said, as he greeted Eddie and hit rocks with him. The nucca just kind of gave me the half nod, then finished riding Eddie's dick. I took a seat on the bleachers in the east side section. All the nuccas off the east side of Detroit had their own section in the gym, cafeteria, weight pile, phones and TV. And so did the west side nuccas. All the other little hick towns and cities had to get in where they fit in. If they ass didn't fit, they just was hit. They had to watch whatever we wanted to watch, wait til we finished working out, use the phone, shower, everything. And today was no different as all the Flint, Saginaw, Pontiac, Kalamazoo, and Adrian, Michigan nuccas sat scattered out on the bleachers, some calling next.

Today it was East side versus West side. The game was serious because the West side was our rival, just like in the streets. Nuccas was placing bets and talking cash money shit, as the ref stepped to the center of the floor and tossed the ball up into the air, with the east side winning the tip. "Give me the ball," Eddie ordered from the top of the key. He caught and shot the ball without putting it on the floor. The crowd went nuts. "E-Money!" Someone hollered as the shot hit nothing but bottoms.

Troy was point guard for the West side. A little stocky baldheaded black nucca with mean handles. He came down doing coast to coast, shaking Eddie and leaving him at the three-point line. Up and under with a reversed layup, Troy answered Eddie's three. Back down the floor, Eddie called for the rock in the low post. He put his weight down and muscled his way to the rack and scored a cheap two point layup. The nucca Troy caught a long lob pass on a fast break and cranked that bitch with two hands. Everybody in the stands was on their feet and hollering Troy's name. Eddie again called for the ball. He was not about to let Troy show him up in front of the entire jail. "Nah, come here and check it up," Eddie said standing baseline. He was talking to Troy. "Ohhh!" the crowd roared.

Troy switched men so he could check Eddie.

"Clear it out," Eddie ordered, waving his hand for everyone under the basket to move. It was personal. "Matter of fact here, nucca, check," Eddie said throwing a chest pass to Troy to check the ball. Troy took off running with the ball toward his end, and threw himself an alley-oop off the backboard and piped that bitch with one hand.

"Bitch ass nucca, you cheating," Eddie walked up in Troy's face at half court.

Everyone in the bleachers stood up on both sides, east and west. I could see all the off-brand nuccas heading for the exit.

"Nucca, if I cheated hit me in my mouth," Troy said not backing down. And that's exactly what Eddie did. He stole the shit out of Troy. Everybody rushed to mid court and got it in. It looked like a swarm of bees out there. I wasn't about to sit on my hands, and get the pumpkin head later on for not riding. I upped the two homemade knives Eddie had given me earlier and rushed into the ruckus. I grabbed the littlest nucca I could find and worked his ass over, stabbing him all in the face. I wasn't using brute force though, 'cause I wasn't trying to catch another body. "Fuck. Shit," I said, nearly falling to my knees. Somebody had stabbed me in my lower back. That shit sent a lightening volt of pain through my entire body, but I was determined not to fall. I swung wildly at no one in particular, just really trying to keep a nucca off my ass until those people came. "Boom! Boom!" Two rounds let off from the guard's concussion rifle.

"Get down!" Man, nuccas weren't hearing no 'get down' shit. It was knives everywhere, and these goofy muthafuckas talking about get down, and stop. It took them about 45 minutes to gain control of the 300 plus nuccas in the gym. Blood was everywhere, and three nuccas laid dead, two from the West side, and Dave from the East side, and all over a basketball game. I was leaking badly and had to be rushed to an outside hospital, where I stayed overnight. The doctor told me, a half inch deeper and it would have been lights out. The nucca who stabbed me had only missed my kidney by half an inch. And I didn't even know who hit me.

Chapter Twenty-Six

Back at Green Oaks, I was locked in my cell for the past two weeks. We were on institutional lock down from the riot in the gym. They had locked Eddie and Troy in the hole for inciting a riot. Eddie sent me word that they were transferring him to Iona Max Center, another juvy prison, because he was the one who had kicked it off, that administration didn't want him back on the yard. He told me to keep all his property and food, and to stay up. Damn, I thought as I balled up the kite from Eddie. I didn't fuck with any of those corn balls around there, and now the only real nucca I had on my team was leaving me. That feeling had become too familiar lately. "I still hadn't heard from Tina or any of the crew. I finally sat down and wrote Tina a letter, telling her that I needed her in my life. But it had been several weeks, and no response. Every time I tried calling the crib the operator would say that the number had been disconnected. 'What the fuck is she out there doing?' I thought.

Being in jail brought me back to when King David used to always tell me, sometimes in life a man has to make his own family. I was starting to see just what he meant by that. And if I was going to make it with my sanity, I had to stop stressing over things, which were beyond my control. One thing Eddie showed me was how to do time. He said to keep busy all day, that way you don't have no time to be stressing. He said, "Before you know it, they'll be calling yo' name to pack it up." "That's right," I told myself while looking in the mirror. "I gotta bid to do. And the world is waiting on me."

When we came up off lock down, I was sticking to my schedule of working out and going to school. I found a job working in the law library as a clerk to help break up my day. Plus, I wanted to teach myself about all the white man's laws, so when I got out I'd be on point, because I already had it in my mind that I was going to get back in the game. However, this go 'round, I was going to play the game how it was supposed to be played, with patience and precision.

Nuccas stopped giving me the dry nod when I passed by. It was now, "Coach! What up dough?" whenever a nucca was in my presence. The word had spread how I stabbed ole' boy all in the face, and that I even took a hit. In Green Oaks, respect was everything, and the only way to get it was to earn it. You couldn't live off another nuccas rep, like I was doing with Eddie. 'There comes a time in every man's life, when he gotta hold his own nuts,' words to the wise from King David. I had put on some weight and my chest was really starting to develop. I was now benching 225 ten times. When I first started with Eddie, I could get 135 off the rack. Now I'm throwing up two and a quarter with no spot. I was doing anything to try to stay busy.

Seven months into my bid at Green Oaks, I finally got a letter in the mail from Tina. My heart skipped a beat as I held the envelope in my hand, the anticipation of not knowing the contents of the letter caused me to tear it open like a present on Christmas morning. The scent from the letter made me close my eyes, as I inhaled deeply. For a moment I was back on the bricks. I opened my eyes and began reading the letter.

Dear Corey:

My son, I know it has been almost a year now since we've last seen each other. And I want you to know that I am sorry for not being there for you. I know you need me right now Corey, and I promise you that I am going to get it together. When can I come to visit you? Please send me a visiting form soon. And our house phone will be back on next week, so call me, baby. Have you been taking care of yourself in there? You send yo' momma a picture, so I can see how you're growing. Stay out of trouble in there, so when it's time for you to come home, you won't be held up. You're not missing anything. The Zone is still the Zone. Your friends are still out here doing you know what. Don't you worry, baby. This will only make you into a better man. You call me next week. I love you. –Tina.

Just like that, my whole routine had been thrown off with that one letter. I was back to thinking about the streets and wondering about what every nucca was out there doing. But the funny thing is, they weren't worrying about me. I didn't care though, I had just heard from Tina. I must've read her letter ten times. I kept stopping at the part when she said she was going to get it together. Deep down, I knew she was talking about smoking crack. That's why she didn't get at me, but she sounded sincere, like she really wanted to get back in my life. I grabbed an ink pen, some paper and rushed over to the desk.

March 3, 1989
Dear Tina:
What's going on with you? Why are you just now sending me a word? I really hope you're alright out there. You know, there's some things I really been wanting to ask you, but I think it'll best be done in person. Yes, you can come visit me. I'ma enclose two visiting forms in case you want someone to ride with you. They got me way up here in the mountains in the middle of nowhere. I really need to see you. That golden smile of yours, I need to see it to let me know it's all going to be alright. What have you been doing? I know you're disappointed in me for what I did, and I promise this will be my last time coming to jail. You know, it was just so much going on that I crashed into a brick wall. That's why I need you, Tina. I hope that we can go back to being the family we once were. Things have changed, but that doesn't mean we have to. I miss you and can't wait to see you. I'll call home next week to see if you got the visiting forms. Ma' take care of yourself out there. And stay in touch. Talk to you soon.

Love,

Coach

*****

    I marked my calendar for next Monday, which was exactly one week from the day I had received Tina's letter. The house phone would be back on by then and I'd be able to call home. Monday came and went. I tried calling our house number like twenty times, hoping for a different answer, but the operator kept saying the line had been disconnected. Maybe it'll be on tomorrow, I told myself. But Tuesday came and went. The same thing, the line had been disconnected. I tried every day for one week, all day I checked the phone to no avail.

I was refusing to believe that Tina had lied to me. The fact that she never called the phone company to turn the phone back on never crossed my mind. I was too busy making excuses for her. Maybe she's got a new number, and she's sending it through the mail. I held onto that thread of hope for the next three weeks. Each day I was at the officers' station sweating the mail bag. I would stand there until he'd passed out every piece of mail, and everyday it was the same story.

"Sorry Townsend, no mail today," the officer would tell me, then I'd go check the phone to see if the number was on.

Tina had fucked my bid up. The past three weeks I hadn't done anything except sweat the mail bag, and listen to the operator. I hadn't worked out, I wasn't paying attention in school, and I had lost my job in the law library. I found myself back laying in my bed starring up at the top bunk stressing.

*****

"Coach, what are you doing?" It was King David. He had been coming to me in my dreams lately. "Son, you've gotta pick yourself up, and keep moving. You can't worry about your mom right now. Ya'll are in two different worlds right now. She's tryna' survive hers, and you gotta survive yours. But you gotta make it. Coach, you gotta make it, son. Don't nobody want to see you make it, trust me. You have to stand on your own two feet and hold your own nuts now, just how I showed you. Get up, Coach. Don't let me down, son…"

"I won't. I won't let you down Pops," I mumbled, still asleep. I knew I was dreaming, and I didn't want to wake up. Being asleep was the only time I got to see King David. In every dream, he'd be kneeled down rubbing his favorite dog, ole' Bruno. He'd be tending to Bruno while schooling me at the same time. "Coach, I'd rather trust a dog with my life than half these nuccas running around here," King David once said. I couldn't understand the interpretation of the dream, I charged it to the fact that we had spent a lot of time together on the pit bull farm. With King David dead, and me in jail, there was no telling what happened to the farm.

I had to pull it together. I couldn't let Pops down. For some reason I felt like he was living through me. And this time around, together, we were going to win!

Chapter Twenty-Seven

September 27, 1993

Exactly five years from the day I had shot and killed those two cats at the State Theatre, the day finally came, I had walked down five calendars like a real nucca's supposed to, once I got in my bid, and accepted things for what they were, time started flying by. My time was up, the world was waiting on me.

At Green Oaks, nuccas didn't broadcast their release dates 'cause there were so many dudes doing all day that you didn't want to press their bid. So, when your date came up, you just kind of disappeared. I sat in receiving and discharge for two hours waiting on my fingerprints to clear, then I was released. I stepped out into the warmth of the sun beaming down on my face, and fell to my knees and kissed the ground. The guard who was driving me to the bus station was laughing at me. His racist ass had the nerve to part his lips and say, "I've seen at least a hundred guys do that same shit, and 95 of 'em done come right back."

"Yeah, well I won't be comin' back. And you can bet that shit," I said climbing into the van.

That yankee couldn't spoil my joy. I was a free man. I was no longer a boy as I went in. I was a grown ass man, 18 years old to be exact as of tomorrow.

I was released one day before my birthday. I couldn't wait to hit the city and see all that had changed. I sat near the window of the Greyhound bus. I watched every tree, bird, rock, car and person the bus passed. I hadn't seen a tree in so long I almost forgot what one looked like. The only thing I saw for the past five years was a brick wall. Green Oaks was surrounded by nothing but stone walls, and wrapped around the exterior were barb wire fences. I tried to block that thought from my mind. I had to tell myself that I was a free man now. No more going to bed when some yankee flashed the lights. I could eat what I wanted, when I wanted to and how much I wanted to. That thought put a huge Kool-aid smile on my face. That and the thick white broad across from me who kept undressing me with her eyes. I could see her through the reflection of the bus window, she was definitely on a nucca's jock. Those thick tanned white legs of hers under her short skirt, made my dick rock up. From the way she was seated, slightly turned in her seat with her legs bust wide open, I couldn't help but see that camel toe.

I turned around in my seat to face baby girl. She was bold with it, not breaking her stare and the shit was turning me on. I motioned my head like, 'come here' and without hesitation she got up and came over, taking a seat next to me.

"What's yo' name?" Damn, she was smelling good.

"Jackie."

"I'm Coach," I said extending my hand.

"That's your real name, or your nick name?" she asked, taking my hand.

"I guess you can say both. But uh, where a pretty little thang like yourself headed?" I asked.

"Home. How about you? You look like you just getting out?"

"How can you tell?" I asked.

"You got them Wranglers on for one. And plus you got that glow."

"Where you from?"

"Detroit. What you thought 'cause I'm white, that I had to be from some hick town?"

"Nah, it ain't like that. I can definitely tell you got some game about ya' self. Where are you coming from?"

"Not too far down the road from where you coming from."

"You just got out, too?" I asked, looking Jackie up and down in disbelief. There was no way a young fine thang like her was just in anybody's jail. "How long you been gone?"

"Only six months, but it feels like ten years. I done missed the whole summer. What about you?"

I let out a deep breath. "Man, it's been five years."

"You been gone five years, straight?"

"Yeah…"

Jackie's eyes lit up with lust. She began licking her lips, and as if she had read my mind she asked, "you want some pussy?"

Without waiting for a response, Jackie grabbed me by the hand. "Come on," she said leading me to the bathroom. She locked the door behind us, then pushed me up against the toilet. I felt the warmth of Jackie's mouth as she neared the head of my dick. She was on her knees and had pulled my pants down to the floor. With my throbbing hard dick in her hand, she teased the head with her tongue, then inhaled me slowly taking the whole nine inches down her throat. I squeezed the back of her head in satisfaction, and gently guided Jackie's head back and forth.

"Ahhh….Sh-shit.." I sighed, as I felt myself about to bust. I sat Jackie down on the toilet, and put the dick back in her mouth. She sucked me soft, swallowing every ounce of nut, and boy was I backed up. I hadn't been out a good two hours and I had already accomplished one of my goals, which was to get my nuts out the sand.

Me and Jackie chopped it up the rest of the drive. She was on some we shit already. Everything was we this, we that. I had to tell her straight up. "Look Jackie, you good people and all, but I'm just coming home after doing five years. I gotta get my life in order. I'm not looking for no relationship right now."

"Oh, so you not gone stay in touch with me?" she asked copping an attitude.

"I didn't say that. We can hook up and kick it, but we both need to get our shit together. I don't even have a number to give you. I don't know what to expect when I get home, or even if my home is still there. I ain't heard from nobody in five years. I'm starting from the bottom, you feel me?"

"Yeah," Jackie said. Her eyes were filled with compassion. She had no idea what I had been through, but she seemed to understand where I was coming from.

*****

The bus pulled into the downtown Greyhound terminal and my stomach instantly filled with butterflies. Me and Jackie were on our feet and at the door waiting when the bus came to a stop. We were the first ones off the bus, each wearing a plastered Chucky Cheese smile, happy to be back home. The smog in the air smelled like a steak. Damn, it felt good to be back in the city. People were hustling and bustling in and out of the terminal. Jitneys cabs lined the curb waiting for customers and traffic was bumper to bumper.

"So, I guess this is it," Jackie said breaking my trance.

"What did I tell you?" I asked, as I grabbed Jackie's hand and led her over to the sidewalk.

"Give me a number where I can reach you."

Jackie handed me a folded piece of paper, she had already penned her information. "Use it," she said kissing me on the cheek. "And take care of yourself, Coach," she said, hopping in the back of a Checker cab.

I tucked the piece of paper into the pocket of my tight straight leg Wranglers and climbed into the back seat of a Jitney cab.

"You got some dough, young blood?" The driver asked turning down the radio.

I had $70 to my name that they gave me in discharge. I dug into my pocket and gave the driver two 10 dollar bills.

"Where you going, around the corner? Young blood, I can't do nothing with this," the old man said as he tried to pass me the money back.

"How much you gon' charge me to drive me to 7 Mile and Caldwell?" I asked.

"That's way on the east side, man."

"How much?" I was getting mad. I felt like the old bitch nucca was trying to work me.

"Fifty dollars," the driver said.

"Here," I said with an attitude, as I stuffed the money into his hand.

"Ten, twenty, thirty, forty, fifty. A'ight, let's ride," the old bitch said turning the engine and pulling into traffic.

We were in a burgundy Ninety Eight with deep crush velvet seats and skirts on the back wheels. This old bama was rockin' a butterfly collar silk shirt, with a must yellow Dob that was once white. He chain-smoked these stankin' ass Winstons and kept digging up under his seat for his pint of Wild Irish rose. He'd take a nip, then tuck the bottle back under the seat. The only good thing he had going was the music. "Turn that up, old head."

"Boy, what you know 'bout this here. That's Frankie Beverly and Mayes," he said turning up the radio.

"*We Are One*," the lyrics poured out of the speakers. I hadn't heard any oldies since my transfer to Green Oaks. All they had were country stations up there in the mountains. I closed my eyes, and envisioned me back on top, where I belonged.

Twenty-Eight

"Bitch, if you ain't got no money, then beat it."

"Dump, you know I'm good for it. Just give me two dimes til later on."

"The only thing you good for is lying and sucking dick. And since I'm tired of you lying to me, how 'bout you suck this dick."

"But you know I don't like doing that," Tina said looking around the room shamefully.

"Since when did you start having pride. Oh, I know what it is, you shamed 'cause all these crack head muthafuckas is in here. Tell you what, come on," Dump said, getting up from his chair. He grabbed Tina by the hand and led her to the back.

*****

"Hey yo, Black, who is that nucca right there getting out of that car?" asked Rome. He and Black were posted on the hood of Rocko's BMW.

"Who, ole' boy with them smooth booties on?" Black asked as he passed the blunt to Rome. "Shit, I don't know. Look like he going over to Tina's crib.

******

I couldn't believe how foul Tina was living. Empty beer cans and trash filled the front porch, so did huge black plastic trash bags, which stunk like shit. I covered my face as I knocked on the front door.

"Come in," a female voice said. I turned the knob and stepped into the smoke filled living room.

Crack smoke filled the air, there was so much smoke that I almost choked to death. I left my shirt over my face to try and block the smell of burning crack.

"Who is you?" A woman seated to my left in a loveseat asked, looking me up and down.

There must have been at least ten crackheads in there. For the most part, I had gone unnoticed with the exception of ole' girl who was quizzing me.

"You looking for somebody?" she asked.

"Yeah, where is Tina?" I asked.

"Tina!" The woman yelled at the top of her lungs, "Somebody's here to see you!"

*****

"Hmm... Hmm," Tina moaned, while sucking Dump's dick. She knew how to get him off. All she had to do was look him in the eyes and moan like it was good "Hmm..." she moaned, then slurped on the head of Dump's dick as he began cumming. "Shit..." Dump whispered, grabbing the back of Tina's head, forcing his entire dick back down her throat. "Ahhh..." he sighed, reaching his peak. "Here," he said, throwing Tina two dime rocks.

She didn't even bother to clean herself up; she packed her pipe in record time and was beaming up to Scottie. "I'ma see you later," Dump said, straightening his clothes before he stepped out of the room.

"A'ight, you muthafuckas. Tomorrow is the first, and if you tryna jump on one of these sweet deals, come see me personally," Dump said, as he turned the corner into the living room.

I knew that voice anywhere. In a way, I was happy to see him, but on the other hand, why? I asked myself. I pulled my shirt off my face as we locked eyes.

"Coach?" Dump said slowly, looking me up and down.

"What's up Dump?" I said cracking half a smile.

"Boy, come here," Dump said rushing over with open arms. He hugged me tight and kissed me on the side of my head. "Stand back and let me take a look at you. Damn, you done blew up. You was in there hitting them weights, huh?"

"Yeah."

"Voice all deep. Talkin' bout, yeah…You got a goatee. Damn, you look just like your father, boy… Tina! Get yo' ass out here girl," Dump ordered. "I know you remember ole' Kathy," Dump said, pointing to ole' girl who had been questioning me. Ain't no way the chick sitting on the sofa was Kathy. Not the little thick bow-legged, bad ass Kathy that I remembered. This chick was skinny as E-mothafucka and her hair was matted to her scalp.

"Hey, Coach." She said smiling.

"What's good Kathy?"

"Why you out here screaming my damn name like you crazy?" Tina asked. She stopped dead in the middle of the living room and put her hands to her face. "Oh, my God. Corey, baby."

"Come on, all you crackhead muthafuckas, out! Let's give them some privacy," Dump said as he booted everyone out. "I'ma see you in a minute, Coach" he said, before closing the front door.

I was crushed, standing there looking at the woman before me who was supposed to be my mother, a woman who was once so beautiful, a person I held in such high esteem, loved and respected. All that vanished at the sight of Tina. She looked an absolute mess standing there with a faded Winnie the Pooh nightgown on and some black spandex, which were no longer tight because she was so skinny. She had bags under her eyes, like she'd been on a crack binge for years and her hair was wrapped in an old silk scarf. I went from being hurt to being furious. I was so enraged that I wanted to seriously put hands on Tina. "So, this is what you've been too busy doing, huh. This is why you couldn't come see me, or have the phone turned on?" I asked pointing to the cluttered living room. Liquor bottles, and ashtrays filled the coffee table. There were burn holes in the leather sofa, and spilled drinks on the rug.

"Corey, I miss you." Tina had tears streaming down her face.

"You what? You miss me? You sho' have a funny way of showing it. Look at you. Look at our home. If daddy could see you, he'd turn over in his casket. I can't believe this shit," I said, walking past Tina and into the kitchen.

Dirty dishes filled the sink. And all the eyes on the stove had been removed, I guess so the crack heads could base up using the light from the stove. The refrigerator was leaking and empty as I inspected it. The kitchen table where we used to have breakfast was missing. It was just an empty space there. Tina had followed me into the kitchen, standing at the entrance.

"I'm sorry Corey," she said crying.

I wasn't trying to hear that shit. Leaving me for dead was one thing, but to shit on Pops and all his hard work, in my eyes, was unforgivable. She had just basically turned our crib into a spot. But that shit was over, starting today.

"Corey, I'm sorry," Tina pleaded.

I turned and looked at Tina and said, "Is that all you can say, is you're sorry? Well guess what? You're right, you are sorry."

There was a knock on the front door.

"Nah, I'ma get it," I said brushing past Tina. I thought it might be one of her crack smoking buddies, I was gone let they ass know off top to stop coming by the crib. I swung the door open wildly, with my murder mask on, I yelled "What?"

"Whoa...Play boy. Calm down, it's me, Black."

I had to let my pupils readjust for a moment, and regain my senses. I stepped out of the house and onto the front porch, closing the door behind me.

"What's good, my nucca?" Black asked. He extended his hand and tried to give me some dap, but I frowned my face up at the nucca. "Damn, what's up my nucca. It's like that?" Black asked stepping back.

"Nah, it ain't like nothing," I said. I could see Rome and Rocko about to cross the street.

"Then, why you tripping. We still crew, right?" Black asked.

"Nah, nucca we ain't crew. Crew don't leave his manz for dead when he doing a bid. And crew hold they manz down."

"What up dough?" Rocko said, flashing a wide grin, as he tried to give me some love. I shunned his ass, too. Rocko, was just as stunned as Black. "Fuck you tripping on, Coach?" Rocko asked.

"Not one of ya'll nuccas got at me, not one time. The whole time I was upstate, you nuccas ain't sent me shit, not a kite, money order, nothing."

"Man, you know how the game go," Rome said.

Why did he go and say that. "Oh, do I? You mean like yo' rat ass making statements on me, saying that I was the one who killed them two nuccas. I got the paperwork," I snapped.

Black and Rocko turned their heads to Rome, who had the tight face. Everybody was waiting on him to deny it, but he didn't.

"Ain't no need in you tucking yo' head back at him, Rocko. Nucca, I got your statement too. Ya'll the reason I pled out 'cause ya'll nuccas was gone testify against me," I said.

"What?" Black said, looking at both of them nuccas in disgust. "Tell me you bullshittin'?" Black asked not wanting to believe that he'd been hanging with two rats all this time, doing God knows what with them.

"Tell em', Rocko. Tell em' how you identified me as the shooter. And how you and Rome were going to take the stand on me."

"Nucca, ain't nobody tell you to start shooting in the first place. You think I was 'bout to go down for some dumb shit you did, nucca you got me fucked up. And let me tell you something else, Nucca, don't nobody owe you shit. When you go to jail you already know what it is." Rocko said in his defense.

"Yeah, I know you two nuccas ain't to be trusted. Matter of fact, nucca get off my porch," I said.

"Fuck you think you talking to nucca." Rocko said, trying to hold his ground.

We squared off chest to chest. All the weed and liquor stunted Rocko's growth. He couldn't do shit with me if he wanted to. I'm looking down on the nucca with my chest stuck out, 'bout ready to put the beats on him, but Black stuck his hand between us.

"Ya'll nuccas chill out," Black said, stepping between me and Rocko. Rome's scared ass had stepped back out of swinging distance. He knew his bitch ass was next if it went down.

"You know what, nucca, you got that, come on," Rocko said, waving his hand. Rome's flunkie ass was right on his heels, but Black remained posted. Rocko stopped by the curb and looked back at Black, "Oh, so you riding with him?"

"It ain't 'bout who I'm riding with. Coach is my nucca. And ya'll two nuccas violated making them statements," Black said.

"Nucca, fuck you too. You know what it is," Rocko said, as he crossed the street and went up in the house next door to Dump's crib.

"That nucca just mad right now. He'll calm down, and it'll be back to normal," Black assured.

"I don't think it'll ever be the same, Black." I took a seat on the steps.

Black sat next to me on the steps. "My nucca, you know I would never cross you, not even to save my own life. I didn't make no statements on you."

"I know you didn't Black. /But why you ain't get at me though? I was gone five years and ain't hear from not one of ya'll. So, what I'm 'pose to do, just come home and be fake with myself and start back fucking with the same nuccas that shit on me?"

"I feel you, but you know I can't read or write. I could have shot you some money and shit, but man it's fucked up out here. The only nucca eatin' around here is Rocko. He got the Zone on smash, all the blocks. It ain't like it used to be."

"And then you know what's killin' me the most, is Tina. Ain't nobody wrote and told me this how she's out here living. I know nuccas probably serving her and everything."

"I swear to you my nucca. I ain't never sold yo' Moms nothing. Because I wouldn't want ya'll to do it to me. You know both of my peoples smoke, so I know how you feel."

For real, I couldn't even be too mad at Black 'cause like King David told me, I was trying to survive my world, just like Black was trying to survive his. Black dug into his pocket and pulled out a bankroll. "Here, my nucca. Get on your feet." He gave me all the money.

"I can't take yo' last, Black" I said tryna' hand him the money back.

"Nah, I insist. I got some work, so don't worry about me. I can tell by the look in yo' eyes that you bouts to blow. And when it happens, I want to be right there with you."

I smiled at my nucca, then embraced him. We hit rocks like we used to. "Good lookin' my nucca."

"I know it's been a minute, but I ain't forgot my manz B-day. Yo' shit is tomorrow, so what you want to get into?"

"Celebrating is the farthest thing from my mind right now. It's time to get this money, again."

"No doubt," Black said smiling. My nucca knew I had a plan.

"Who is that coming outta that house?" I asked.

"That's Amanda," Black said, as he turned to face the house Rocko and Rome just went into.

"That's Amanda?" I asked in shock.

She didn't look the same. She was busted to say the least. She was wearing open toe sandals, some daisy duke shorts, and a tank top which accentuated her C-section gut. She had a small baby on her arm and another one by the hand as she walked down the stairs of the house and to the BMW parked at the curb. "Nucca, that ain't Amanda," I said laughing.

"It is. Watch this. Amanda!" Black called out, and sure enough she looked over at us.

"Who is that?" she asked, after putting the kids in the car.

"Don't tell her it's me over here," I whispered. I didn't want her to see me with these Wranglers on.

"It's Black. Bring me a 40 of Old E back."

"You better give me some money."

I got you when you get back. I gotta catch a few custos," Black said.

"You betta have my money when I get back," Amanda said climbing in the car.

I was tucked low on the porch as she drove by. "Whose car is that?" I asked.

"Rocko's. I told you the nucca is eatin', he got all kind of whips back there."

"So, what is Amanda doing driving his car?" Black got all quiet on me.

"Oh, you gone give me the silent treatment now, huh?"

"What's up my nucca?"

"I know how you feel about Amanda, my nucca, so I don't want you to shoot the messenger," Black said, looking off into space.

"What up?" I asked, sitting up.

"Them two kids she was dragging to the car, she had 'em while you were gone. But that ain't all. Both of them lil' fucks is Rocko's babies. Soon as you got your time, the bitch jumped on Rocko's dick 'cause he started getting money. I told the nucca it was some slimy shit, but you know how nuccas think with their dick instead of their heart.

I was stuck. Black had just rocked my world with that one. I wasn't tripping though, it is what it is, I told myself as I listened to Black continue to fill me in on the latest. Who all had died and gone to jail. We kicked it on the porch all day, just reminiscing going back down memory lane, and watching the never ending traffic as custos copped their shit and left. The Zone hadn't missed a beat. I guess the old saying was true, the game don't change, just those that play it.

Chapter Twenty-Nine

I was lying on the sofa in the pool house, staring at the money Black had given me earlier, it was spread out across the coffee table. Altogether it only came up to $750. When Black first handed it to me, I thought it was about five grand, but it was all small bills. I was thankful for the gesture though, 'cause I knew Black had given me his last. I let out a deep breath in frustration. Back to square one, I thought. I knew what I had to do, which was all I knew how to do, sell dope. I was going to take that $750 and put it to work. 'First thing in the morning, I'ma find me some work and I'ma get this money,' I told myself before closing my eyes.

*****

"See you made it," King David said smiling up at me.
"Yeah, Pops I made it outta there," I said.
"Why you sound so down, son?"
"It's mommy. She's at the lowest point in her life, and feels helpless. I can't stand to see her like this."
"What did I tell you? You have to survive your own struggle, Coach. Get yo' self together first. Don't you worry about your mom for now; get up, Coach. Don't let me down. You hear me?"
"Yeah, Pops. I won't."
We were in the pitbull farm, as we were every time King David came to see me in my dreams.

"Go get him, son, and remember what I told you. Trust a dog, before you trust a nucca with your life," King David said.

My eyes popped open and I sat up. He had been trying to tell me something all this time. I grabbed the money off the table, stuffed it into my pocket and hit the door. It was pitch dark outside, so I really couldn't see anything as I jumped the fence into the farm. All the dog houses were empty, I guess they had all died off while I was on lock. Either that, or Tina sold them for some crack. I looked closer and saw that Bruno was still on deck. He came out of his house wagging his tail happily, as if he remembered my scent. "Bruno..." I said rubbing his chest and head. He was badly malnourished, and he stunk like he hadn't had a bath in years. His eyes told me that he had only held onto life because he was waiting on me.

I unchained Bruno, then moved his dog house to the side. And sure enough, just as I thought, there was a wooden board underneath the straw, which surrounded the dog house. I fell to my knees and began brushing the straw aside, then yanked the board up. About four feet down I could see a large metal box peeking through the dirt.

I jumped down into the hole and strained as I lifted the box out of the hole. I climbed out of the hole and brushed the dirt off the lid of the box, then flipped the latch back. I couldn't believe my eyes. The box was filled from the bottom to the top with stacks of hundred dollar bills. I slammed the box shut and stood to my feet. I looked around to make sure no one was watching me, then scanned the farm for something to help me get the box back to the pool house.

There, I thought, my eyes fixated on the wheel barrel leaning against the back privacy fence. I lifted the box into the wheel barrel and exited the farm through the back fence into the alley.

"Come on Bruno," I said, pushing the barrel through the backyard and into the pool house.

I locked the door behind me and closed the blinds, then raced over to the box. I pulled back the lid and began tossing stacks of money onto the coffee table. At the bottom of the box was a lone manila envelope with my name on it. I tore the envelope open and took a seat on the sofa, and began reading the letter inside.

*****

Dear Coach:

Son, I knew you'd figure it out. I know you probably thought I'd left you and your mom for dead, but you can see now why I didn't leave your mom with the money. She would have blown it in two days (laugh). Consider this my will, and you're the sole beneficiary. I would never leave you in a cold world with nothing, son. Between the knowledge I left you with and this here money, you should be just fine. Kiss your momma for me and take care of her for me. She's all you got now. Do what you have to out there to survive. Get yo' self together first, but as I taught you, don't ever forget the importance of family. Make me proud son. I love you.

-Pops

*****

I was in tears reading King David's letter. To me they were his last words. All that money sitting on the table meant nothing to me. I would burn it in a heartbeat to have my father back. "I won't let you down, Pops. I promise." I folded the letter and put it back into the envelope. I pulled myself together, then started counting all that money stacked up on the table. It didn't take me long because King David already had it in $10,000 stacks with a rubber band around each bundle. It came up to $2,000,000 on the nose. I paced back and forth looking at all that dough. I was making plans on how I was going to first fix the house back up. Tina had completely let it go to the dumps. And I was going to try and save Tina if I could. I couldn't let Pops down. And besides that, Tina really needed me. But first, it was time to jump clean and shine on them sucka's. I dug up the floor boards in the bedroom beneath the carpet, and stashed the majority of the bread. I laid across the bed with Bruno just looking up at the spinning ceiling fan. I couldn't wait until morning.

Chapter Thirty

I had pulled an all-nighter. I couldn't get to sleep for anything in the world last night, and to be real I wasn't trying to. I was out the door at 7:00 on the dot. I knew all the businesses would be open no later than eight, and I wanted to get fresh, it was my B-day, and King David had given me the best birthday present ever, 2 million in cold cash. I ain't gonna lie neither, that shit was burning a hole in my pocket. I walked up to 7 Mile and flagged down a passing Checker cab. Still wearing my smooth booties I left Green Oaks in, I handed the driver a hun'd dollar bill, and told him to take me to Eastland Mall on 8 Mile and Kelly Road.

"This that old money," the Nigerian driver said with a smile as he eyed the bill.

"I know," I said looking into the rearview mirror at him.

"I want you to wait for me, while I grab a few things. Just leave the meter on." I hopped out of the cab, and walked into the mall. I went straight to Max Green's boutique. They always had that new fresh shit in there. That's where me and the crew used to do our shopping before I got knocked.

"May I help you?" this bad lil' yellow bone asked me as I stepped inside the store.

"Yeah, what you got new up in here?" I asked.

"Everything we got is new," she said, sounding a lil' smart.

"Oh yeah, well, in that case I'll take one of everything in a size 34-36 and 4X shirt, since it's all new."

Ole' girl looked me up and down as if I was playing and as if I was broke.

"Maybe this will help," I said pulling ten g's out of my smooth booties.

"I am so sorry."

"Don't apologize. I know you thought a nucca was broke, it's all good. Just let me get those clothes in a 34-36 and 4X shirt."

"Right away," she said spinning off. "Would like to try any of these on?" she asked, pulling clothes off their racks.

"I tell you what. Put me an outfit together, something I can wear out of here, and just bag the rest up." I spoke in a boss tone of voice.

She put together this Marc Buchannan outfit, and matching Pelle Pelle leather jacket. I stepped out of the dressing room looking like new money. The only thing missing was some fresh kicks. She stepped behind the register and rang up everything. "That'll be $3,2280.13" she said looking at the register.

"That's all?"

"Yeah."

"How much for you?"

"I have a boyfriend."

"That's cool. I'll take care of you and that nucca," I shot while counting out the money.

"I ain't never heard that one," she said blushing.

"Write your number down, and we gone hook up a lil' later," I said handing her the money, with a lil' something extra.

"What's your name?" she asked, writing her math on the back of my receipt.

"Coach."

"Well, Coach, I'm Carmen. You betta use it," she said handing me the receipt.

"A'ight lil' momma," I said heading for the door.

I pulled the same stunt in Foot Locker on the lil' bowlegged chocolate brand named Ava. I balled out and bought like ten pair of fresh sneaks, and a few fitted hats. I promised her too that I would call her later and we'd hook up. I stepped out of Foot Locker in my new Jordan's lookin' like a cool mill. Every chick I passed by was breaking their neck, and I was hollerin' at all of them. I was trying to get my black book back up, and so far I had six numbers.

I copped a pager, then bounced. Ole' boy was still parked at the curb when I came out.

"You ready?" he asked popping the trunk.

"Yeah," I said tossing all the bags in the trunk. The meter was on two hundred and some change.

"Here you go," I said passing ole' boy three more hun'ds.

"Where to now?" he asked.

I looked across the street at the sign which read, Exotic Cars. "Take me over there," I said pointing.

As we pulled into the car lot, I locked eyes on this cocaine white 500 Coupe Benz. It was sittin' on some chrome deep dish hammers and had a kit on it. "Damnnn..." I said climbing out of the cab, in hot pursuit of the Benz. I looked in at the peanut butter guts and wood grain interior that lined the dash board and door panels. There wasn't a price tag on it, just two numbers in the windshield marking the year-'93-that boy was brand spanking new.

"You wanna take her for a ride?"

I spun around to face the man talking. He was an older Arab dude with salt and pepper hair. He was dressed in a tailor made suit with loafers on, and wore a gold iced out Presidential Rolex watch. Everything about him said money.

"Sure," I almost stuttered, "But I don't have a license right now."

"I'll drive, that way yo get a better feel for the car," he said.

The man yelled something in Arabic. A young boy came flying out of the dealership with a license plate in his hand. He slapped it on the back of the Benz, and the old man said, "Shall we?" While waiving his hand towards the car.

We both climbed inside the car and sunk down into the plush leather seats.

"Seat belt please," the man said.

I fastened my belt as he cranked the car up. It was so quiet that I didn't even know that it was running. He backed out, and turned onto 8 Mile Road heading deep east. He turned down Jefferson next to the lake, and opened the Benz up to 60 mph. It got low and hugged every curve of Jefferson, as we cruised back up to Moross. I had seen enough. I had to have it!

"How much?" I asked, as we pulled back into the dealership.

"Sixty thousand."

"I'll take it. But listen, I am not what you call legit."

"Don't worry about it kid. I'll take care of you. We'll cover the paperwork to make it seem like its being covered in payments."

"Cool. Do you think you can help me get some tags too?"

"Kid, don't worry about it." The old man led me inside the dealership.

"Let me ask you something," I said, taking a seat in the man's office.

"Anything kid. What's on your mind?"

"How come you took me serious about buying the car? How'd you know I wasn't wasting your time?"

"I've been in this business a long time. You see those lumps in your pocket? I saw them soon as you got out the cab."

I couldn't do nothing but smile. The old man had game... I sat back while he got all the paper work together. "You know I can help you get that license for an extra grand," the old man told.

I smile from ear to ear because I didn't have time to go to nobody's driving school to get my license. King David taught me how to drive since I was ten years old. I agreed to his price.

"Come inside. We'll take a picture of you and you will have your license tomorrow. I've got my connects everywhere," the old man said while laughing, as if he was connected to the streets.

"You still have to come back and see me in two weeks, and I'll have your plate for you. Until then, the temporary tag will do just fine," the old man said, patting me on the back.

I unloaded all of my bags from the cab into the trunk of the Benz, and asked ole' boy if he wanted to follow me to my house while the old Arab drove me to my house in my brand new Benz. The car was too hot for me to drive it without a license, and I didn't want to take that chance. I jumped in the passenger seat of my new Benzo while the old man took the wheel. I cranked up the sounds to Tupac's *'I Get Around'* pouring through the speakers. I opened the sunroof as the old man pulled into traffic.

"Round and round. Round we go…" I sang along to the song while dancing in the mirror, I was stopped at a red light.

I asked the old man to pull into Diamond Glow Car Wash on 7 Mile and Mt. Elliot. I wanted to get the Benzo beamed up before I hit the Zone. I had to shine on them suckas, Rocko to be specific. Oh yeah, and that dirty bitch Amanda.

"Here you go my man." I handed the worker a twenty. "Keep the change," I said rolling my window back up. After my car rolled through the automated wash tracks, the old man pulled over to the side to get my tires hit up with some Amor All. Two nuccas were drying the beads of water off, while one dude hit the tires.

"A'ight you good," Ole' boy said waving me off.

I rolled the window down to give him and his man a tip. It was Eddie.

"Eddie!" I yelled, asking the old man to throw the car in park while I jumped out.

"Coach?" Eddie said, dropping the rags in his hand.

"Yeah, nucca. Come here and show me some love," I said.

We embraced like two long lost friends.

"Man, when you get out?" asked Eddie.

"I got out yesterday."

"And you doing it like this already. That's you?" Eddie asked looking at the Benz.

"Yeah man. Long story. But what's up with you, how long you been out?" I asked.

"Shit, I been out for a minute now. I'm just working and tryna' stay out of jail, ya' feel me?"

"I feel you my nucca. And you know you're my nucca for real. I can't have you working up here while I'm out here shining."

"Shit, nucca gotta survive."

"We 'bout to do more than survive. Here," I said digging into my pocket and handing Eddie a wad of hundreds. "You looked out for me up in the Oaks, and you kept it real, so the least I can do is return the favor. We done been to the bottom together, now let's go to the top. Come on," I said climbing back in the Benz. Before Eddie got a chance to climb in the back, I asked him, "Do you have a driver's license?" He looked at me like I was stupid for asking. "Hell yeah, I got a license," he said. "Then, you're driving, my nucca," I told him.

I asked the old man to jump in the cab that was waiting for us while we went through the car wash. I paid the cab driver to get him back to the dealership. Eddie jumped in the driver's seat and we burned out!

Chapter Thirty-One

The scene couldn't have been more perfect. It was just like I imagined so many nights while lying in my bunk at Green Oaks. The block was packed with nuccas and hoodrats, everybody playing high post leaning against their whips with the sounds pumping. I leaned my seat back and turned the sounds up, as Eddie brought the Benz to a slow creep. One by one nuccas were turning their heads and pointing at my shit.

"Whoa…I told ya'll nuccas, my nucca ain't broke," Black shouted, as he tailed the Benz to the curb. I jumped out fresh to death, knowing I was that nucca. All eyes were on me, and I could feel the hate piercing through my back.

"My nucca, tell me this you," Black said giving me dap.

"Yeah, it's me," I said popping the trunk to get all the stuff I bought at the mall.

"I knew yo' ass was holding, nucca." Black laughed, as he helped me with the bags.

"Is she looking?" I asked Black, with my head in the trunk.

"And you know it."

I was talking about Amanda's boot mouth ass.

"All you need now my nucca, is some shine. I know you gone hit Greenfield Plaza."

"Yeah, but that shit can wait." I closed the trunk. "Come on, E." I said, as Eddie got out the car.

"Who this?" Black asked, sizing Eddie up.

"You remember Eddie, he went to Farwell with us back in the day. E, saved my life up in Green Oaks, so he's crew," I said. Eddie hit 'em off with the nod. "Let's take this shit inside," I said.

"Girl, Coach ass is lookin' too good. I know you gone get back with him," Shante said. She was sitting on Rocko's porch with Amanda. They had been sweatin' my ass since Eddie bent the block in my new Benzo.

"I ain't stuntin' his ass. Rocko's my man," Amanda said, lying through her teeth.

"Hmm, hm. You mean he ain't stuntin' yo' ass, and it serves you right, how you did him was fucked up."

"Bitch, you need to get a bag of business and stay the hell outta mines. I can have that whenever I get ready," Amanda snapped.

"Did you see them nuccas faces when you pulled up? That nucca Rocko damn near shit on his self. All the hoes was like, who is that? I know we gon' ball out tonight for your B-Day. Everybody is hitting Belle Isle tonight for Rocko's party, you coming?" asked Black.

"Hell nah," I said carrying the bags of clothes into the bedroom. "I'm focused on one thing right now, money. Let them lames have their lil' party. We gon' shine when it counts. Look!" I said taking a seat on the sofa with Black to my right and Eddie to my left. "We 'bouts to get this money like no nucca in the city has ever done. Now I know ya'll two don't know each other, but that's cool. All that's fenna change. This is the crew right here. Ya'll the only two nuccas I trust and that I'm fuckin' with. I gotta shoot a move outta town, but I want ya'll nuccas to hang out and get to know each other. Here!" I said giving Black the keys to the Benz. "Ya'll go and stunt on them fools for me. Hopefully when I get back, we'll be on for life...."

"Where you going, my nucca?" Black asked.

"I gotta get my mom some help. I won't be gone but a few days tops. E, you welcome to whatever's in them bags. Gon' and jump fresh, and I'ma see ya'll nuccas in a few days." I hit rocks with Eddie and Black, before getting up.

I walked into the main house in search of Tina. I found her in the living room with Kathy. They both had this dumb ass geeky look on their faces, like they were in need of some crack. "Kathy, let me holla' at my mom in private," I said. Kathy grabbed her stem off the table. "I'ma see you later Tina. I'll be across the street." I closed the door behind Kathy and flopped down on the sofa next to Tina.

"You still mad at me?" Tina asked breaking the silence between us.

"You know I can't stay mad at you," I answered, as I rubbed Tina's head. "You will always be my mom no matter what. It just hurts me to see you like this."

"I know baby. I'ma get it together," Tina said, turning to face me. She had tears in her eyes, and that look which said 'I'm tired.'

"I know you want better ma, and I'm going to help you through this. We're going to get some help, I promise," I said, dropping a lone tear. I leaned over and kissed Tina on the forehead and pulled her close to me. I just held her tight for hours. I wanted her to know that I was there for her, and that she'd bounce back.

Chapter Thirty-Two

I called my uncle Robert, Tina's brother in Cali. I hadn't talked to him since I skipped town on him like six years

ago. I explained to him all I'd been through, and what
Moms was currently going through. He was eager to help.
"What can I do, Coach? You know I'll do anything for my
sis."

"I want to send her to rehab, but I don't want her to be
tempted to leave the center, so I was thinking maybe it
would be best to send her out there."

"Enough said. I'm on top of it," Uncle Robert said.

*****

Uncle Robert had mad connections. The next morning,
there were were two first class tickets to California waiting
on me and Tina at the customer service booth inside the
Metropolitan Airport. I stopped by the old Arab's dealership
to pick up my brand new license before heading out to the
airport. We didn't pack any clothes, I promised Tina we'd
do our shopping once our plane landed. I was a little
nervous and sweating under my arms because I was wearing
a thermal top, two T-shits, and a sweater. I was trying to
camouflage the $50,000 I had wrapped around my chest
with Glad plastic wrap. Tina had another $50,000 strapped
to her. She played it cool though, she had made dozens of
trips like that before with King David. We made it onto the
plane without harassment and took our seats. I let Tina get
the window seat, she was just like me, a big ole' kid
wanting to look down at all the passing cars and people. I
grabbed her hand and kissed it. "When you get back, you're
going to be bigger and better than ever, Ma." I believed
every word of it.

"Thank you, for believing in me, Corey," Tina said, as her
eyes welled with tears.

I wiped them from her pretty face, and pulled her close to me. "Don't let me down." King David's voice echoed in my head.

Uncle Robert was waiting outside the terminal with a sign bearing our names, just like he had six years ago.

"There he is," I said to Tina, pointing to Robert.

"Oh, my God. How do I look?" Tina asked, examining herself in the reflection of the terminals sliding glass door.

"Come on. You look fine, Ma."

"Tina! Ahh…" Uncle Robert broke out running toward Tina like a flaming faggot, arms open and hips swinging side to side. He scooped Tina up into the air and spun her around in circles.

Finally, Robert sat Tina down, then kissed her on the forehead. "Look at you, girl. We gon' have to put some meat on these bones. And we most definitely gots to do some shopping," Robert said pulling on Tina's clothes.

I had stepped as close as possible to them. I didn't want unck to break out into another gay ass sprint on me.

"Coach, look at you. Hmm.. The ladies ain't ready for all this." Unck said, rubbing my chest. "Boy. If you weren't my nephew. Le me stop," he laughed.

"Boy, you is too crazy," Tina said, laughing.

"I see you still at it, huh unck. You still throwing those wild parties?" I asked."

"Three nights a week and you betta know it. Come on, let's get outta here." Unck said, leading the way to his brand new hunter green Range Rover.

"You stay in something slick, unck." I sunk into the butter soft leather back set.

"You know I gotta stay fresh on these hoes," Unck said, pulling out into traffic.

He and Tina were in the front seat giggling like two school girls, catching up on old times. It had been decades since they had seen each other, but the love was still there.

*****

"Robert, this is your home? Coach, told me that you were living large, but this is a castle," Tina said, as we pulled up to unck's estate. He flipped all his old cars and traded them in for late models. The Corvette and Porsche were tucked off to the side in the sun.

"Yeah, baby girl. Bro' doing alright. My castle is your castle for as long as you need it," Robert said, opening the front door and waving his hand for Tina to step in.

"Wow!" Tina said, taking in all the fine detail and plush furniture. "What you say you do for a living Robbie?" Tina joked.

"I told you, girl. I design computer software for major corporations."

"You must be designing it well. 'Cause yo' ass is living large. When you gone settle down? I know you tired of living in this big ole' house by yourself," Tina said, walking into the gourmet kitchen.

"You know your baby brother is a playa, all capitals," unck said, laughing. "But come on and let me get you settle in. then we can do some shopping, 'cause tomorrow your scheduled to begin treatment. I already got everything set up. Come on," unck said, grabbing Tina by the hand.

"Hold on. Ma., let me get that." I said.

Unck's eyes damn near popped out his head as Tina lifted her shirt. He saw all that money peeking through the plastic. "Boy, what you doing with all that money?" unck asked, as Tina handed me the stacks.

"Never leave home broke. This that street money," I said.

"Well, when you're ready. Let yo' uncle show you how to turn that into some corporate money." Unck said.

"A'ight, but in the meantime, Let me hold the keys to that Range Rover, so I can go do some shopping.

"Be careful," Unck said as he tossed me the keys.

I kissed Tina on the cheeks, and then bounced.

Chapter Thirty-Two

I was going to hit the Melrose and do some shopping, but first I had to check and see if the reason I had came to Cali was still in play. I pulled in front of white boy Nick's father's house and parked at the curb. I didn't see anyone out front, and the blinds to the house were closed. In the driveway sat a low-rider truck sitting on some 13" Dayton's. The truck looked like it had switches 'cause it sat low to the ground. The license plate was custom fit, and it read WBN. I juggled with the letter in my head, and then it hit me. That was white boy Nick's shit. I jumped out the Range and walked up the long driveway. I could see someone peeking out the blinds at me as I climbed the stairs to the porch. Before I could ring the door bell, the front door swung open.

"Who you looking for?"

It was Nick that fool hadn't recognized me. It had been six years and some change, and I had buffed up, had facial hair now. The fool didn't know who I was, but Nick still looked the same. He still had bad acne, but was on his pretty boy shit at the same time. He was still frail as hell, only difference was he grew a few feet. I decided to play a quick game on ole' Nick.

"I'm looking for the owner of that low-rider parked in the driveway."

"I'm the owner," Nick said. "What's up?"

"That truck is hot, that's what's up. It's been tagged and resold. It was stolen from my uncle's car lot out in L.A. and I have the paperwork to prove it," I said, freestyling.

"Man, you're outta your fuckin' mind. I bought that truck stock, and had it tricked out."

"That's what I'm telling' you. The parts are hot too."

"My man, you've got the wrong truck. All my parts were ordered by phone from customs."

I couldn't hold back the laughter, 'cause Nick was turning red, and I could tell that he was about to curse me out any second.

"What the fuck's so funny?" Nick asked.

"You don't remember me, do you?"

"Nah, who are you?"

"Fool, it's me, Coach."

"Oh, shit. What up dough," Nick said, hitting rocks with me. Man, look at you. You big as shit. I looked up and found out you were up in Green Oaks man. I wanted to get up with you, but didn't know how. What's up?"

"I came to check on you. You know you're my dawg for life. Even though I cut out on you at the airport."

"I ain't stuntin' that shit, I would've done the same thing. But what's up, what are you doing back in Fresno?" Nick asked stepping onto the porch, and closing the front door. We sat on the swinging love seat and kicked it. He hadn't said one word about that key I stole, and from his body language I didn't think he even knew it was missing.

"Do you remember what you showed me that day on the plane?" I asked, cutting the chase.

"What? That kilo of coke?"

"Yeah."

"I remember. What about it?"

"I know that was a long time ago, but does your Pops still fuck around?" I asked.

"Shit, ain't nothin' changed but the date. How you think I'ma pushin' that low-rider? What you tryna' get on?"

"Hell yeah."

"Say no more. I'ma holla at my dad, he's pretty cool about the shit. For real, I been handling most of the business, but he still flies the shit."

"When you gone holla' at him?" I asked.

"Shit, matter of fact, he's in there right now. Let me go holla at him right quick," Nick said, getting up from the swing and leaving me on the porch. About five minutes later, Nick stuck his head out the front door. "Come on in, my dad want to holla' at you."

I followed Nick down into the garage out back, where Torch was tinkering with his Harley Davidson. He stood up and wiped the oil from his hands onto his filthy wife beater, then extended his hand to me.

"Dad, you remember Coach?" Nick said.

"Yeah, the one who ditched us at the airport." Torch laughed, as we shook hands.

"How are you doing, sir?"

"Cut that sir shit out. You making me feel old. I told you long time ago to call me Torch. So, what's up? Nick tells me you're looking to score some coke. I hope you're talkin' some serious numbers, 'cause I don't mess around with no petty crap."

"Nah, I wouldn't waste your time."

"So, what are you looking for?"

"I'm looking to cop like 20 bricks. You think you can handle that for me?"

"Twenty kilos ain't a lot of dope, but it sure cost a lot. You know that's gonna run you close to $200,000. Maybe a lil' cheaper since you're buying twenty at one time. You got that kind of money, kid?"

I pulled up my shirt and began unwrapping the plastic. I sat the $50,000 on the hood of Torch's Camero, then dug in my pockets and put the other $50,000 on the hood.

"That's $100,000 right there. When I get the 20 keys I'll give you the other $100,000."

Torch's eyes lit up with greed, as he scooped the money up into his arms. "I just have to ask you one question, though, Coach. And I don't want you to take any offense," Torch said.

"What's up?"

"You're not working with the cops, are you?"

"Hell no."

"The DEA?"

"No."

"FBI or ATF?"

"Dad, leave Coach alone. He's good people," Nick said.

"I'm just checking. You can never be too careful in this business. Okay, so you want twenty kilos. How are you going to get them back to Detroit, assuming that that's where you'll be taking them?" Torch asked.

"I was hoping you'd be able to take care of that."

"You know normally I wouldn't fly such a small order, but since it's on my route anyway I'll do it. But it's going to cost you an extra grand for each kilo."

"I got you."

"Let's see, I leave for Detroit in two days. You know where the City Airport is, right?"

"Yeah, on Connors."

"Right. That's where you're to meet me. Give me your number. And whatever you do, don't be late. I hate sitting at the airport on the tarmac with dope on me. I just want to drop 'em off, and get back in the sky."

"Got it." I said, trying to hold back a smile. I was in.

"A'ight, I'll see you in a couple of days, Coach," Torch said, as he disappeared into the house with the money.

"Man, good lookin' out my dude." I hit rocks with Nick.

"Ain't nothin'- besides, I get commission on them shits. So, blow up fool."

We hit rocks again and laughed.

"I got an idea, why don't you come back to the city with me. We can get this money together. I know you tired of this so-called life."

"Yeah, for real. Only reason I stayed out here this long is because my mom got married to some dick. I just been out here chillin' with my dad, you know."

"I'm not saying move back to Detroit, but go back and forth. I really could use some brains on the team. Fool, if all this shit goes right, we gone be larger than life."

I could tell by the look in Nick's eyes that he was hanging onto my every word. He wanted to be a part of something grand!

"We gone get so much money that our names will be ringing for years. Just think, everybody a be callin' you white boy Nick, and the white boy with all the money and hoes."

"Yeah," Nick said, thinking about the picture I was painting.

"Fool, we gone be living legends," I said.

"Let's get it," Nick said, hitting rocks with me to seal the deal.

We hit up all the boutiques on Melrose. Nick and I had jumped fresh into some crispy Polo outfits with some Gucci loafers. Unck was throwing a party later on and I wanted to be that fly young nucca all the hoes flocked to. I copped some Gucci shades and a Cartier watch to set the outfit off. Nick's corny ass had been out in Cali too long, he was losing his swagger. The fool was stuck on them ugly ass Chuck Taylor's. He bought a new pair of red ones to match his outfit, and some dumb ass motorcycle hat.

"Yeh, we got's to hurry up and get you back to the D. You done started wearing Chucks, and ride switches. Man, next thing you'll be waving a red flag round this bitch," I joked.

"Never that," laughed Nick, as we jumped back in the Range and headed home.

Cars were starting to pull up at unck's crib. The sun was dying down and the party was about to be on. Nick and I hit the door carrying our bags inside. There were three young white chicks talking in the living room. "Who is that?" Nick asked as we stopped and stared at the PYTs.

"I don't know, but I got the one on the left," I said, setting my bags down and walking over to the sectional sofa where the girls were chillin'.

I flopped down between ole' girl I wanted and another girl. "Damn baby, what's your name?" I asked sparking a conversation with the young lady.

Nick was going for his. He was all on the other two chicks. I don't know what he was saying, but he had them laughing. We chilled and sipped champagne while the house continued to fill with the guests.

"Coach, where have you been all day?" Unck said, stepping into the living room.

Tina was right behind him and was looking sharp in her new dress and heels.

"I did some shopping, and went to holla' at an old friend of mine.

"You remember Nick, don't you?"

"Oh yeah, ya'll went to school together, right?"

"Yeah, we just chillin'. Enjoying these tenderonies you feel me?" I said, nibbling at ole' girl's neck.

She squirmed and giggled. "Stop!" she said, slapping me on the leg.

"Oh brother, anyways…Coach, I need for you to do me a favor and greet the guests as they come in. Take their coats and hang 'em up for them."

"Come on unck, I'm entertaining," I said.

"Corey you can finish entertaining after you do what your uncle asked you to," Tina said laying down the law.

I reluctantly got up and looked back at ole' girl one last time. Nick was taunting me as he pulled all three girls close to him. He had his arms wrapped around them, and waved his pinky at me, like "bye".

I was at the front door greeting all of Unck's weird ass friends and taking their coats for them. "Hey, how are you?" I asked one of them, while wearing a plastic smile.

"Well alright, then, buddy, enjoy the party," I said in a white man's voice to this one geeky looking white dude. If I had to be at the door, I was at least going to have some fun bidding off the guests as they arrived.

"Damn" I said to myself, as this bad little Spanish broad got out of a red Mustang. She was heading dead toward me looking like a movie star, with her hair swishing with every stride she took. I zeroed in on her face and couldn't believe it, it was Gloria's fine ass, Unck's assistant.

I licked my lips real quick and cleared my throat, as she approached the double doors of the house.

"Long time no see, stranger," I said, while blocking the entrance of the door.

"Do I know you?" Gloria stepped back and removed her sunglasses.

"Oh, so you gone act brand new on me, huh?"

"Excuse me. You must have me mistaken for someone else," Gloria said as she tried to move past me.

"Hold on sexy. Nah, I got you just right. I know it hasn't been that long, look at me."

Gloria looked at me like I was retarded or something, and I could tell she was getting irritated.

"Coach, why you out here bothering this pretty girl?" Tina asked standing behind me.

"Coach? Oh, my God. Come here and give me a hug," Gloria said, finally recognizing me.

"Betta watch it now, girl, I ain't that little boy you remembered," I said joking as we hugged.

"You so crazy," Gloria said hitting me on the arm. "Look at you. All grown up and handsome."

"Gloria, I want you to meet my mom, Tina. Tina, this is Gloria, Uncle Robert's assistant."

"Excuse me, I am an associate now, thank you very much," Gloria said correcting me.

"Damn, it has been six years, huh?"

"Nice to meet you Tina," Gloria said shaking Tina's hand. We all stepped inside. Fuck what unck was talking about,

Gloria was in the building and I wasn't about to let some lame snatch her up.

"Let me take your coat." I peeled Gloria's short jacket off her. I was looking down her back, she still had that onion back there.

"You still looking good, Gloria."

"Thank you," she said blushing.

"Come on, let me fix you a drink," I said, heading for the bar.

"I'ma need the whole damn bottle," Gloria said, as she followed me.

"Long day at work?"

"That would be an understatement."

I pointed to a bottle of Alize.

"That's perfect," Gloria said.

I grabbed two glasses and the bottle of Alize, and stepped from behind the bar. "Come on, let's go somewhere quiet, so you can finish telling me about your day."

We stepped out back on the patio. On our way, I hit Nick off with the pinky wave as I escorted Gloria by the hand.

"Ahh…" Gloria said as we sunk down into two plush patio chairs. She kicked her shoes off and grabbed the bottle from me, then poured us two glasses.

"So, finish telling me about work," I said breaking the ice.

"I don't want to talk about work. I just want to chill and enjoy your company. What have you been up to, Coach?" Gloria asked, taking a deep swallow of Alize. She guzzled the entire glass, then poured herself another one.

"Well, I've been to the top and back since we've last seen each together. When I went back home, things were great for a while, but I got into some trouble and ended up doing some time."

"That must have been terrible. How long were you in jail?"

"Five years. I just got out the other day."

"What did you do that had you sitting in jail for five years, Coach?"

"Something too stupid to go into, but I feel bad about it now."

"Well, I'm just glad you're out now."

"Five whole years on lock down without a pretty face like yours"

"You poor thing. So, that's why I haven't seen you. I had asked Robert about you, but he never would go into detail. I'm glad you're doing well."

"Yeah, it's all good. I'm just tryna' piece my life back together right now. Besides work, what's new with you?"

"That's the problem, nothing's new. Right now, I feel like I'm at work. I only come to these parties to mix and mingle with these clowns to help build my contacts. Robert insists that if I want to make it further, that I have to network. I hate being phony, though smiling and what not. I really started not to come tonight," Gloria said, downing another glass.

"Well, I'm glad you did," I said.

Gloria looked over at me and blushed. "You know what? So am I."

We locked eyes for a moment, which was what I had been waiting on. The buzz from the Alize was kicking in, and if the feelings were real, she wouldn't refuse me, I told myself as I took the lead. I leaned over the small table which separated us, and kissed Gloria softly on the lips.

She didn't refuse me; she closed her eyes and went with the flow. I held the side of her face with as much affection as I could while tonguing her down. I came up for air, and kissed her lips once more. I looked her in the eyes and told her "You are so beautiful. Come on," I said standing and grabbing a hold of Gloria's hand. "Don't forget the bottle." We started through the kitchen and out into the hallway leading to the steps. Nick watched as I walked silently, giving him the pinky wave.

I escorted Gloria to my room and locked the door behind us. "Come here," I said softly. I was standing with my back to the door. She set the bottle down on the dresser, then seductively walked over to me. We locked lips, passionately kissing each other's face. I tore at her clothes like a mad man, as she did the same. Within seconds, we were both standing there in nothing but our underwear. I was in my boxer's, and she had on a black thong, but no bra. My dick was standing straight out. Gloria noticed, and she pulled my dick through the hole of my boxer's. She jacked me off while looking in my eyes.

I couldn't take that shit a second longer. My blood was boiling, and I had dreamed about fucking Gloria so many nights while at Green Oaks that I couldn't believe it was really about to go down. I peeled the thong off Gloria and picked her up carrying her over to the bed. She smelled so good, like she was fresh out of the shower. I sat her on the edge of the bed and got down on my knees wrapping her legs around my shoulders. Gloria gripped my head as I began mouthing her clit. She grunted something in Spanish, as I made long circles around her clit with my tongue. "Papi," she squealed. I had her right where I wanted her, hot and bothered. Her pussy was gleaming wet like the inside of a clam. I didn't let her get off that nut that was building up. I could tell by the way her clit kept drawing back behind its sheath, she was almost there. I wanted her to explode while I was deep inside her. I rolled Gloria over to her stomach and put a pillow under her pelvis so that her ass sat up a little, giving her an arch in her back. Still standing at the edge of the bed, I slowly slid the head of my dick in. "Ahhh... Papi." Gloria sighed, as I inched forth in search of her G-spot. There it is, I thought as the head of my dick touched a small piece of tissue. Gloria dug her nails down into the sheets as I started deep stroking, concentrating my every stroke at the center of her G-spot. She couldn't take it. She tried to crawl to the top of the bed, but I was mounted on that ass, gripping both ass cheeks firmly and thrusting away.

"Ohh... Oh!" Gloria screamed in deep satisfaction. She was having multiple orgasms, as I kept a steady consistent pace. The softness of Gloria's ass, and the sight of it slapping against my stomach had me at my peak. I knew in just a matter of a few strokes, I'd be skeeting everywhere. I couldn't make my mind up whether to pull out, or bust inside her. I looked down at Gloria who was looking back with a mean fuck face and her eyes closed. I couldn't stand it. "Ah, shit Oh fuck..." I uttered, as I shot a lug in Gloria. I continued to pump until my dick went soft, but I didn't pull out. I lay on top of Gloria all out of breath, breathing hard and kissing on the back of her neck. It didn't take but a few minutes before I was back up and digging her guts out. We fucked all night while the party was going on down stairs. I must've bust like five nuts fucking with

Gloria. She just did something to me that made my sex drive go into overdrive.

The next day, I had to reluctantly kiss Gloria goodbye. Nick and I had to be back in Detroit when his dad got there with the coke.

"When am I going to see you again?" Gloria asked. She drove me and Nick to the airport.

"Real soon. Real soon," I said, not knowing exactly when soon would be.

"Well, you be careful. And I hope soon is soon," Gloria said kissing me, before I headed through the tunnel to board the plane.

Chapter Thirty-Three

"Who is this?" Black asked, looking Nick up and down, giving him the ice grill.

"Chill out, Black," I said putting my arm around his neck. "That's my man, white boy Nick. He's official, trust me," I said as we climbed in the backseat of my Benz.

"You missed me?" I asked.

"What kind of question is that to be asking?" Black said, getting behind the wheel.

"I wasn't talking to you. I was talking to the car," I said laughing.

"You burnt out nucca," Eddie said passing a blunt back to me. "What up dough?" he said hitting rocks with Nick. "What's ya' name?"

"White boy Nick."

"Eddie. But everybody calls me E-double."

"Where you find slick at?" Eddie asked looking back at me.

"You gon' get enough of picking up every stray dog you see on the side of the road." Black said.

"Oh, so I'ma stray dog, too, huh?" laughed Eddie.

"Nah, you's road kill." laughed Black.

"Nucca, fuck you," Eddie said firing up another blunt.

"Ya'll two simple nuccas getting along just fine, huh? That's what's up. But check it, my man Nick here is the final addition to the crew. He's a real nucca," I said.

"Don't you mean, cracker," Black said, then burst out laughing.

You's a fool," laughed Eddie.

"Don't mind these two ignorant nuccas. They high right now, they don't mean nothing by it."

"It's all good, I got jokes too," Nick said.

"Don't do it," I warned Nick. "Just let it go."

"What the fuck is all these tents and shit doing out here?" I asked, as Black turned down the block. I could see army sized green tents perched on the sidewalks of both sides of the street. The fire hydrant was going, as little kids ran back and forth through the water. People were everywhere, and they had the street blocked off.

"Black, I hope this ain't what I think it is," I said as we pulled into my driveway.

We all got out the car, and who do I see coming my way, Felicia.

"Muthafuckas said you been out almost a week, and I'm just now seeing you. A bitch thought I'd be the first one you holla'd at," Felicia said stopping in front of me.

"That's what I thought too." I was speaking of my long bid at Green Oaks. But anyway, what up dough?

"Shit, out here enjoying the festivities of your coming home party."

I turned and looked at Black. He just gave me that dumb ass grin, then shrugged his shoulders.

I had told him that I didn't want no party. I didn't want to be fucking with no one who had shitted on me.

"So, what you gon' do now that you're home? I see you riding new already. You must have had that money put up, huh?" Felicia asked.

"You know I'ma do what I always do, get money," I said.

"I know you got a spot for me on the team."

"You see these three nuccas," I said pointing to Black, Eddie, and Nick. "This is my team right here."

"So, you ain't fuckin with me?" Felicia asked, crossing her arms and turning up her nose.

"That's what I been tryna' tell you. Not on no level. I don't even know why..." My words were cut short at the sight of Amanda heading our way.

She stopped next to Felicia and sucked her teeth while looking me up and down.

"So, we ain't speaking, Coach?" Amanda asked with an attitude.

"You gotta lot of nerve, you know that."

"I'ma let you two love birds be alone. Coach, you ain't gon' stay mad at me neither," Felicia said, excusing herself.

"What is you trippin' on?" Amanda asked, as if she didn't know.

"If you don't know, then I don't neither," I said, as Rocko came stepping up. He tried to hit rocks with me, but I just looked at his hand until he withdrew it.

"Damn, my nucca you gon' stay mad at me 'bout that lil' shit. What? You ain't fuckin' with me no more?"

"That's what I been tryna' tell you. That's what I been tryna' tell all ya'll asses!" I yelled, looking around at all the phony faces. Rocko's face got tight. He thought that I was supposed to just forget that rat shit he did, like it was all good. He just didn't know how many nights I couldn't get to sleep, as I tossed and turned in my bunk, fretting over whether or not I should put them hot balls in his ass.

"What is he trippin' on?" Amanda asked.

"What? You ain't tell her? He ain't tell you?" I asked Amanda.

"Tell me what?"

"I swear to God, you betta tell her before I do!" I yelled.

"Nucca fuck you," Rocko said, as he took a wild swing at me. He caught me one on the side of my head, and I side stepped as he tried to land another punch.

I was so angry. 'This nucca just stole me,' I thought. We were in the middle of the street dancing, Rocko throwing jabs trying to keep me off his ass. Finally, I saw an opening and I took it, I let the nucca land a two piece to my dome, so I could get up on this ass. Why did he do that? I scooped his legs from under him, as he tried back stepping. I balled his little ass up in a knot and power drove him through the windshield of his BMW.

"Oh, my God!" I heard someone yell. "He's going to kill him," they said, as I put the beats on Rocko. I was pounding his head into the hood of the car, denting it with every thrust.

"Let me through here," Dump said, pushing his way through the crowd, which had gathered around me and Rocko.

I felt someone put their strong hands on my shoulders, then I was yanked back. I caught my footing and squared off with Dump in the middle of the street. I was so zoned out, that for a minute I didn't recognize who he was. "Oh, so now you gone hit me," Dump said. I dropped my guard realizing who he was. My heart was racing and my adrenaline was pumping. I wanted to fight some more. Rocko got up off the car, and in a last hope to save face he pulled a chrome 9 mm from his pants, and staggered up behind Dump. I put my hands in the air, like whatever. With not an ounce of fear, I dared him to shoot me. "Shoot nucca. I'm tellin' you what God knows, you betta kill me,"

I said. Dump reached over and lowered the gun to Rocko's side. "Ya'll two is bigger than this." Dump said, taking the gun from Rocko.

"Nah, we were." I said turning to walk towards my crib with my real crew in tow.

"Everybody, take a seat," I said as we stepped into the house.

Once Black, Nick, and Eddie were seated, I began speaking. "Listen, that lil' shit that just happened, nevermind that. I want to holla' at ya'll about how we bout's to get this money. Like I said, this right here is crew. The only thing I ask and expect is loyalty. With loyalty, the rest will come. I've been in sticky situations with all of ya'll, and not one of ya'll folded on me, which is why your crew in my eyes. Now I know that ya'll don't know one another, but I'm asking for the love ya'll got for me to get to know one another. We gon' need loyalty to each other if we gone get this paper…"

"How we gon' do that?" asked Eddie.

"Me and Nick got a connect on the work. The shit is butta, and it's dirt cheap. We got twenty bricks comin' tomorrow, but we gone stretch them shits to thirty and open up as many spots we can around this bitch. And Eddie, you can sew yo' hood up as well. For the first two flips, I'ma need all the money back, so we can get our weight up. After that, everybody is gone get paid. I already paid for the work, so we good on that. I just need ya'll nuccas on deck with me."

"What you need me to do?" asked Black.

"You and Eddie gon' be in charge of running all the spots, finding workers, securing custos, security, and collecting money. Nick, you already know your job is to secure shipments and storage of the work. And I'ma be the chief and accountant. My job is to keep ya'll with the work, and flip our money. Give me a good six month run, and we'll all be millionaires. So, if you're with me, put your hand on top of mine.

"Remember. Loyalty," I said, looking each of them in the eyes.

*****

Our meeting was interrupted by a knock on the door. I got up cautiously and peeked out the blinds. 'What the fuck she want?' I thought as I opened the door.

"What up Kathy. You know Tina ain't here right now."

"I know. I'm not looking for her."

"So, who you lookin' for?" I asked. Kathy was scanning the faces seated at the round table in the dining room.

"Can we go somewhere and talk. There's something I need to tell you, but in private," Kathy said.

"Huh, sure," I said, letting Kathy in.

"Hey, ya'll, I'ma be out back by the pool. Holla' if you need me." I led Kathy outside.

"Coach, there's something I've been wanting to tell you for years, but you were just too young at the time, and I didn't want to see you get yourself hurt."

"What is it about?"

"King David."

Pops name made me stop in my tracks. Me and Kathy had been doing laps around the back yard, I stopped in front of the pool. "What about King David?" I asked.

"Coach, Craig didn't kill your father."

"Well, who did?" I asked sternly.

"If I tell you this, you gotta promise me you're not going to be upset with me."

"I promise. Now, who?"

Kathy let out a deep breath, then said, "Dump."

I didn't believe her. My body had filled with rage. I reached out and grabbed a hold of Kathy by the arms. "Look at me, Kathy. Are you telling me the truth?" I asked, looking in her eyes searching for something.

"Coach, I am not lying to you. I swear."

"Then, how do you know this? Who told you this?" I demanded, now shaking Kathy violently."

"I was in the house when Dump, Keith and Cane were talking about it, before and after KD's death. Dump said that it was his time to be king, and that David had to go. That's when David's body turned up the next day."

"But did Dump tell you that he did it?"

"In so many words he did. He never would outright and say that he killed David, but I could see it in his eyes."

"And why are you tellin' me this now. Is it because Dump ain't treating you right no more, what is it, huh?"

"I always told myself when you got old enough that I was going to tell you. It has nothing to do with me. Remember that night I gave you that bath?"

"Yeah."

"And what did I tell you?" I told you that you were the next king."

I let go of Kathy's arms. I couldn't believe what I had just learned. But I wasn't about to let it ride. "Look, this is what I want you to do." I broke down my plan to Kathy. "Soon as he falls asleep, page me 187." I dug in my pants pocket and gave Kathy $200.

The plan was for Kathy to slip some sleeping medicine in Dump's drink and once he went under she was to page me.

Chapter Thirty-Four

"Come on, Coach. Let's hit downtown and fuck with some hoes. Cause you know tomorrow its gone be all work after we meet up with my dad," Nick said.

"Nah, I'ma chill out at the crib. But ya'll three nuccas go ball out and get to know each other. I got some shit I gotta handle tonight."

"A'ight. But next time you coming," Eddie said.

I hit rocks with the crew and watched them safely to the car. They piled in the 500 and skated off. I closed the door and leaned against it for a moment. I was so ready to get this nucca, my dick was hard. I paced the living room floor in my all black get-up, constantly looking at the clock on the wall. It was 12:30 and Kathy still hadn't hit me up. I peeked out the front window over at Dump's crib after hearing a car door slam. It was Keith and Cane leaving. The car started and they pulled away. "Come on Kathy," I said, as I went back to pacing the floor.

Beep. Beep. Beep. My pager lit up. It was sitting on the coffee table. I raced to pick it up, it read 187, 187, 187.

I pulled my hoody over my head, cocked my hammer and slid out the door. The block was dead, not a soul was outside. Perfect, I thought crossing the street like a black cat. Kathy was standing in the half opened door as I climbed the stairs. "Where is he?" I whispered.

"He's in the bedroom tied up, just like I promised." Kathy advised, stepping to the side to let me in.

"What about, Rocko?"

"They all went clubbin' and Keith along with Cane just left. Besides Dump, I'm the only one here."

"Good job, here." I said, handing Kathy a half ounce of crack. Her eyes lit up at the sight of all the crack. She grabbed the sack and took a seat at the living room table.

I crept toward the back of the house with the mag in my hand. I peeped through the crack of Dump's bedroom door. I could see his fat ass all sprawled out across the bed. He was lying on his back. His feet and hands were tied to the headboard and baseboard.

I was having flashbacks of Dump speaking at King David's funeral, him having breakfast with me and Tina, and him having me kill Craig. Tears of hate streamed down my face as I pushed open the door and stepped into the room.

I stood at the foot of the bed with my .9 mm pointed directly at Dump's slobbing face. I had the trigger about half way pulled, but released it. I wanted his bitch ass to know who had killed him. I walked around the side of the bed and slapped the shit out of Dump with the cold steel barrel of my gun. His eyes rolled in the back of his head, and then he came to.

"What the fuck?" he yelled in agony and fear, as he noticed the sheets tied around his ankles and wrists.

I flicked the light on and pulled back my hoody.

"Coach?" Dump asked. "Boy, what the hell you doing?" He tried to sit up. "Take this shit off me, right now!"

"Shut yo' bitch ass up. You ain't runnin' nothing."

"What is this about, earlier? That shit with you and Rocko?"

"Nah," I said raising my gun to Dump's head. "It's about you and King David."

Dump's eyes locked with the bullet exiting the barrel of my gun. Boom! A lone shot rang out, blowing a hole straight through Dump's forehead. His brains flew out the back of his skull and rested on the pillow beside him. Boom! Boom! Boom! I put three more shots in Dump's chest just for good measure. "That's for Craig, bitch!" I yelled at Dump's lifeless corpse. I was furious. He deserved to die a much worse death. I had let the bitch off easy, I thought heading out the room. Kathy was still at the table stuck. She was so high, that I don't think she even heard the shots. I stepped to her as she sat in her chair, eyes bucked. I put the barrel of my gun to her forehead, and waited for her to look me in the eyes. She had this look on her face, that said, "Me too." Her eyes welled with tears, as she knew I wasn't bullshitting. "What, you thought I was gon' leave you to tell it?" I asked, then pulled the trigger. Boom! I knocked a patch out of Kathy's head. Her body flew back out of the chair and crashed to the floor. I stood over her and put two more slugs in her back, then bounced. The way I saw it, the bitch knew all this time who killed my daddy, yet, she was over at my crib everyday getting high with Tina. Bitch was in total violation.

I scanned the block before stepping out of the house. Not a soul in sight, I shot across the street to the crib. I couldn't wait until morning came when Dump's body would be discovered....

Stay tuned for Part II
The Rising
Coming soon

Sample chapter from
Kwame: An American Hero.
Available now!

The streets are calling

Kwame's war against the most ruthless drug gang in Brownsville, led up to his one-man attack of the hardest penetrated fortress there ever was in the hood. If he could penetrate that fortress so easily by himself, he wondered how the cops could act like it didn't exist. The two men standing guard at the door didn't even see him coming. The loud thump of a punch to the throat of the 6ft-5-inch giant guarding the door with his life, had the breath taken right out of him with that one punch. He stumbled to the ground without any hope of ever getting back up. His partner noticed the swift and effective delivery of the man's punch, and thought twice about approaching him. Running would be the smartest option at this time, but how cowardice that would be? The attacker was but five feet ten inches tall and perhaps one hundred and ninety pounds in weight. The security guard didn't have time on his side and before he could contemplate his next move, the masked attacker wearing army fatigues, unloaded a kick to his groin that sent his 6ft-7inch frame bowing in pain while holding his nuts for soothing comfort.

Another blow to the temple followed, and the man was out permanently.

At first glance, Kwame didn't stand a chance against the two giants guarding the front door. One weighed just a little less than three hundred and twenty five pounds, and the other looked like an NFL lineman at three hundred and sixty pounds. However, Kwame was a trained Navy SEAL. He came home to find that the people closest to him were embroiled in a battle that threatened their livelihood daily. His sister, Jackie, became a crackhead while his mother, Janice, was a heroin addict. Two different types of drugs in one household, under the same roof, were enough to drive him crazy. Kwame didn't even recognize his sister, at first. She had aged at least twice her real age and his mother was completely unrecognizable. He left her a strong woman when he joined the Navy six years prior, but he came back to find his whole family had been under the control of drug dealers and the influence of drugs, and Kwame set out to do something about it.

The two giants at the door was just the beginning of his battle to get to the high level dealers who controlled the streets where he grew up. As he made his way down the long dark corridor, he could see women with their breasts bare and fully naked, bagging the supplies of drugs for distribution throughout the community. Swift on his feet like a fast moving kitten, Kwame was unnoticeable. He could hear the loud voices of men talking about their plans to rack up another million dollars from the neighborhood through their drug distribution by week's end. The strong smell of ganja clouded the air as he approached the doorway to meet his nemesis. Without saying a word after setting foot in the room, he shot the first man who took notice of him right in the head. Outnumbered six-to-one, magazine clips sitting on the tables by the dozen, and loaded weapons at the reach of every person in the room, Kwame had to act fast. It was a brief standoff before the first guy reached for his 9Millimeter automatic weapon, and just like that, he found himself engulfed in a battle with flying bullets from his chest all the way down to his toes. Pandemonium broke and everybody reached for their guns at once. As Kwame rolled around on his back on the floor with a .44 Magnum in each hand, all five men were shot once in the head and each fell dead to the floor before they had a chance to discharge their weapons. The naked women ran for their lives as the barrage of gunshots sent them into a frenzy. The masked gun man dressed in Army fatigues was irrelevant to them. It was time to get the hell out of dodge to a safe place, away from the stash house. Not worried too much about the innocent women, Kwame pulled out a laundry bag and started filling it up with the stacks of money on the table. By the time he was done, he had estimated at least a couple of million dollars was confiscated for the good of the community. The back door was the quickest and safest exit without being noticed. After throwing the bag of money over a wall separating the stash house from the next house, Kwame lit his match and threw it on the gasoline track that he had poured before entering the house. The house was set ablaze and no evidence was left behind for the cops to build a case. It was one of the worst fires that Brownsville had seen in many years. No traces of human bones were left, as everything burned down to ashes by the time the New York Fire Department responded.

Kwame had been watching the house for weeks and he intended on getting rid of everything, including the people behind the big drug operation that was destroying his community. Before going to the front of the house to get rid of the security guards, he had laid out his plan to burn down the house if he couldn't get past them. A gallon of gasoline was poured in front of all the doors, except the front way where the two bouncers stood guard. His plan was to start the fire in the back and quickly rush to the front to pour out more gasoline to block every possible exit way, but that was his last option. His first option was to grab some of the money to begin his plans to finance the local community center for the neighborhood kids. His first option worked and it was on to the next house.

When Kwame came home to find his mother and sister almost a shell of what he left behind, he was determined to get rid of the bad elements in his neighborhood. Mad that he had to leave home to escape the belly of the beast, Kwame came back with a vengeance. He wanted to give every little boy and little girl in his neighborhood a chance at survival and a future. He understood that the military did him some good, but he had to work twice as hard to even get considered for the elite Navy SEALs. The military was something that he definitely didn't want any boys from his neighborhood to join. For him, it was his best option and in the end, he made the most of it. Guerilla warfare was the most precious lesson he learned while in the military, and it was those tactics that he'd planned on using to clean up his neighborhood. Kwame wanted to do it all alone. A one man show meant that only he could be the cause of his own demise. There'd be no snitches to worry about, no outside help, no betrayal and most of all, no deception from anybody. Self- reliance was one of the training tactics he also learned in the Navy and it was time for him to apply all that he learned to make his community all it could be.

Getting rid of that stash house was one of his first missions. Kwame had seen the crack houses sprouting all over the neighborhood and it would take precise planning on his part to get rid of them one by one, without getting caught by the police. Kwame also knew that he wasn't just going to be fighting the drug dealers, but some of the crooked cops that were part of the criminal enterprise plaguing the hood as well. At this point, Kwame was one up on the "Benjamins Click," one of the most dangerous drug gangs in

Brownsville, Brooklyn. It was just the beginning of a long fight, but the history behind what led to this point is the most fascinating aspect of Kwame's story.

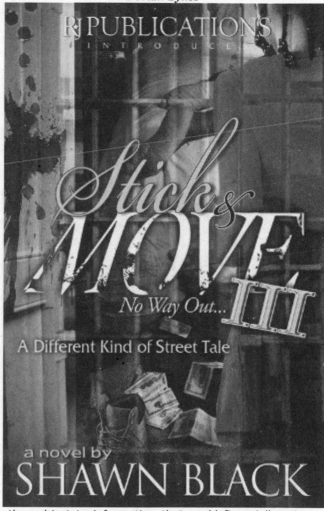

Serosa becomes the subject to information that could financially ruin and possibly destroy the lives and careers of many prominent people involved in the government if this data is exposed. As this intricate plot thickens, speculations start mounting and a whirlwind of death, deceit, and betrayal finds its way into the ranks of a once impenetrable core of the government. Will Serosa fall victim to the genetic structure that indirectly binds her to her parents causing her to realize there s NO WAY OUT!

In Stores!!!

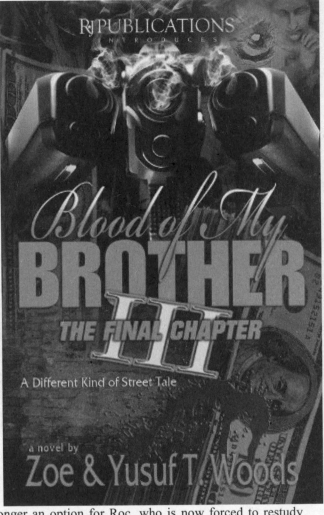

Retiring is no longer an option for Roc, who is now forced to restudy Philly's vicious streets through blood filled eyes. He realizes that his brother's killer is none other than his mentor, Mr. Holmes. With this knowledge, the strategic game of chess that began with the pushing of a pawn in the Blood of My Brother series, symbolizes one of love, loyalty, blood, mayhem, and death In the end, the streets of Philadelphia will never be the same...

In Storess!!!

After Chasin' Satisfaction, Julius finds that satisfaction is not all that it's cracked up to be. It left nothing but death in its aftermath. Now living the glamorous life in Miami while putting the finishing touches on his hybrid condo hotel, he realizes with newfound success he's now become the hunted. Julian's success is threatened as someone from his past vows revenge on him.

In Stores!!!

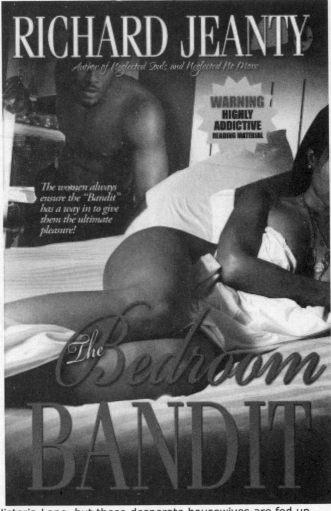

It may not be Histeria Lane, but these desperate housewives are fed up with their neglecting husbands. Their sexual needs take precedence over the millions of dollars their husbands bring home every year to keep them happy in their affluent neighborhood. While their husbands claim to be hard at work, these wives are doing a little work of their own with the bedroom bandit. Is the bandit swift enough to evade these angry husbands?

In Stores!!

NEGLECTED SOULS

Motherhood and the trials of loving too hard and not enough frame this story...The realism of these characters will bring tears to your spirit as you discover the hero in the villain you never saw coming...

In Stores!!!

Jimmy and Nina continue to feel a void in their lives because they haven't a clue about their genealogical make-up. Jimmy falls victims to a life threatening illness and only the right organ donor can save his life. Will the donor be the bridge to reconnect Jimmy and Nina to their biological family? Will Nina be the strength for her brother in his time of need? Will they ever find out what really happened to their mother?

In Stores!!!

Betrayal, lust, lies, murder, deception, sex and tainted love frame this story... Julian Stevens lacks the ambition and freak ability that Miko looks for in a man, but she married him despite his flaws to spite an ex-boyfriend. When Miko least expects it, the old boyfriend shows up and ready to sweep her off her feet again. She wants to have her cake and eat it too. While Miko's doing her own thing, Julian is determined to become everything Miko ever wanted in a man and more, but will he go to extreme lengths to prove he's worthy of Miko's love? Julian Stevens soon finds out that he's capable of being more than he could ever imagine as he embarks on a journey that will change his life forever.

In Stores!!!

The police in New York and other major cities around the country are increasingly victimizing black men. The violence has escalated to deadly force, most of the time without justification. In this controversial book, noted author Richard Jeanty, tackles the problem of police brutality and the unfair treatment of Black men at the hands of police in New York City and the rest of the country.

In Stores!!!

Just when Darren thinks his relationship with Tina is flourishing, there is yet another hurdle on the road hindering their bliss. Tina saw a therapist for months to deal with her sexual addiction, but now Darren is wondering if she was ever treated completely. Darren has not been taking care of home and Tina's frustrated and agrees to a break-up with Darren. Will Darren lose Tina for good? Will Tina ever realize that Darren is the best man for her?

In Stores!!

Ronald Murphy was a player all his life until he and his best friend, Myles, met the women of their dreams during a brief vacation in South Beach, Florida. Sexual Jeopardy is story of trust, betrayal, forgiveness, friendship and hope.

In Stores!!!

Tina develops an insatiable sexual appetite very early in life. She only loves her boyfriend, Darren, but he's too far away in college to satisfy her sexual needs.
Tina decides to get buck wild away in college
Will her sexual trysts jeopardize the lives of the men in her life?

In Stores!!!

Faith Jones, a woman in her mid-thirties, has given up on ever finding love again until she met her son's best friend, Darius. Faith Jones is walking a thin line of betrayal against her son for the love of Darius. Will Faith allow her emotions to outweigh her common sense?

In Stores!!!

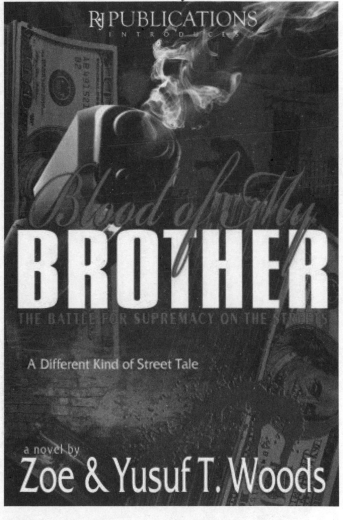

Roc was the man on the streets of Philadelphia, until his younger brother decided it was time to become his own man by wreaking havoc on Roc's crew without any regards for the blood relation they share. Drug, murder, mayhem and the pursuit of happiness can lead to deadly consequences. This story can only be told by a person who has lived it.

In Stores!!!

Violence, Intimidation and carnage are the order as Nathan and his brother set out to build the most powerful drug empires in Chicago. However, when God comes knocking, Nathan's conscience starts to surface. Will his haunted criminal past get the best of him?

In Stores!!

RJ PUBLICATIONS
I N T R O D U C E S

Stick & MOVE

A Different Kind of Street Tale

a novel by
SHAWN BLACK

Yasmina witnessed the brutal murder of her parents at a young age at the hand of a drug dealer. This event stained her mind and upbringing as a result. Will Yamina's life come full circle with her past? Find out as Yasmina's crew, The Platinum Chicks, set out to make a name for themselves on the street.

In stores!!

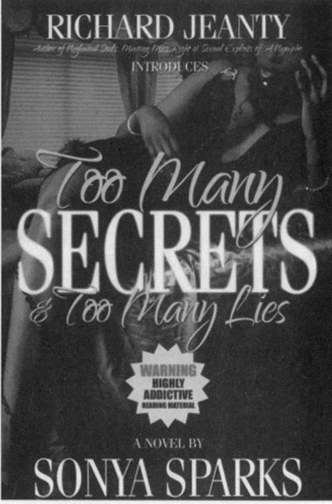

Ashland's mother, Bianca, fights hard to suppress the truth from her daughter because she doesn't want her to marry Jordan, the grandson of an ex-lover she loathes. Ashland soon finds out how cruel and vengeful her mother can be, but what price will Bianca pay for redemption?

In stores!!

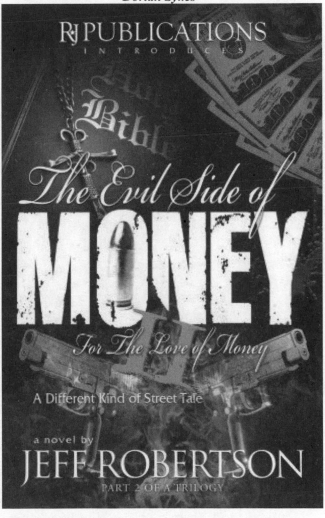

A beautigul woman from Bolivia threatens the existence of the drug empire that Nate and G have built. While Nate is head over heels for her, G can see right through her. As she brings on more conflict between the crew, G sets out to show Nate exactly who she is before she brings about their demise.

In Stores!!!

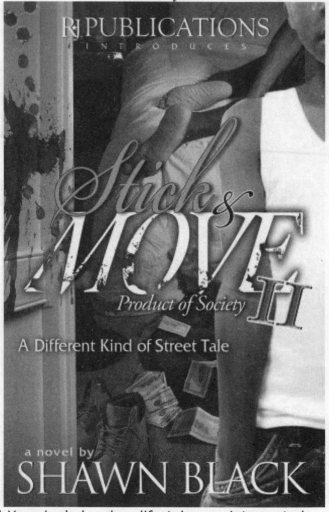

Scorcher and Yasmina's low key lifestyle was interrupted when they were taken down by the Feds, but their daughter, Serosa, was left to be raised by the foster care system. Will Serosa become a product of her environment or will she rise above it all? Her bloodline is undeniable, but will she be able to control it?

In Stores!!

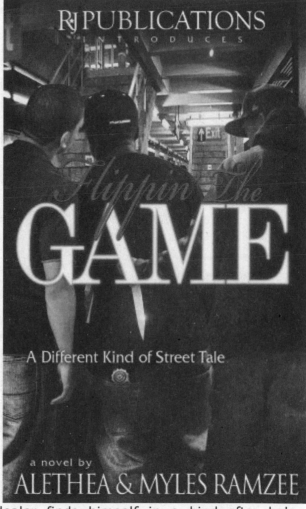

RJ PUBLICATIONS
I N T R O D U C E S

Flippin The
GAME

A Different Kind of Street Tale

a novel by
ALETHEA & MYLES RAMZEE

An ex-drug dealer finds himself in a bind after he's caught by the Feds. He has to decide which is more important, his family or his loyalty to the game. As he fights hard to make a decision, those who helped him to the top fear the worse from him. Will he get the chance to tell the govt. whole story, or will someone get to him before he becomes a snitch?

In Stores!!!

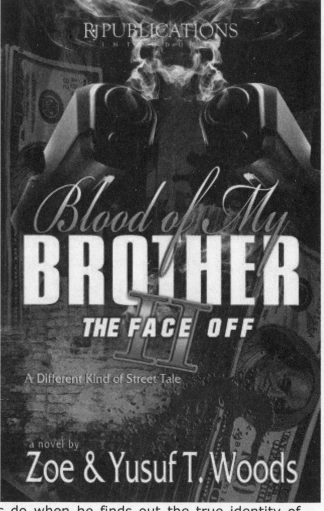

What will Roc do when he finds out the true identity of Solo? Will the blood shed come from his own brother Lil Mac? Will Roc and Solo take their beef to an explosive height on the street? Find out as Zoe and Yusuf bring the second installment to their hot street joint, Blood of My Brother.

In Stores!!!

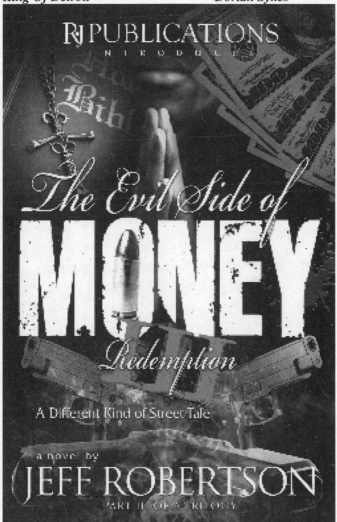

Forced to abandon the drug world for good, Nathan and G attempt to change their lives and move forward, but will their past come back to haunt them? This final installment will leave you speechless.

In Stores!!!

Nafiys Muhammad managed to beat the charges in court and was found innocent as a result. However, his criminal involvement is far from over. While Jerry Class Classon is feeling safe in the witness protection program, his family continues to endure even more pain. There will be many revelations as betrayal, sex scandal, corruption, and murder shape this story. No one will be left unscathed and everyone will pay the price for his/her involvement. Get ready for a rough ride as we revisit the Black Top Crew.

In Stores!!

Dave Richardson is enjoying success as his second book became a New York Times best-seller. He left the life of The Bedroom behind to settle with his family, but an obsessed fan has not had enough of Dave and she will go to great length to get a piece of him. How far will a woman go to get a man that doesn't belong to her?

In Stores!!!

Deon is at the mercy of a ruthless gang that kidnapped him. In a foreign land where he knows nothing about the culture, he has to use his survival instincts and his wit to outsmart his captors. Will the Hoodfellas show up in time to rescue Deon, or will Crazy D take over once again and fight an all out war by himself?

In Stores!!!

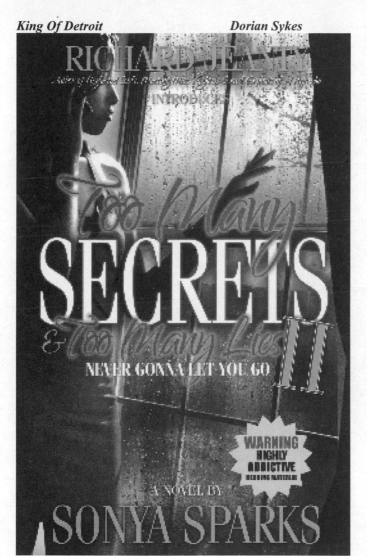

The drama continues as Deshun is hunted by Angela who still feels that ex-girlfriend Kayla is still trying to win his heart, though he brutally raped her. Angela will kill anyone who gets in her way, but is DeShun worth all the aggravation?

In Stores!!!

Buck Johnson was forced to make the best out of worst situation. He has witnessed the most cruel events in his life and it is those events who the man that he has become. Was the Johnson family ignorant souls through no fault of their own?

In Stores!!!

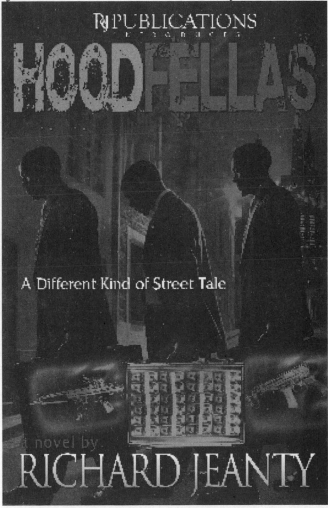

When an Ex-con finds himself destitute and in dire need of the basic necessities after he's released from prison, he turns to what he knows best, crime, but at what cost? Extortion, murder and mayhem drives him back to the top, but will he stay there?

In Stores !!!

What happens when someone falls insanely in love? Stalking is just the beginning.

In Stores!!!

Pharaoh decides that his fate would not be settled in
court by twelve jurors. His fate would be decided in
blood, as he sets out to kill Tez, and those who snitched
on him. Pharaoh s definition of Going All Out is either
death or freedom. Prison is not an option. Will Pharoah
impose his will on those snitches?

In Stores 10/30/2011

Kwame never thought he would come home to find his mother and sister strung out on drugs after his second tour of duty in Iraq. The Gulf war made him tougher, more tenacious, and most of all, turned him to a Navy Seal. Now a veteran, Kwame wanted to come back home to lead a normal life. However, Dirty cops and politicians alike refuse to clean the streets of Newark, New Jersey because the drug industry is big business that keeps their pockets fat. Kwame is determined to rid his neighborhood of all the bad elements, including the dirty cops, dirty politicians and the drug dealers. Will his one-man army be enough for the job?

In Stores December 15, 2011

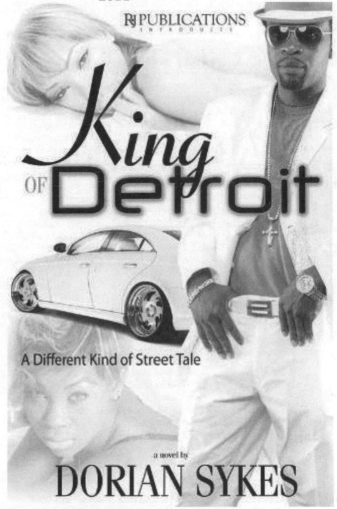

The blood-thirsty streets of Detroit have never seen a King like Corey Coach Townsend. The Legacy of Corey Coach Townsend, the Real King of Detroit, will live on forever. Coach was crowned King after avenging his father s murder, and after going to war with his best friend over the top spot. He always keeps his friends close. Coach s reign as king will forever be stained in the streets of Detroit, as the best who had ever done it, but how will he rise to the top? This is a story of betrayal, revenge and honor. There can only be one king!

In Stores February 15, 2012

Use this coupon to order by mail
1. Neglected Souls, Richard Jeanty $14.95 Available
2. Neglected No More, Richard Jeanty $14.95 Available
3. Ignorant Souls, Richard Jeanty $15.00, Available
4. Sexual Exploits of Nympho, Richard Jeanty $14.95 Available
5. Meeting Ms. Right's Whip Appeal, Richard Jeanty $14.95 Available
6. Me and Mrs. Jones, K.M Thompson $14.95 Available
7. Chasin' Satisfaction, W.S Burkett $14.95 Available
8. Extreme Circumstances, Cereka Cook $14.95 Available
9. The Most Dangerous Gang In America, R. Jeanty $15.00 Available
10. Sexual Exploits of a Nympho II, Richard Jeanty $15.00 Available
11. Sexual Jeopardy, Richard Jeanty $14.95 Available
12. Too Many Secrets, Too Many Lies, Sonya Sparks $15.00 Available
13. Stick And Move, Shawn Black $15.00 Available
14. Evil Side Of Money, Jeff Robertson $15.00 Available
15. Evil Side Of Money II, Jeff Robertson $15.00 Available
16. Evil Side Of Money III, Jeff Robertson $15.00 Available
17. Flippin' The Game, Alethea and M. Ramzee, $15.00 Available
18. Flippin' The Game II, Alethea and M. Ramzee, $15.00 Available
19. Cater To Her, W.S Burkett $15.00 Available
20. Blood of My Brother I, Zoe & Yusuf Woods $15.00 Available
21. Blood of my Brother II, Zoe & Ysuf Woods $15.00 Available
22. Hoodfellas, Richard Jeanty $15.00 available
23. Hoodfellas II, Richard Jeanty, $15.00 03/30/2010
24. The Bedroom Bandit, Richard Jeanty $15.00 Available
25. Mr. Erotica, Richard Jeanty, $15.00, Sept 2010
26. Stick N Move II, Shawn Black $15.00 Available
27. Stick N Move III, Shawn Black $15.00 Available
28. Miami Noire, W.S. Burkett $15.00 Available
29. Insanely In Love, Cereka Cook $15.00 Available
30. Blood of My Brother III, Zoe & Yusuf Woods Available
31. Mr. Erotica
32. My Partner's Wife
33. Deceived I
34. Deceived II
35. Going All Out I
36. Going All Out II 10/30/2011
37. Kwame 12/15/2011
38. King of Detroit 2/15/2012
Name_____
Address_____
City_____   _____State_____Zip Code_____

Please send the novels that I have circled above.
Shipping and Handling: Free
Total Number of Books_____Total Amount Due_____
        Buy 3 books and get 1 free. Send institution check or money order (no cash or CODs) to: RJ Publication: PO Box 300771, Jamaica, NY 11434
For info. call 718-471-2926, or www.rjpublications.com allow 2-3 weeks for delivery.

Use this coupon to order by mail
39. Neglected Souls, Richard Jeanty $14.95 Available
40. Neglected No More, Richard Jeanty $14.95Available
41. Ignorant Souls, Richard Jeanty $15.00, Available
42. Sexual Exploits of Nympho, Richard Jeanty $14.95 Available
43. Meeting Ms. Right's Whip Appeal, Richard Jeanty $14.95 Available
44. Me and Mrs. Jones, K.M Thompson $14.95 Available
45. Chasin' Satisfaction, W.S Burkett $14.95 Available
46. Extreme Circumstances, Cereka Cook $14.95 Available
47. The Most Dangerous Gang In America, R. Jeanty $15.00 Available
48. Sexual Exploits of a Nympho II, Richard Jeanty $15.00 Available
49. Sexual Jeopardy, Richard Jeanty $14.95 Available
50. Too Many Secrets, Too Many Lies, Sonya Sparks $15.00 Available
51. Stick And Move, Shawn Black $15.00 Available
52. Evil Side Of Money, Jeff Robertson $15.00 Available
53. Evil Side Of Money II, Jeff Robertson $15.00 Available
54. Evil Side Of Money III, Jeff Robertson $15.00 Available
55. Flippin' The Game, Alethea and M. Ramzee, $15.00 Available
56. Flippin' The Game II, Alethea and M. Ramzee, $15.00 Available
57. Cater To Her, W.S Burkett $15.00 Available
58. Blood of My Brother I, Zoe & Yusuf Woods $15.00 Available
59. Blood of my Brother II, Zoe & Ysuf Woods $15.00 Available
60. Hoodfellas, Richard Jeanty $15.00 available
61. Hoodfellas II, Richard Jeanty, $15.00 03/30/2010
62. The Bedroom Bandit, Richard Jeanty $15.00 Available
63. Mr. Erotica, Richard Jeanty, $15.00, Sept 2010
64. Stick N Move II, Shawn Black $15.00 Available
65. Stick N Move III, Shawn Black $15.00 Available
66. Miami Noire, W.S. Burkett $15.00 Available
67. Insanely In Love, Cereka Cook $15.00 Available
68. Blood of My Brother III, Zoe & Yusuf Woods Available
69. Mr. Erotica
70. My Partner's Wife
71. Deceived 1/15/2011
72. Going All Out 2/15/2011

Name_____

Address_____

City_____State_____Zip Code_____

Please send the novels that I have circled above.
Shipping and Handling: Free
Total Number of Books_____Total Amount Due_____
       Buy 3 books and get 1 free. This offer is subject to change without notice.
Send institution check or money order (no cash or CODs) to:
RJ Publications
PO Box 300771
Jamaica, NY 11434
For more information please call 718-471-2926, or visit www.rjpublications.com
Please allow 2-3 weeks for delivery.